DECISIVE MEASURES

DECISIVE MEASURES

John Nichol

Hodder & Stoughton

First published in Great Britain in 2000
by Hodder and Stoughton
A division of Hodder Headline

A CIP catalogue record for this book is available
from the British Library

Hardcover edition ISBN 0 340 75117 7
Trade paperback edition ISBN 0 340 76968 8

Typeset by Hewer Text Ltd, Edinburgh
Printed and bound in Great Britain by
Mackays of Chatham plc, Chatham, Kent

Hodder and Stoughton
A division of Hodder Headline
338 Euston Road
London NW1 3BH

*To the Murphy family, without whom my work,
travels and research would be impossible. Bernard,
Elaine, Hannah and Ross: thank you all.*

Foreword

Sierra Leone has been devastated over the past few years by some of the most brutal internecine fighting and civil war that even the continent of Africa has ever witnessed. Much of the country's mineral wealth is extracted by foreign corporations and the majority of the profits are repatriated by them. Mercenaries also operate in the country, protecting the corporations' substantial investments. The story that follows is pure fiction, however, and no resemblance to any organisation or individual, living or dead, is intended.

John Nichol
May 2000

Prologue

The sunset was already reddening the sky and casting long shadows across the hills when the radio crackled into life again. 'Echo 14. Hostiles reported 179502. Investigate.'

I suppressed a groan and acknowledged the order. We had already been flying for over eight hours, sortie after sortie over a land already scarred by fighting, arriving always too late, to find another village in ruins, another pillar of black smoke reaching up into the sky.

I banked the heli around and headed north-east over the dusty Macedonian hills. I dropped to low level as we approached the border, and began twisting and turning, hugging the contours of the land. We soared to clear a last mountain ridge and then dropped into the target valley.

Ahead was a familiar scene: a small hamlet, a cluster of houses sheltering in the lee of the hills, surrounded by a dense belt of woodland. I could see columns of smoke and the orange flicker of flames piercing the jagged outlines of ruined houses. Of the inhabitants there was no sign.

I put the heli into a broad turn around the hamlet, my eyes raking the open ground and the edges of the woodland, alert for the flash of gunfire from the deepening shadows or the telltale plume of smoke from a rocket launch. Still no figures moved.

Then, out of the corner of my eye, I glimpsed a group of rectilinear outlines in the shadows among the trees – trucks or maybe even tanks using the wood for cover. My flesh crept, but I maintained the same course until we had passed out of sight beyond the end of the wood. I radioed base. 'Possible hostiles sighted. Over.'

Then I jabbed the intercom. 'Keep alert, guys. There are at least six vehicles among the trees. I'm making another pass along the edge of the wood. Echo Thirteen, follow me through.'

I heard a thud behind me as the gunner slid open the door of the cab and swung his gun to cover the target. I swooped in low and fast past the edge of the wood, using my peripheral vision to search for the outlines among the trees. The branches were whipped to and fro by the downwash from the heli, but I tried to ignore the movement, focusing only on what lay beyond. Once more there was no sign of people and no firing, only the tantalising, half-hidden shapes.

I had now made out eight distinct forms under the trees and a long tapering black cylinder angled upwards at 45 degrees. It could have been the barrel of a tank gun; it could equally have been a fallen tree.

I passed beyond the end of the wood and banked in a tight turn, as my wingman followed me through. The intercom crackled as he completed his pass. 'Definite hostiles,' he said. 'Let's go for it.'

I hesitated. 'Negative. Am not sure. Going in again.'

As we dropped back towards the wood, I lowered the collective, washing off some of our speed. A flash of the dying sunlight reflected from my co-pilot's helmet as he turned to look at me. 'Jesus Jack,' he said. 'How much of an invitation are you going to give them?'

'We've got to be sure.'

'We'll be sure enough when we're dead.'

As we reached the midpoint of the wood, I flared the heli, putting it into the hover. The force of the downwash threw the branches aside for a moment and I at last saw movement – figures sprinting towards the vehicles. I hauled up the collective and rammed the cyclic forward, sending us speeding up and away from the wood.

I reached for the radio. 'Figures and vehicles sighted.'

The answer came back before I had posed the question. 'Clear engage.'

Still I kept circling. My wingman's voice came over the intercom. 'What are we waiting for?'

I gnawed at my lip. When I glanced across at my co-pilot, his gaze was still fixed on me. 'Well?' he said.

Abruptly I made the decision. 'Engage.'

I headed out in a wide loop and then dropped to minimum level, accelerating back in towards the wood, the ground blurring beneath me.

'Arming weapons.'

The reply came a fraction of a second later. 'Weapons armed.'

We were into the long shadow of the wood and the trees rose like a dark wall ahead of us. I held the heli level for a few more seconds as I stared into the cross-hairs. They intersected on the largest shape inside the trees and I pulled the trigger once, twice.

There was a 'whoosh' as the rockets streaked from the pod. I hauled back on the cyclic and sent the heli soaring up into the sky. A moment later, there was a massive explosion and a bubble of oily flame and black smoke belched upwards through the trees. The gun thundered as the door gunner raked the edge of the wood. There was no answering fire.

I saw my wingman complete his attack run as I banked for another pass. I dropped in low, the turbines screaming, my finger once more tightening on the trigger. The cross-hairs came together on another dark shape, but a micro-second before I fired, a figure burst from the undergrowth at the edge of the wood, a human torch burning from head to toe. The long black skirt flapping around the woman's legs was a sheet of flame.

I jabbed the intercom button. 'Abort. Abort.'

I hauled on the cyclic to pull us up, peering down through the Perspex screen. The woman was still wreathed in flame, her arms raised, her hands spread wide in supplication. She threw her head back. I saw her scorched face and her mouth opening in a silent scream. Then the flames closed around her, obliterating her from my sight. She slumped to the ground, a shapeless, burning mound of rags.

I turned for base, the ground blurring before my eyes as tears trickled down my face.

Chapter 1

A wall of stifling heat and humidity hit us as the door of the aircraft swung open. Sweat beaded my forehead at once as I watched two Africans in threadbare overalls pushing a rusting flight of steps towards the plane.

Tom leaned past me and stared out at the airfield. From his expression he was less than impressed. Over forty years old, and a career RAF man, he was finding the adjustment to the harsh realities of life on the outside a hard one to make. 'That must be the welcoming committee,' he said as a cloud of flies formed around us.

'Welcome to the real world, Tom, better get used to it. There's no more soft postings, Officers' Mess and squadron dinners for us, and no more people to hold our hands and tidy up after us. We're on our own now.'

'And how.' He scowled and the ever-present frown lines

deepened on his forehead. 'God, what a dump. Remind me what we're doing here, Jack.'

'We're doing the only job we know, making a few quid for ourselves and upholding Her Majesty's vital interests at the same time.'

He gave a sour smile. 'Vital interests spelt D-I-A-M-O-N-D-S. If they're that vital, why doesn't Her Majesty send some of her own boys to look after them? No, don't tell me, let me guess: because some things are better done at arm's length. Mustn't soil those white gloves with anything too messy, must we?'

I met his gaze. 'Listen, it's a job of work. We agreed to the terms when we signed the contract. It's a bit late now for regrets.'

The steps clanged into place. We hurried down and walked across the potholed concrete towards the terminal building, a scaled-down version of a glass and concrete 1960s shopping centre. The years had not been kind to it. The façade was stained and crumbling and its windows were filthy, cracked and starred with bullet holes.

Tom's thinning, sandy hair was darkened and plastered to his head by sweat, which ran down his forehead and dripped from his eyebrows into the dust at his feet as we crossed the scorching concrete. I could feel my shirt sticking to my back.

Although the shed-like arrivals hall was out of the direct sunlight, it felt little cooler. A solitary fan turned in slow, lethargic circles, barely disturbing the clouds of flies. We stood for a moment letting our eyes get used to the gloom after the blinding glare of the sun.

Two soldiers in grease-stained uniforms got up and put on their hats as we approached. They pored over our passports and visas, examining each page in turn, then dropped them onto the table in front of them, making no move to return them. We waited in silence, searching their impassive faces for some clue to the next move.

A group of African men, women and children, most in torn clothes and ragged T-shirts, stood on the far side of the steel gates beyond the arrivals hall, staring at us without apparent interest or curiosity. Then there was a commotion and the group parted to allow through two men. They pushed open the gates and came striding towards us.

The leader was a powerful figure, his skin tanned to mahogany from long exposure to the sun and his sandy hair flecked with grey. A broad grin showed beneath his walrus moustache. Ignoring the soldiers, he walked over and slapped the two of us on the back. 'Glad you made it, boys. Grizz Riley. You can't imagine how pleased I am to see you here. I was beginning to think we'd never get another heli crew.'

As he spoke his companion, a paunchy African with a gold tooth and a shiny mohair suit, began talking to the soldiers in low confidential tones. I recognised the type, a local fixer paid to smooth our way with a few crumpled notes past police, customs and the other local piranhas nursing greedy expectations at the sight of a Westerner.

I heard the words 'Decisive Measures', and the rustle of leone bills. Pocketing the bribe, the two soldiers, now all smiles, handed us back our passports and waved us through.

Grizz led us outside to a battered pick-up. A bullet-headed, square-jawed soldier in faded fatigues stood guard over it. His blond hair was cropped so short that his scalp showed through it, and a network of scar-lines gleamed white against the tanned skin. He remained unsmiling, scrutinising each of us in turn.

'Another new kid on the block,' Grizz said.

'Jack Griffiths,' I said, holding out my hand. 'Pleased to meet you.'

The soldier scowled, but shook my hand. 'I'm Rudi,' he said in a thick Afrikaans accent.

Rudi and the fixer got in the front while we climbed into the back with Grizz, settling ourselves among the piles of bergens, weapons and ammunition. A few heads turned to watch us drive off, the rest continued to stare through the chainlink fence at the now empty arrivals hall, still waiting – though for what, no one seemed to know.

It was an uncomfortable ride. The airport road was potholed and badly scarred by tank tracks. The rusting, burned out wreck of one tank had been bulldozed off the road and then left to rot, its gun barrel pointing aimlessly at the sky.

We reached a junction with the main road up the peninsula towards Freetown. Its surface was marginally better and we accelerated away towards the capital. The sun was now directly overhead and I was glad of the breeze and the patches of dappled shade as the road weaved through the fringes of the rain forest. At intervals there were clusters of mud-and-thatch huts, and an occasional concrete building set back from the road. Sun-bleached signs still advertised bars, shops and cafés, but all now appeared to be closed, and many were smoke-blackened and pocked with the marks of gunfire.

We climbed to clear a thickly forested ridge and saw Freetown sprawling over the hills below us, a mosaic of bare earth, grey concrete, palm thatch and multi-coloured tin roofing, all overlaid with a layer of red dust.

Beyond the capital, palm-fringed, white sand beaches, which stretched south along the peninsula as far as I could see, looked deserted. This was clearly no place for tourists. Commanding the heights of the ridgeline were rows of colonial houses raised above the earth on stilts and shaded by breadfruit and cotton trees.

Grizz followed my gaze. 'It was named Hill Station by the British,' he said.

Like their former occupants, the houses had once been white, but they were now faded to a dull khaki brown, stained by rivulets of damp. All of them were surrounded by high brick walls or tin sheet fences topped with shards of broken glass and coils of razor wire.

I could see mango and breadfruit trees growing in the lush grounds of the Presidential Palace on Signal Hill, but the white walls, unrepaired from years of coups and counter-coups, were pitted with the marks of rounds and shellfire.

Lower on the steep hillside the slopes festered with an ugly, sprawling shanty town, running all the way down to the creek at the bottom of the hill. The shacks were built of packing cases and scrap wood, and roofed with patches of rusting corrugated metal or palm fronds.

'They're without heat, light, water or sanitation,' Grizz said. 'They burn dung, garbage and even old tyres for fuel. When the wind's in the wrong direction, the stink is unimaginable.'

Ahead of us, a few overloaded, battered pick-ups drove down the hill into the city, laden with firewood and farm goods to sell. As we rounded a bend on the steep descent, we came to a juddering halt. A pick-up and a beaten-up old Mercedes taxi had collided at the point of the bend. Both drivers were out of their vehicles remonstrating with each other.

As they argued, a human tide began pouring out of the shanty town on the hillside just below the road. Ignoring the drivers' protests and tearful pleas, the mob began looting the vehicles, stripping them of everything they could carry. The Mercedes driver tried to save his car radio, but he was punched to the ground and a man carried it off into the maze of shanties, waving it triumphantly above his head.

Drivers coming up the hill stopped, sized up the situation, and as one man, they either reversed back down again or pulled three-point-turns and disappeared in clouds of dust. A moment later, there was a blare of horns and a police car appeared around the corner. It braked to a halt and sounded its siren. The looters barely glanced up from their work of stripping the cars. No policemen emerged from the car and after a moment it, too, reversed down the hill.

Grizz glanced at me. 'Welcome to Sierra Leone,' he said. He reached for his rifle, stood up and fired a short burst into the air. Then he lowered the barrel, pointing it directly at the looters. There was a moment's stunned silence, then they fled in panic, many dropping their booty as they ran.

Grizz waited as the car owners scooped up what possessions they had been left and shoved them back into their broken vehicles, then they too disappeared down the hill and we drove on into the city.

At the Kissy roundabout we turned west through the Lebanese district and drove down East Street past the bus station, the mosque and the empty government book store. There was no pavement and the high brick walls of the Pademba Road prison rose straight up from the edge of the street.

The US Embassy, a three-storey white building overlooking Cotton Tree roundabout, looked intact from a distance, but even its walls were pocked with gunfire. A group of burly, heavily armed Marines stared out suspiciously from inside the gates.

The decaying façades of once imposing colonial buildings lined the broad streets at the centre of Freetown, but City Hall was a crumbling wreck, its windows shattered and rubbish piled to the sills of every ground-floor room. Surrounding it were rows of shabby, two-storey buildings. Many of the concrete flat roofs had been crudely repaired with rusting tin sheets. Tattered washing hung from lines suspended across the street at first-floor level, and most of the houses looked to have a firepit in the yard in place of a kitchen.

We pulled up in Garrison Street by a row of battered shops with buckled and scorched steel shutters. The streets stank of shit and rubbish and were clogged with beggars. There were rats everywhere, the only creatures who looked well fed.

I peered into the shops as we walked past. Most were run by Lebanese traders, but few had any goods to offer; only a handful of tins and fly-blown packages stood on the otherwise empty shelves.

The general store at the end of the street was slightly better equipped, though the goods seemed more appropriate to a frontier town than a capital city. There was soap, mosquito coils and nets, candles, kerosene lamps, axes, bush knives and the shovels and sieves used by gold-panners.

Grizz busied himself stacking supplies which Rudi took out and loaded onto the pick-up while the store owner ran around scribbling notes on a pad. We left the fixer to argue about the price, and Grizz led us around the corner and up a low rise to a hotel. It resembled a Soviet apartment block and, with a perversity that seemed beyond the call of duty, it had been built back to front. The entrance and balconies faced inland and the bathrooms and toilets looked out over the sea.

The check-in involved another prolonged scrutiny of our passports and a marathon form-filling session. Grizz left us at the desk. 'When do we start work?' I said.

He smiled. 'Decisive Measures are generous employers. You get one night's acclimatisation and R & R. Then we go up-country to the Bohara mine first thing in the morning. I'll leave you guys to sort your kit and recover from the flight. I'll be back at six to give you a briefing and then show you what passes for a good time in these parts.' He winked and sauntered out.

My room was everything I expected: the lights didn't work, there was the waxed-paper rustle of cockroaches from the bathroom and a stench that made me reluctant to investigate further. The bedroom was high-ceilinged, with a tiled floor and shutters. There was a rusting fan at the centre of the ceiling, although there was rarely the electrical power to turn it. The French windows to the balcony were cracked and starred with bullet holes; it was not a good omen.

A kerosene lamp stood at the bedside, and the bed was draped with a mosquito net. I turned back the covers and stared suspiciously at the sheets. They did at least look clean. I lay down and closed my eyes.

I woke soaked with sweat, my heart pounding, the thunder of gunfire still resounding in my ears. Only the noise of the cicadas broke the silence of my room. As I lowered my head back to the pillow, cursing the nightmare that had frightened me awake, I heard the banging of fists on the door and Grizz's voice shouting, 'Come on, you lazy bastard, get the lead out. I've nearly worn my knuckles off on this door.'

I croaked a reply.

'Twenty minutes, in the lobby,' he said.

I heard his footsteps recede down the corridor. I dragged myself out of my bed and, more in hope than expectation, I tried the light switch. This time it worked and cockroaches scattered for the cover of the drain as I walked into the bathroom.

I turned on the shower and stood under the dribble of brackish water for a few minutes, then towelled myself dry. I pulled on jeans and a clean long-sleeved shirt, rubbed on some foul-smelling insect repellent and then headed down the stairs, not wishing to try my luck with the lift.

I found Grizz, Rudi and Tom sprawled in armchairs in the lobby, staring out through the plate glass window at the skyline.

There had been a slow build-up of cloud throughout the afternoon, climbing the wall of the mountains and piling higher and higher into the sky, building the thunderheads that would bring the evening rain. Now the sun had almost set and lightning was sparking over the mountains.

As the sky darkened, the lights all over Freetown went out. Tom started and looked round in alarm. Grizz had not moved a muscle. 'Just another power failure,' he said.

For a moment the city was in darkness, then scores of generators fired up in a metallic chorus, counterpointing the croaking of the frogs in the swamps.

We walked through to a small meeting room off the lobby. Beneath a recent white paint job, the marks of smoke damage and the crudely repaired outline of an impact from a heavy round or rocket were clearly visible where the wall met the ceiling.

We settled ourselves into chairs as Grizz closed and locked the door. He strode to the front of the room. 'Rudi, you can sleep through the first bit if you want, unless helicopter-spotting is one of your hobbies.'

He turned to Tom and me. 'Have you guys flown together before?'

'You mean apart from the training course on the Huey?' I said. 'Not for a while. Tom trained me at Finnington though, nearly ten years ago.'

'It won't be a problem,' Tom said. 'We both know our own jobs.'

Grizz nodded. 'I certainly hope so. Okay, as I'm sure you've been told, you'll be flying a Huey XI. The terrain is very difficult here; it's all ridges and valleys, so the helicopter is absolutely vital to the resupply and support of the garrison at the Bohara mine. You'll be based here in Freetown, but your job is to keep Bohara supplied with everything from mining equipment and ammunition to food and medical supplies.

'The Huey comes to us via at least one African dictatorship and it's twenty years old, but it's been upgraded many times along the way and I can vouch for its condition. It has uprated engines, a door-mounted mini gun, a nose gun and forward firing rockets, and chaff and flare dispensers. It's also been fitted out for flight with night vision goggles.'

'What about the rebels?' Tom said. 'What have they got?'

Rudi stirred and began to show some interest.

'They're backed by Liberia,' Grizz said, 'and a lot of their weapons come through that regime. They have plenty of AK rifles, a few RPGs and a couple of heavy machine guns. They also captured a ZFU anti-aircraft gun from the government some years ago, but it's never been used and we're uncertain whether they have either the ammunition or the know-how to fire it effectively. The Liberians do have Hinds, however, and there are rumours that at least one has been allocated to the rebels. If true, that obviously poses a serious risk.'

He paused. 'Now you'll have read plenty about Sierra Leone in the papers and you'll be hearing plenty more from me over the next few days, but in some ways the reality here surpasses anything you've heard. Nothing you've been used to anywhere else applies. The government is in theoretical control of the country, but in practice its writ barely runs as far as the outskirts of Freetown. There are a couple of million displaced people – that's a third of the population. Fifteen thousand of them are minus at least one limb.'

He gave a bleak smile. 'It's a little habit the rebels have. Limbs and lives have no value here. Only one thing counts: diamonds are everybody's best friends. The government owns the mines but is powerless to protect them without the help of private military companies like Decisive Measures, and like everybody else, the companies take their reward in gemstones. Don't get the idea that we operate on a lavish budget though, we operate on a shoestring.'

'So apart from a share of the diamonds, what are the rebels fighting for?' I said.

Grizz shrugged. 'Just that. They're the only rebel movement I ever heard of that has no ideology worth the name. They want to defeat the government, but only so that they can take control of the diamond producing areas. The rebels are undoubtedly bloody and brutal fighters but they're not particularly well equipped; the Liberian regime that backs them creams off the vast majority of the diamond wealth that the rebels steal or smuggle out.

'The regular army is supposed to be on our side, but despite the diamonds, this is the poorest country in the world and the soldiers certainly aren't growing too fat for their uniforms. When they're paid at all, it's very sporadic and they're also going hungry; their ration of rice was cut recently by fifty per cent. They're supposed to get one bag of rice a month, plus their clothing and their gun, but the senior officers keep back as much rice as they can, then sell it on the black market. In a country that is crying out for food, they've effectively become rice merchants, not soldiers.

'A cut in rice rations was what started the last revolution – the January Uprising – in which six thousand were killed in Freetown alone. So many bodies were thrown in the river they were bobbing up months later in Skull Bay just around the point; you can guess how it got its name.

'An American company was operating here. They're mining engineers apparently, or at least that's what it says on their letterhead.' He grinned. 'It's a CIA front. They were resupplying and helping to retrain the armed forces, but as usual at the first sign of trouble the Americans have downed tools and gone home.

'In short, we can rely on no one but ourselves here. No one else is going to help us. If it all goes to ratshit, the British government and the UN won't want to know. There will be no SAS or US Marine rescue parties flying in to save our arses. We either look after ourselves and each other or we go under.' He paused. 'That's the bad news; the good news is that for the moment we're in a lull in the fighting. The capital is quiet and the rebel offensive in the north-east has stalled. That's more because of the rainy season than the resistance of the government forces, however, and with the dry season almost upon us we must expect an upsurge in rebel activity.

'For the moment, though, Decisive Measures is simply tasked with keeping the Bohara diamond mines running as smoothly as possible. Your job is to get the supplies and the personnel out there to enable them to do so. That's it. Any questions? Then let's go and have a beer.'

We went out into the hot, humid night. It was low tide and the sickly, foetid smell of mud and mangroves filled the air. I heard the whine of mosquitoes and pulled my shirt cuffs tighter around my wrists.

Women sat impassive at the side of the street. Their goods — dried fish, rice, cassava roots, chillies and potato leaf — were spread in front of them on palm leaves laid in the dust. Their hungry, pot-bellied children played around them as they waited. Street hawkers passed by, offering single cigarettes and magazines that were either second-hand or stolen by post office clerks. A few street food sellers offered local delicacies like bush-rat and potato leaf plasas.

Here and there a solitary street light flickered into life as the mains power was restored, but most were broken, their wiring stolen and sold for scrap, or cannibalised for other uses.

We passed several burned out and derelict houses. Those that remained intact had iron barred windows, stout locks and razor wire fences. The walls were still clapboard, however. There might be no way in for a sneak thief, but if the rebels came again, it looked like they would find it easy to kick the houses down.

Grizz led us out along the road fringing the beach. It was lined with restaurants. From the nameboards over the doors, most of them, like the shops, were run by Lebanese. Many were long deserted, but at one the owner still presided over his bamboo-fronted bar, perched on a rusting stool, his paunch spilling out of his torn, stained T-shirt. The lack of tourists and businessmen had not dented his trade, however, for his bar was full of expatriate mineworkers, traders, soldiers and government officials, and a scattering of dull-eyed whores.

The walls of the bar were blackened with damp and the only decorations were mildewed posters of strangely light-skinned Africans advertising American cigarettes and Japanese cars.

The menu was limited: groundnut soup and rice. I ordered food and beer for all four of us, and the owner gave me a gap-toothed smile as he added my leone notes to a huge roll held by a rubber band. He waved a fly whisk across the bar as if in benediction, briefly disturbing the black cloud of flies hovering over us. The beer was local – the only label on the bottles was a picture of a yellow star in a blue oval – but it was cold and tasted fine.

I took a leisurely look around the room. There was only one other white face there, a sallow, lank-haired man who sat in a corner flanked by two burly black men in combat fatigues. Both had machine pistols in holsters slung over their shoulders. Their employer held a bag clutched to his side. He rarely lifted his gaze from it and kept his hand resting on it at all times.

'Who's he?' I said.

Grizz shrugged. 'He claims to be a missionary, but I've never seen a missionary hanging out in bars, nor one with a bag full of diamonds.'

'That explains the two goons with the Uzis, then.'

Grizz took a swig of his beer, lit a cheroot and blew a smoke ring at the ceiling. Then he glanced at Tom. 'So what brings you here, Tom? Apart from the money, of course. Bottom line, that's what we're all here for, isn't it?'

Tom sipped his drink while he considered his reply. 'Money and boredom, I suppose,' he said. 'I've been pensioned off by the RAF, but it's a bit early in my life to be getting out the pipe and slippers, so I thought I'd give this a go.'

'Any family?'

'No. Well, I've two children, but they're grown up now. One lives in Australia and the other's in New York.'

'And your wife's back in England?'

As Tom stared down into his beer, the overhead light deepened the furrows in his forehead and he looked even older than his forty-five years. 'She left me a few months ago.' He said it with the same expression of surprise he must have shown when she broke the news to him. 'It would have been our silver wedding this month.'

Grizz studied him for a moment. 'So your break-up would have been another reason for a change of scene for you?'

Tom didn't reply. After a moment, Grizz switched his attention to me. 'What about you, Jack? You're too young and handsome to have been pensioned off. So what's the story? Rub up some air marshal the wrong way?'

'Something like that.'

Grizz waited for me to continue. As the silence lengthened, he smiled to himself. 'Fair enough. It's none of my business, anyway, as long as you do your job here.' He shot a glance at Rudi. 'And you're certainly not the only one working for Decisive Measures who's got a bit of a history behind him.' He paused. 'So . . . got any wives or children?'

'Not last time I looked,' I said. 'What about you?'

'Plenty of each — three wives, four children. All in the past tense now, though.'

'Even the children?'

'Oh, I send them a card on their birthdays and things, but I'm abroad so much of the time they've almost forgotten who I am by the time I turn up. It only upsets them if I do go to see them. It's better all round if I stay away.' He tried to force a smile, but his eyes belied it.

'And you, Rudi?' I said.

'Fifteen years in the South African Defence Force fighting bush wars against the ANC. I quit the day Mandela was sworn in. Since then I've been working as a mercenary.'

'Any family?'

He shook his head and ended the interrogation by walking over to the bar. By the time he returned with more beer, Tom, Grizz and I had moved the conversation onto less personal ground, talking about previous ops and mutual acquaintances.

Rudi stayed aloof from the chat, downing a succession of cans of beer and replying in monosyllables to any remarks directed at him, but his watchful eyes showed that he missed little of what was said. I found my gaze straying back to him, feeling more than a little mistrust and dislike for him, though I had nothing to base it on but my own instincts.

Finally, as if he had crossed a personal threshold or we had passed some secret test, Rudi banged another four beers down on the table and gave a broad smile. He took a long pull on his drink, then put his feet up on the table and rocked his chair back.

He lit a cigarette and blew a cloud of smoke into the air. 'This could be God's country, Jack — perfect beaches, gold, diamonds, any woman you want for the price of a pack of cigarettes, and just enough trouble from the rebels to keep us in work. You couldn't have a better posting.'

His speech was now a little slurred, and though he smiled he had the air of a man who could change moods in a second at a wrong word or gesture. I had known plenty of guys like him in my time in the forces and usually avoided them like the plague; we had enough battles to fight at work, without going looking for them in our time off as well.

As Rudi was warming to his theme, a taxi pulled up outside. A few moments later two women entered the bar. Both were tall and striking. One had long, black hair cascading around her powerful shoulders, and her mouth, lipsticked in vivid red, looked like a gash against skin so dark it seemed blue-black in the dim light. The other was model thin with close-cropped, dark brown hair that still looked damp from the shower. She had coffee-coloured skin and her eyes were a piercing blue. I could not take my eyes off her.

'Jesus,' Rudi said, staggering to his feet. 'Some good-looking whores at last.'

He headed off across the room and had just reached the two women when Grizz returned from the bar with another round of beers. He took in the scene and winked at us. 'This should be entertaining.'

Rudi's bulky figure loomed over the two women as he propositioned them, waving a ten dollar bill he produced from his pocket. The black woman simply ignored him, turning her back and talking to the barman. The other heard Rudi out in silence, eyeballing him without blinking. Then she took the ten dollar bill he was proffering, tore it in quarters and dropped it on the floor at his feet.

'Even if I was a whore,' I heard her say, 'it would take more than you could earn in a lifetime to persuade me to sleep with an ox like you. But I'm not a whore, I'm a paramedic. Part of my job is to patch up dumb mercenaries when they get shot. I look forward to making your acquaintance again, but only under those circumstances.'

Rudi stared at her, the veins knotting in his forehead. I started across the room, afraid that he might strike her, but he dropped his gaze and began scrabbling in the dust for his torn-up bill. Then he turned and shambled back across the room.

His crestfallen look turned to a scowl as he saw us suppressing our laughter. He swore in Afrikaans. 'That bitch needs teaching a lesson.'

Grizz raised an eyebrow. 'That bitch is a bloody good medic.' His voice remained low and even, but it carried an edge of menace. 'Now have a drink and take your beating like a man. There's plenty of whores will take your money without hitting on women who won't.'

Rudi reverted to a sullen silence, draining his beer in one gulp.

'So who is she?' I said.

Grizz shrugged. 'She's called Layla and like I said, she's a paramedic. She works for Medicaid International, but she's seconded to us part of the time. She deals with any medical problems at the mining compound and also holds clinics in the surrounding villages.' He smiled. 'And don't waste your time; we've all tried.'

I saw her move to the bar. 'I'll get the next ones,' I said.

I walked over and stood next to her as I ordered the beers, then glanced across at her. 'Hi, I'm Jack,' I said. 'I fly helicopters. I gather we'll be working together now and again.'

She looked me up and down. 'I'm Layla.' Her accent was English but with a faint lilt. 'I don't think so. I work with mercenaries as little as possible. My job's to save lives.'

'So's mine.'

'Sure,' she said. 'Just like your friends over there.'

'Do you always judge people by the company they keep?'

She shrugged. 'Out here, it's as good a guide as any.' She walked back to her table, leaving me staring after her.

I went back to the others. Rudi was still mechanically downing one beer after another, and his mood was turning increasingly ugly.

Grizz glanced at him and then at us. 'Maybe we could round the evening off with a couple of beers back at the hotel,' he said.

Rudi shook his head, his eyes still fixed on Layla and her friend. 'Not me. I'll see you later.'

Grizz shrugged. 'You guys with me? Then I'll just hit the can and we'll be out of here.'

On his way back from the stinking lean-to that acted as the communal toilet, I saw him stop and speak to Layla. She turned and looked at Rudi, then frowned and nodded.

Grizz walked back over to us. 'Let's go.'

Tom and I followed him outside through the baffa – the outside drinking area attached to the bar. It had a tin roof, but the sides were open to let in the breeze. After the stifling heat of the bar, the relative coolness of the baffa was welcome enough, despite the attentions of the mosquitoes. The taxi that had brought Layla and her friend was still waiting, parked with the lights off at the roadside a few yards away. Grizz signalled to it and we climbed in.

'Wait a moment, please,' Grizz said.

Tom gave him a puzzled look. 'What for? Rudi said he was staying put.'

He smiled. 'I think you'll enjoy this company more than Rudi's.'

As we waited, the mosquitoes and the bats foraging for moths disappeared, and a moment later the evening rain began to fall. In seconds it was battering down, blanking out the view and turning the brown water coursing down the road to foam. The roof of the baffa seemed to buckle under the weight of the rain, which cascaded over the edge like a waterfall.

Layla and her friend appeared in the doorway of the bar. They hesitated at the sight of the rain, then glanced behind them and ran for the taxi. By the time they had reached it they were soaked to the skin, their hair plastered to their scalps.

Layla jumped in next to me, her wet clothes clinging to her showing every contour of her body. As her friend also squeezed onto the crowded back seat, Layla was pressed against me. My nostrils were full of the musky aroma of her perfume, and I could feel the soft swelling of her breast against my arm. The heat of her body seemed to burn all the way down my side and I hoped that the darkness of the cab's interior hid from her how aroused I was.

The taxi moved off along the road, inching through the flood lapping around the sills of the car. The wipers barely interrupted the torrents of water pouring down the windscreen. I glanced behind us. The huge figure of Rudi was visible for a second, framed in the lit doorway of the bar, staring after us. Then the curtains of rain blocked him from view.

We were halfway back to the hotel when the storm ended as abruptly as it had begun. The floods began to ebb away and a watery moon appeared as the clouds parted and the chorus of frogs resumed. Even this late in the evening, I saw traders come shuffling out of the buildings and doorways where they had been sheltering. They began setting up again, lighting candles and storm lanterns to illuminate the tables and cardboard boxes on which they spread their wares.

The hotel bar was deserted but still open. 'Anybody fancy a last drink?' I said, unsuccessfully trying to hide my disappointment when Layla exchanged a glance with her friend, then shook her head.

There was the hint of a smile in her eyes. 'Nothing personal. We've all got an early start in the morning.'

'Have we?'

'You guys are the helicopter pilots, aren't you?'

'Yes, but—'

'Then don't stay up all night drinking. I'm flying up to Bohara with you in the morning to run a clinic at the mine.' For the first time all evening, she gave me a genuine smile. I could still smell a faint trace of her perfume in the air long after she had disappeared up the stairs.

Chapter 2

We set off early the next morning. Layla rode up front with Grizz. Tom and I were once more perched in the back with Rudi, who was even more monosyllabic than usual. He ignored Layla completely as he climbed up and took his seat right at the back of the pick-up.

The glass had been knocked out of the small window in the rear of the cab, allowing us to talk to Grizz and Layla, though we had to shout to be heard above the roar of the engine and the jolting as we bounced over the rutted and potholed roads.

Grizz drove through the empty streets of the town centre, but when we reached the Kissy roundabout, instead of taking the road I expected, he continued straight on. 'This isn't the way to the airport,' I shouted as he accelerated away

'I know. That's because the helicopter isn't kept there.'

We passed through the belt of dismal shanty towns surrounding the capital, the smell of the smoke from cooking fires mingling with the stink of refuse and decay, ragged people moving among the shacks. They turned to watch us pass, their faces blank. 'Every rebel offensive sends a few more thousand fleeing to Freetown,' Layla said. 'They all end up in the shanty towns. There's no work or land here, but there's safety of a sort.'

We passed the last of the shanty towns and were out into open country. The road ran along the fringes of dense jungle and swamp, winding through the rain forest before beginning its climb into the hills. The tree canopy often met high overhead above the potholed road, but as we rose higher, the forest thinned and the first deciduous trees showed among the dull green of the jungle species.

The tarmac gave way to a surface of red earth and crushed rock as the road climbed steadily towards the mountains. Looking back from the ridge I could see the capital sprawled around the foot of Mount Auriol, the colonial houses ranged along the ridges of Juba Hill and Signal Hill, and the vivid splashes of colour – the painted roofs of shacks and shanties clinging to the slopes – among the green-capped peaks and steep valleys cascading down towards the sea. I picked out the huge cotton tree in the centre of Freetown, the burnt orange walls of the prison and the squat ugly blocks of Wilberforce Barracks. Beyond were the beaches of Man of War Bay and the lighthouse at Cape Sierra Leone.

We drove on. A small town of mud houses lined the rutted, dusty road, its surface potholed and fissured by rainwater and floods. We passed a ruined, fire-blackened building.

'That was the only petrol station between the coast and the Bohara mine,' Grizz said.

I looked again and saw its ancient petrol pump lying broken on the ground with a huge crater replacing the below-ground storage tank.

Ahead I saw the first spreads of savannah grassland, punctuated by the clustered mud huts and tiny vegetable plots of
small villages. The savannah looked lush and fertile, studded
with breadfruit, pawpaw, guava, mango, tamarind and locust
trees, but the villages were few and sparsely populated.

A handful of women and naked children working in the fields
stopped to watch us pass, their expressions wary, poised for
flight. Many of the mothers looked little more than children
themselves.

'Why so few people?' I said. 'Is it the fighting?'

'Partly,' Layla said. 'But we've also entered the region of the
tsetse and black flies. We're treating river blindness very
successfully now, but sleeping sickness still decimates the
population here.'

We drove on between walls of elephant grass as high as a man
rising on either side of us. The road curved to the left out of
sight, and as we reached the apex of the bend, Grizz hit the
brakes hard. Ahead of us a tangle of tree branches had been
thrown across the road. Beyond it stood a row of armed men.

I shot an uneasy glance at Grizz as I reached down to touch
the stock of the rifle beneath my feet. Rudi already had his
cradled across his lap, and I heard a soft click as he eased off the
safety catch. There was no way of telling whether the men were
soldiers or rebels, since all wore the same battered uniforms,
topped with whatever lurid T-shirts or other clothes they had
managed to loot. They stood in silence, fingering their weapons
and gazing at us with baleful hostility.

'I think they're government men,' Grizz said, out of the corner
of his mouth. 'Not that it makes much difference. They're
hungry and they haven't been paid. That's enough to make
anyone bad tempered. Give them some smokes.'

I reached for one of the packs of American cigarettes stashed in the back and held it out over the side of the pick-up as Grizz drove slowly forward to the makeshift barrier. The leader of the soldiers stepped forward, took the cigarettes and weighed them in his hand as if estimating their value. He remained unsmiling, his disdainful gaze ranging over each of us in turn, but after a few moments, he nodded and signalled his men to move the barrier.

As we moved off, Rudi kept the muzzle of his rifle trained on the group of men, swinging himself slowly round as we nosed through the narrow gap in the barrier, until he was facing back over the tailgate. I could see a muscle working in his cheek.

'It's okay, Rudi,' I said. 'It's sorted.'

As the men disappeared from sight, obscured by the dust trail we were laying, he turned to look at me. 'Are you telling me how to do my job?'

'No, of course not. I only meant—'

He cut across me. 'Two things you should know. Never turn your back on those black bastards.' He paused. 'And never, ever try and tell me how to go about my work again.'

'Okay. You're the man.' I dropped my gaze and found myself staring into the muzzle of his rifle. He gave a cold smile, clicked off the safety catch and laid the rifle aside. I couldn't suppress a shiver. He noticed it and his smile broadened, then he turned away, staring out over the side of the pick-up.

Tom looked at his watch. 'How much farther is it?'

Grizz pointed up the road ahead of us. 'The turn-off's just over this rise.'

We left the main road for a broad, rutted dirt-track leading away through the bush. It dog-legged right and left, and as we swung round the second bend, I saw a stretch of rusty wire fencing and a pair of open double gates, sagging at such an angle that it seemed unlikely they had been closed in years. The legend on the peeling, sun-faded signboards was just about legible: 'Sierra Leone Defence Forces, Camp 17.'

Tom shook his head. 'And this is the secure area?'

Grizz didn't reply.

Beyond the fence was a broad expanse of beaten earth and concrete hard standing. Grass and even small shrubs grew up through the cracks, and the barrack huts and buildings beyond the concrete were so ruinous it seemed inconceivable that the base could still be in use, but a squat soldier appeared from the collapsing guard house and pointed a Kalashnikov in our general direction. His scowl changed to a smile as he recognised Grizz and he made a brave attempt at a regimental salute.

Without slowing down, Grizz returned the salute and I tossed him a pack of cigarettes as we bounced and jolted our way on across the base. We rounded the corner of a barrack block and came to a halt by a helicopter parked on the concrete hard standing. It was an old American Huey, and even through the camouflage net covering it, I could see that it was rusting and riddled with holes.

'We're not flying that,' I said. 'Are we? It looks like a wreck.'

Grizz smiled. 'It is. The one you're flying is inside the hangar.' He pointed towards a building that looked like a World War Two Nissen hut, an arch of corrugated tin sheeting walled with mud bricks. Another soldier dozing by the doors leapt to attention and was rewarded with another pack of cigarettes.

Grizz kicked at the rotting wooden doors to loosen them, then we dragged them open. 'Same model,' he said, 'just better nick.'

Rudi had already turned the pick-up round and backed it up close to the doors. He ran out the winch cable and connected it to the helicopter and we began half-dragging and half-pushing it out of the building. The rotors were tied down, but even so, it cleared the doorframe by no more than a couple of inches.

I looked it over. It was covered in a thin layer of red dust and its body panels were a jigsaw of repaired and reclaimed pieces, suggesting it had had a hard and bullet-riddled life, but the rotor hubs were greased and when I opened the engine covers, the turbines looked clean and well maintained.

'It looks better than the other one, at any rate,' I said. 'Where's the engineer?'

Grizz smiled. 'You're looking at him.'

'I thought you were the door gunner,' I said.

'That too. Versatility is the first rule of these kind of ops.'

'So why keep it here? What's wrong with the airport in Freetown?'

'If we left it there, it would be impounded and flogged off by the first government minister who was short of a few quid. This way it's under our control.'

'Hardly,' I said. 'It's still guarded by government soldiers.'

He smiled. 'But the government doesn't pay them. We do. If the President says one thing and I say another, they'll do what I say.'

Rudi jumped down from the pick-up and spat in the dust. 'Besides, they know we'll kill them if they don't,' he said.

Tom glanced at me as Rudi disappeared into the gloom of the Nissen hut.

'I know,' I said. 'But he's not employed for his charm, is he?'

Rudi returned rolling a drum of aviation fuel and began topping up the tanks as Tom, Grizz and I began a detailed check of the heli. Layla settled herself to wait in the shade, but within a couple of minutes a queue of soldiers had formed next to her. All complained of aches and pains and pestered her for drugs and medicine. They wore a baffling variety of uniforms, collaged together with multi-coloured T-shirts and sandals cut from old tyres. Their weapons were a similar mixture, but the guns did at least look clean and well maintained. I suspected that might be down to Grizz, not to the army.

It took us an hour to make the initial checks on the heli. The oil pressure on one of the engines was a little low and as Grizz tinkered with it, trying to solve the problem, I strolled over and sat in the dust next to Layla, who had just sent her last patient away.

'You had quite a queue there, considering they didn't even know we were coming,' I said.

'It's the same wherever I go.'

'So what do you do?'

She met my gaze. 'Treat the sick ones as far as I'm able, and give the others a placebo – a dummy medicine.'

'And if you run out of drugs?'

She shrugged. 'Then they all get a placebo. You'd be amazed how well it works.'

'Even on the sick ones?'

'Especially on the sick ones.'

We sat in silence for a while. 'What brought you to Sierra Leone?' I said.

'I'm a medic.'

'I know, but why here?'

'Why not? They need all the help they can get. There are two million displaced people here, tens of thousands left orphans because their parents have been killed, and an infant mortality rate of almost one in five live births.

'It's all the more appalling because Sierra Leone should be one of the richest countries in the world; it has platinum, gold, iron ore, chromide, rutile, bauxite and above all diamonds. But, by any measurement you care to use, it's the poorest country on earth.

'The national wealth's all held by foreign corporations or in Swiss bank accounts. By the time mining companies – she glanced at me – 'and their mercenaries, and the president, the army officers and government officials, the rebels and everybody else with a snout in the trough have had their share, there's precious little left.

'Know what they call the mining district? The Wild West. Officially, two million carats of diamonds are being exported every year, but even on the most conservative estimates, for every one legally exported, another two are smuggled across the border. There are no diamonds in Liberia and yet there are more diamond merchants in Monrovia than there are in Amsterdam.

'Of course, some of the theft is institutional. The government has no foreign currency reserves, so instead it gives away its remaining assets at knock-down prices. Decisive Measures and its associate company are paid in mineral rights. They now get sixty per cent of the diamonds. Once they'd done that deal, they lost whatever interest they had in fighting the rebels. All they want to do is protect their diamond concessions.'

I was surprised by the vehemence in her voice. 'But the mines bring work as well.'

'Very little. The skilled jobs all go to expats and the mines are so mechanised that there's very little unskilled work.' She paused. 'When you've seen a little more of the way things are here, you'll understand my anger.'

'And Medicaid International?'

'Are willing to get involved in places where no one else will. We can't change things but we can at least help to ease the misery of people who have nowhere else to turn.' She gave me a defiant look. 'That probably sounds pompous to you.'

I shook my head. 'But how is it different from the Red Cross? Isn't that what they do?'

'No. The Red Cross is fine in many areas, but at the cutting edge, in places where the greatest threat to the citizens isn't an earthquake or a flood or a volcano but civil war or the brutality of the state, they're ineffectual. They'll do their best to make the political prisoners more comfortable, but they won't work to free them, nor utter a word of condemnation of those who have imprisoned them.'

'And Medicaid International will?'

She hesitated and her piercing blue eyes studied me before replying. 'Not as much as I might sometimes wish, but that's why it was formed: as a more radical and interventionist organisation than the Red Cross.'

She frowned, as if angry with herself for being drawn out on the subject. 'That's enough about me,' she said. 'What persuaded you to join the mercenaries?'

'They don't like to be called that, but—'

'But that's what they are, hired killers.'

'So are all soldiers.'

'And pilots.'

'And pilots.' I paused, seeing yet again in my mind the burning woman with her arms outstretched. I hurried on, trying to banish the image from my mind. 'Yes, sure. We're all trained to fight and kill; it's the last resort, but that's our job and sometimes we have to do it. In peacetime we're hated for it and in wartime people love us for it. But we're doing our government's bidding.'

'Mercenaries aren't.'

'Some aren't. Private military companies like Decisive Measures are. They're here to defend the diamond mines, but by doing that, they're also keeping the rebels at bay. They're like the armed forces, but at one remove, that's all, doing the jobs the UK doesn't want to be seen doing for itself.'

She looked across at Rudi, who was cleaning and oiling his rifle. 'Like killing Africans.'

'That's not why I'm here. You couldn't be more wrong. I'm here because I don't want to see . . .' My voice trailed away. 'Anyway, Decisive Measures would say they're here to protect Western interests.'

It sounded hollow to me even as I said it and she was quick to pounce. 'If those interests were in Europe – white Europe – the West would send its own troops, not mercenaries. They were quick enough to intervene in Bosnia and Kosovo. In Africa, no one cares.' She held my gaze. 'The lesson is obvious, isn't it?'

'You're very cynical.'

'But I'm also right, aren't I?'

I changed tack. 'Listen, I'm a trained military pilot. I've left the RAF; what else can I do?'

'Why did you leave?'

I ducked the question. 'It's a job, it's money, but please don't call me a hired killer. I'm just flying people around, dropping guys on patrols, ferrying in supplies; it's like driving a bus or a truck.'

She gave a sour laugh and pointed to the rocket pod under the body of the Huey. 'And where you come from buses are fitted with those, are they?'

I gave a rueful grin. 'Only on Saturday nights, after the pubs close.' I felt ridiculously pleased when I won an answering smile from her, but it was short-lived.

'So let me get this straight,' she said. 'You're just a driver who drops these guys off at their destination and what they do after that is none of your business? Come of it, Jack. You don't absolve yourself of responsibility just because your finger isn't on the trigger. If you're part of it, you share the guilt.'

Her look challenged me to argue, but I knew she was right and I couldn't meet her gaze. 'But if you feel so strongly about this,' I said, trying to shift the subject away from me, 'why do you work with Decisive Measures yourself?'

She searched my expression before replying. 'Because it's the lesser of two evils. We have no helicopters and very few vehicles. So I treat Decisive Measures' mercenaries and the expat workers at the Bohara mine, because it also enables me to treat the African workers there and run clinics at some of the villages in the surrounding bush.' She stared at me. 'But that doesn't mean I condone what Decisive Measures does.'

Grizz wandered over, wiping the oil from his hands with a piece of rag. He stretched and yawned. 'Don't let Layla pile too much guilt on you, Jack. Mercenaries have been a part of Sierra Leone for centuries. Chiefs, merchants and traders all hired professional warriors; the Mende tribe rented themselves out as fighting men to anyone who would pay them in tobacco, cloth or rum. They relied on rape and plunder for their real rewards, and they soon became so powerful and lawless that they grew beyond the control of any one faction.' He gave a bleak smile. 'Sound familiar? It should; nothing's changed.' He paused. 'Now if you and Comrade Layla have finished your dialectical discussion, I've got a helicopter I'd like you to fly.'

Tom and I began the pre-flight checks. I reached under the belly of the helicopter and released the drain valve. As fuel dribbled out, I checked it for signs of water and impurities, then resealed the valve.

As Tom removed the tie-down strip from the tail rotor, I climbed onto the roof, checking the rotor hub, the control rods, the transmission mounts and above all the 'Jesus nut' at the top of the mast. If it came unstuck the whole assembly would fly off, leaving me piloting the airborne equivalent of a breeze block.

I scrambled down into the cockpit. The dusty, scratched Perspex canopy was etched with the fine lines of stress patterns, casting a blurred halo around every object seen through it. I settled myself into the tiny, bone-hard seat and looked around the cockpit. Tom and I had only a three-week familiarisation course on the Huey behind us, but already it felt as familiar to me as the driving seat of a family car.

I connected the helmet and radio and we ran through the first round of cockpit checks. Then I gave the wind-up signal to Tom and pressed the starter. The turbines coughed like a man clearing his lungs with the first cigarette of the day, and puffs of blue-black smoke drifted away behind us. Then they fired, roaring into life.

I shifted the lever into flight idle and the rotors began to turn, ponderously at first then accelerating to a blur. The noise increased to a thunder and a cloud of dust rose around us, obscuring the compound.

We made the last round of pre-flight checks, a rapid-fire exchange of question and response – fuel, hydraulic pressures, oil temperature, battery temperature, turbine outlet temperature, torque gauge – and I made a particularly suspicious scrutiny of the tachometer oil pressure gauge. Whatever Grizz had done seemed to have solved the problem.

Checks complete, I flicked the intercom switch. 'All ready?'

The answers came back at once. 'I'm ready,' Tom said.

'Ready in the back,' Grizz said.

I glanced behind me and caught a glimpse of Layla's face. I gave a thumbs-up sign and she smiled and nodded in response.

I raised the collective and heard the whine of the turbines and the thunder of the rotors increase overhead. Again, a dust cloud rose around us, billowing outwards, obscuring the ground, and I felt the heli lift on its springs. I held it for a second in the no-man's-land between earth and sky, and then raised the collective again. We lifted clear of the ground, the heli juddering in the turbulence from the downwash.

The noise and vibrations decreased as we reached cleaner air, free of the ground effect. I held it in the hover while I made a further round of checks, then made a leisurely, climbing turn around the base before heading east towards Bohara. The Huey was an old model, the workhorse of the US forces in Vietnam, but it was solid, well engineered and reliable. I had no real worries about its age, but every individual heli had its own quirks and characteristics, and I wanted to be aware of them now, not in the middle of a future emergency.

The feel of the rudders was a little mushy, but the response of the cyclic and collective to my touch was crisp and positive. I glanced across at Tom. 'Happy?'

'As happy as I can be seven hours' flying time from the King's Head.'

We made the short hop to Freetown airport and loaded the heli with supplies from Decisive Measures' chained and padlocked steel storage bunkers. Then we took off again, flying out over the shanty towns, tracking the road we had taken that morning. We passed the base and flew on due east over a plain of elephant grass studded with villages of brown huts as round and fat as mushrooms pushing out of the red earth.

Clumps of tall trees cast dark shadow pools onto the baking earth and a broad river wound its way down from the distant mountains. Its banks were lined with trees, but beyond their shade, the surface of the water sparkled like silver in the glare of the sun.

Layla leaned through from the cab, resting an arm on the back of my seat. 'What do you think?'

'Looks great, doesn't it?' I said.

'From here, maybe,' Tom said. 'Get down there with no heli, and just the tsetse flies, mosquitoes and rebels for company and see how great it is.'

Layla stared at him. 'Perhaps you should reserve judgement until you've actually seen the place and met the people.'

'I don't need to. I already know what it's going to be like.'

'It must be nice to be so certain about everything.'

'Don't worry about him,' I said. 'He's got a mind like a steel trap — it's permanently closed.'

She stayed where she was, standing silent, watching me flying the Huey. 'It looks unbelievably complicated,' she said.

I glanced over my shoulder and smiled at her. 'It's not really. When we're airborne there are only four controls that matter — the rudders, the throttle, the collective and the cyclic.' I pointed towards the floor of the cockpit. 'The rudders are controlled by those foot pedals.

'On my left-hand side' — I waggled the control slightly — 'is the collective. It increases and decreases the pitch angle of both the main rotors at the same time — pull it up and the heli rises, lower it and the heli goes down. The throttle grips are on the end of the collective — you twist on more power as you raise the collective and twist it off again as you lower it.

'The cyclic is this long thin stick that comes out of the cockpit floor between my legs.' I paused. 'No bad jokes, please. The cyclic alters the pitch angle of the rotors on one half of their cycle and feathers them on the other half.'

I clocked Layla's blank look. 'Sorry,' I said. 'It's hard to break a lifetime habit of technobabble. What it boils down to is whichever way you tilt the cyclic — forward, backward, left or right — the disc of the rotors, and therefore the heli itself, will tilt in the same direction.

'That's really all there is to it . . . except that, just to make life even more complicated, none of the controls can be operated in isolation — not if you want to stay airborne anyway. Movements of the cyclic and the collective have to be synchronised; if they're not, you either find yourself diving into the ground or climbing so steeply you either stall or flip over.'

We flew east for another hour, as the terrain grew steadily higher and rougher below us. The valley bottoms remained fertile, but on the upper slopes, sparse, sun-scorched grasses and stretches of bare rock predominated.

Finally we climbed towards the last steep ridge separating us from the Bohara valley. As we cleared the ridgeline, I gasped at the desolation of the scarred, apocalyptic landscape revealed below us. The head of the valley was still forested, but as far as my eyes could see, nothing grew in the entire lower valley.

Whole forests had been felled, the ground cleared and levelled and then stripped to the bedrock. A river had been diverted from its natural course and a huge dam built, flooding a vast area with water that was a vivid, sickly shade of orange. Man-made mountains of crushed rock, the tailings from the mine-workings, rose hundreds of feet, bare of any vegetation, and punctuated only by a couple of rusting, abandoned dredges.

A few ant-like figures scurried around the monstrous machines gouging and rending at the ground. Enormous draglines ripped at the diamond-bearing gravels, biting out tens of tons of rock at a time. Massive dumpers moved in an unending procession down to a smoke-belching mill, where they dumped the gravel onto conveyor belts as wide as roads, which disappeared into the gaping maw of the plant.

More conveyor belts moved the debris away, building fresh spoil heaps that seemed to grow as I watched them, and a torrent of discoloured water flowed constantly from an opening at the base of the sheer wall of the mill, like a river emerging from beneath the face of a glacier.

A thick pall of dust hung over the whole area, but in the far distance beyond the mine I could see an ugly sprawling town, an island of a few concrete buildings rising from an ocean of mud huts and tar-paper shacks.

Nearer to the mine itself was another, much smaller shanty town surrounding two concentric circles – the perimeter fences of the mining compound. The outer fence was a surreal combination of a US cavalry fort and an army base in Belfast – a wooden palisade of sharpened stakes. It would have been no surprise to see men draped over it with arrows protruding from their torsos, but instead it was topped by a tangle of barbed wire.

Some distance inside the palisade was an altogether more modern fortification: a chainlink perimeter fence topped with coils of razor wire surrounding an inner compound. Right at its heart was a helipad of beaten red earth.

Chapter 3

I circled the compound, determining the best approach path for the landing site, clear of the worst obstacles and heading into the wind. I had done it so many hundreds, even thousands of times, that it was automatic, almost instinctive.

I came in at a steep angle, steadily decreasing the air speed as I lowered the collective. I increased the backward pressure on the cyclic, and pushed the nose of the heli upwards, flaring towards the landing. The downwash threw up such a dense cloud of red dust that I had to use the artificial horizon indicator to hold the craft level. Turbulence from the ground threw the helicopter around as we descended the last few feet. I levelled the nose just before we touched down, but still made a heavy landing, thumping down onto the springs.

I shut down the engines, stripped off my flying helmet and wiped the sweat from my forehead as the wind from the slowing rotors blew away the last traces of the dust cloud. Then I climbed stiffly down from the cockpit to join the others.

A tall, dark-haired man was waiting to greet us. He was in civilian clothes, but he wore them like a uniform; everything from his immaculately parted and combed hair, to his rolled down sleeves and sharp-creased trousers marked him out as an ex-army officer.

'Welcome to Bohara,' he said. 'I'm Colonel Henry Pleydell, CEO of Decisive Measures, but don't worry' – he did his best to twinkle at us – 'this is just a flying visit. I'll not be here keeping an eye on you chaps all of the time. We're here to protect the integrity of this site and ensure the smooth running of this, one of the world's largest diamond mines. That' – he gestured beyond the fence to the town just visible in the distance – 'that was a cluster of half a dozen huts when diamonds were discovered here. It's now a town of 75,000 people, the biggest in the country after Freetown. The main street was originally the dumper line for trucks taking gravel to the processing plant. You can see how far we've come – in every sense – since then.'

He spoke with the same ponderous, pompous quality as a golf club president proposing the loyal toast at the annual dinner. Tom glanced at me and rolled his eyes, but Pleydell was not to be stopped in mid-flow. 'Most of the processes are automated. There are few hand operations because of the chances for pilfering they allow, but there are also thousands of illegal miners.'

His lips pursed in distaste as he uttered the words. 'They work at night in the hope of avoiding our security and they make a bloody nuisance of themselves. Areas levelled for mechanical mining one day are often scarred with hand-dug pits by the next morning.' He paused. 'Any questions?'

'Just one,' Tom said. 'Isn't one of the world's largest diamond mines worth rather more protection than a fifth-hand Huey and a platoon of' – he paused, looked around him, then chose the polite wording – 'soldiers?'

Pleydell studied him for a moment. 'I wouldn't lose any sleep over that. A platoon of highly trained well-paid soldiers should be more than a match for the rabble the rebels can put in the field. And the Huey is not only a fine aircraft in its own right, it's also streets ahead of anything that the rebels have to offer. Well, if there's nothing else? Then I hope you enjoy your stay here.'

It was hard to tell if he was being ironic. As he turned aside to consult with one of the mining engineers, I took a look around his kingdom. All around the inside of the outer palisade were palm-roofed sheds that looked like Japanese prison huts of World War Two. The wattle-and-daub walls had been crudely constructed and there were small cairns all along the foot of the walls, where the dried mud had been washed out by the tropical rains.

Layla followed my gaze. 'The native workers live in them,' she said. 'The mine operates twenty-four hours a day, seven days a week and the miners work twelve hours on, twelve hours off. They use a "hot-bed" system.' Her gaze flickered to Pleydell, then back to me. 'The day shift sleep in the beds the night shift have just vacated. They're crammed forty to a hut that would comfortably accommodate less than half that number. Some of their wives and dependents live in the shanties just outside the wire. Of course, if the rebels attack . . .'

She broke off as Pleydell began shaking hands all round, then he climbed into a heavily armoured, long wheelbase Landrover. Six mercenaries took up gun positions on it and it drove out of the gates and disappeared down the road in a cloud of dust.

'So it's back to the golf course for the colonel then,' Grizz said, turning away.

I continued my scrutiny of the base. The stanchions of observation towers and floodlights punctuated the chainlink and razor wire fence surrounding the inner compound, and the steady bass thud of generators showed that whatever the power supply problems in Sierra Leone, these lights were never extinguished.

Rusting shipping containers stood just inside the gates, their doors chained and padlocked. One stood ajar and I could see racks of tools and mining equipment. Tanks of diesel and petrol for the heavy machinery and drums of aviation fuel for the helicopter were kept nearby in a padlocked wire cage.

Eight more shipping containers had been stacked together in a double-tiered block in the centre of the compound. Door and window openings had been cut into them with oxy-acetylene torches, and steel grilles had been welded over the windows.

A huge palm-frond roof with a satellite dish protruding through it covered the containers; supported on scaffolding and long bush poles, it gave some shade and shelter from the heat of the sun. The whole ramshackle construction was surrounded by an earth mound, capped with a sandbag wall pierced by firing slits. It was obviously the last redoubt. If the rebels stormed the outer compounds, this is where the mercenaries would make their stand.

A row of single-storey houses built of rendered breeze blocks surrounded it, the accommodation for the expatriate workers. The doors, windows and roofs were also shielded by sandbags, and awnings erected around the sides gave the houses a little shade. There were sun-loungers, swing-seats and barbecues on the stoops, and inside each house, no doubt, were video cassette recorders and wide-screen TVs, freezers full of steaks, and fridges full of cold beer. It could almost have been a prosperous suburb of Virginia on a sunny afternoon, except for what lay beyond the fortified and patrolled perimeter fence.

Beyond the houses, at the far end of the compound, another shipping container had been dug into the ground so that only the top quarter protruded from the earth. Its exposed walls and roof were heavily sandbagged.

'That's the armoury and magazine,' Grizz said. 'The shithouse is just alongside it. Just follow the flies.'

Tom wrinkled his nose. 'I'd hate that stinking shithole to blow while I was taking a dump,' he said.

'It wouldn't be too great for anyone, would it? Those who weren't killed would be covered in shit.'

We walked over to the central building. Layla peeled off to begin her clinic, with a row of Africans waiting patiently in the dust by the piles of wood stacked next to the fire pit where the cooking was done. Some of the men had bloodstained bandages on their arms and legs.

Grizz saw my look. 'Just mining accidents,' he said. 'We haven't had a contact with the rebels for a few months now. They got their arses kicked last time they tried it.'

We filed through a gap in the sandbagged walls and Grizz showed us around the building. The mining company used the upper tier for offices. The front half of the lower tier served as a combined mess hall, satellite TV lounge, briefing room and relaxation area for the mercenaries, and the end section was used as a dormitory. Rudi had already bagged a spare bunk and made himself comfortable. Tom and I chose a couple as far away from him as possible.

Most of the other soldiers were lazing in chairs, watching videos. An arsenal of weapons was propped against the walls around them. We were introduced to them: white officers and NCOs, commanding black troops. There were few of the latter in evidence and I wondered if their quarters were with the black workers beyond the wire. From their accents, the majority of the white soldiers were Rudi's fellow-countrymen, but there were five Englishmen, two of whom claimed to be ex-SAS.

'I'm from Hereford, enough said,' one growled as he crushed my hand in an iron handshake. 'Call me Raz, everybody else does.' He was at least a couple of years younger than me, with keen blue eyes and a square, pugnacious chin.

'That's my mate Reuben,' he said, pointing out another young mercenary with a round, moon face and a disconcerting facial tic that made him blink his eyes in a constant rapid motion. It gave him an air of being permanently surprised. He blinked, raised an arm in greeting, blinked, smiled, blinked again and turned his attention back to the television.

'The thick-looking one is Hendrik,' Raz said, gesturing towards a skinheaded bull of a man, who was picking his teeth with the point of a knife. He gave us a curt nod at the mention of his name. 'Don't let his table manners put you off,' Raz said. 'He's not a bad guy – for a South African.'

The three of them were the only ones who bothered to shift their eyes away from the television screen.

'Friendly boys, your mates,' Tom said.

Raz shrugged. 'They do the job and that's all that counts. If you came here to socialise, you chose the wrong place. It's a good posting if you want to save a few quid; there's fuck-all to spend it on, that's for sure.'

I hadn't worked alongside mercenaries before, but from what I'd heard, even more than regular soldiers or expatriates, they showed a complete indifference to the culture, politics and history of the country in which they operated. They did what they had to do and then went home. They were throwbacks, fighting and fucking on every continent, killing because they were told to kill, lining their pockets where they could, then moving on to the next conflict, the next war-ravaged country. Now I was one of them – in Layla's eyes at least.

We left them to their videos and moved back to the dining area. Grizz reached into the battered old fridge and passed Tom and me a beer.

'There don't seem to be too many recruits from Sierra Leone,' I said.

Grizz gave me a sharp look. 'Don't you start, I get enough of that from Layla. The theory for public consumption is that we're here to train the Sierra Leone forces to defend themselves.' He gave a brief, sour smile. 'The practice is that since most of them don't even get paid enough to piss on, the majority will disappear at the first opportunity and join the rebels or anyone else who offers the chance for a bit of plunder. So there's no point in training and arming them when they're just going to either sell their weapons to the rebels or desert and join them.

'In any case, the army and the rebels often seem to be working hand in glove. You'd be amazed how frequently the army pulls out of a village shortly before a rebel attack. When the rebels have scared away all the villagers they haven't killed or kidnapped, and retreated with all the plunder they can carry, the army moves back in and steals the rest.'

I glanced around and dropped my voice. 'What about those guys you're working with?' I said. 'Are those two real Hereford or bullshitters?'

'Bullshitters from top to bottom. Pleydell was a Guards counter-terrorist expert, if that isn't a contradiction in terms. One of the other guys is an ex-Para – a damn good soldier. The rest are infantrymen or South African veterans of the bush wars against the ANC. They're psychotic fuckers. I'd give them a wide berth, if I were you.'

'Wider than I give Rudi, you mean?'

He smiled. 'No, just the same distance.'

As if on cue, there was a sudden burst of firing from outside. It provoked an instant flurry of activity. Soldiers who had been recumbent a moment before, grabbed their helmets and weapons and sprinted for the door.

One of them, Reuben, was carrying an RPG launcher. He slapped on a round as he ran for the door, but in doing so, he dropped the weapon. As it hit the floor it went off. The grenade blasted upwards, hit the sandbagged metal roof, rebounded and, tumbling drunkenly end over end, landed a few feet away. Grizz had hit the deck the instant it fired. The rest of us had not even had the time or presence of mind to react. We stood there, rooted to the spot, as the seconds crawled by.

It failed to explode. As the ringing in my ears began to subside, I wiped the cold sweat from my forehead and glanced around.

Reuben still stood there. 'Jesus.' Before he could say anything else, Grizz strode across the room and felled him with a single punch. Reuben stared up at him through the fingers he had clamped over his smashed and bleeding nose.

Grizz glared down at him. 'Be glad I didn't shoot you, you stupid bastard. You could have killed us all.' He turned away and ran outside.

There was no further shooting and Grizz and the others soon returned. 'No big deal,' he said. 'A couple of rebels taking a few pot-shots. A patrol's gone out, but they'll have legged it by now.'

I gave it a few moments before I spoke, but my voice still cracked a little. 'Why didn't the RPG explode?'

Grizz glanced up at the dent in the roof. 'Sheer bloody good luck,' he said. 'The grenade's designed to spin a few revolutions before it arms itself – a safety measure to ensure it doesn't blow up the guy who's just fired it. The tin roof must have been solid enough to stop it spinning just in time.'

None of the mercenaries moved to help Reuben, still clutching his broken nose. He stood up and shambled outside, leaving a trail of bright drops of blood in the dust. When he returned, his nose was swathed in a dressing. He avoided meeting Grizz's gaze and sat by himself in a corner.

The sight of the bandage reminded me that Layla had been outside right through the shooting. I hurried out into the bright sunlight. The queue waiting for treatment had dwindled to a handful of people. I stepped back into the shade by the door and watched Layla as she worked, admiring both the patience she showed as she listened to each person's tale, and the speed and skill with which she examined, diagnosed and treated them.

Some of the African workers had brought their wives and children into the inner compound to be treated and even the smallest child, a little boy, showed no fear as Layla examined him, one of her slender hands stroking his forehead to soothe him as she tested his distended stomach wall with the other hand. She gave the parents a reassuring smile, but I saw her bleak look as they turned away with the medicine she had given them.

She started as I stepped out of the shadows next to her. 'Sorry,' I said. 'Didn't mean to startle you. Was that a placebo?'

She nodded. 'But it won't do any good in that case.' I heard a catch in her voice as she spoke.

'Is there anything you can do for him?'

'Not really. In the UK I'd have sent him straight to hospital to be examined by a specialist, but here . . .' She gestured hopelessly around us.

'We could fly him to Freetown.'

She looked up in surprise. 'You obviously haven't read the Decisive Measures manual — no inessential passengers allowed.'

'Sod the manual. If it's a matter of life and death, let's do it and worry about it afterwards.'

'Thanks.' I felt the cool touch of her fingers on my arm. 'But it's not that simple. Even in Freetown there are neither the drugs nor the expertise to cure him, and he'll be far from his parents and his village if – when – the worst happens. It's better that he stays here.'

'So is there nothing we can do for him?'

'Only pray.'

She turned to her last patient, a frightened looking, elderly man. A cloud of flies buzzed around the ugly gunshot wound in his arm.

'The rebels?' I said.

Layla spoke to him in his local language, then shook her head. 'The mine guards. As Pleydell said, there's a lot of illicit mining. Nice people you work for, Jack.' She held my gaze until I looked away.

By the time she had cleaned and dressed the wound, night was falling.

'I've never got used to how quickly the sun sets in the Tropics,' I said. 'I really miss those long summer evenings back home.'

'Me too.' She fell silent, staring up at the darkening sky.

'Where is home for you?'

'Don't laugh, I'm an Essex girl; not the best place to grow up for someone of my—' She hesitated. 'Of my background.'

'What do you mean?'

'What do you think I mean?' She shot me a suspicious look, searching my expression before she spoke again. 'My mother was a nurse. She met my dad when he was in hospital after an accident at work. He'd been an engineer in Guyana; the only job he could ever get in England was on the assembly line at

Dagenham.' She shrugged. 'I don't know. Maybe things are different there now, but it seemed to me that I was always too black for some and too white for others. Of course, when I grew up, most of the guys wanted to get into my pants.' Her look challenged me to argue.

She fell silent and gave a slow shake of her head. 'I don't know why I'm even telling you this. You're no different – just another white mercenary that fancies his chances with me.'

'That's not true.'

'Isn't it?'

I looked around. It was now full dark. A solitary soldier was patrolling the perimeter wire, his boots scuffing in the dust. There seemed to be no one else around. The diggers, draglines and dump-trucks had fallen silent, and though the low rumble of the crushing plant continued in the distance, the night was unnaturally quiet.

The normal noise of the African bush and forest – the chatter of monkeys, the croaking of frogs and the whine and buzz of a billion insects – was absent. In this valley of desolation, almost nothing moved except men and machines.

The night had a strange beauty of its own, however. The stars dusting the sky overhead were mirrored by a myriad pinpricks of soft lights, moving slowly through the mine workings like glowworms in the darkness of some vast cave.

'What are they?' I said.

Layla stirred and turned to look. 'The illicit miners. They work at night by candle- or lantern-light. They dig out the gravel and carry it in baskets on their heads to the nearest stream. They sieve and jig it, then turn it upside down and hand-pick any diamonds.' She paused. 'If they have time before the guard patrols chase them away or shoot them.'

'There must be at least a thousand of them.'

'Why be surprised? There's no other work to be had. Many of them used to farm during the wet season, growing the year's food to supplement the fish they caught in the rivers. Then they'd prospect for diamonds in the dry season. Now the mines have destroyed or flooded most of the farmland, and wrecked the fisheries too. The country was once self-sufficient in rice; now the bulk of it's imported.

'The diamond leases always include clauses requiring the companies to rehabilitate the land, but they're never enforced.' She gestured towards the far side of the valley. 'One area over there was reclaimed and planted with oil palms, but a couple of years later the price of diamonds went up sharply and the palms were ripped up again as they reworked the old tailings. They've never been replanted.'

She searched my face for a moment in the glow of light from the open door of the building. 'If you want to see the real Sierra Leone, come with me tomorrow. I'm doing a clinic in Boroyende, a village a few miles north. Some of what you'll see is far from pleasant – when things are bad here, they're worse than anywhere else on earth – but if you've eyes to see, it can be inspiring too. It'll give you an insight into what the country could be like if the war ever ends and the mines start to be run for the benefit of Sierra Leone, not Britain and America.'

'All right,' I said. 'I'd like that.'

She gave me a dazzling smile. 'Good. Now I'm pretty tired and we have an early start in the morning. I'm going to get some sleep.'

She walked across the compound to one of the single-storey, breeze-block houses. As she closed the door and walked through the house I saw her shadow outlined against the blinds. I stood watching for some time before I went back inside.

Grizz gave me an old-fashioned look when I asked him if I could go with Layla.

'I've told you, you're wasting your time with her.'

'That's not why I want to go,' I said, failing even to convince myself.

'Then why do you?'

'To – to see what it's like.'

'I can tell you that. If you like disease, deprivation and mutilation, you're in for a treat.'

I remained impassive. 'So can I go?'

'Yeah, I suppose so. I could do with the time up here to lick these useless bastards into shape. But don't get captured by the rebels, for Christ's sake. They're not that far from Boroyende and we had enough trouble getting you out here; I don't want to have to start searching for another helicopter jockey all over again. Take a rifle as well as your pistol, and as much ammunition as you can carry. And be back in time to get us back to Freetown before dark.'

As I walked down the room towards my bunk, Grizz's mocking voice came floating after me. 'Oh and Jack? Want Tom to come with you for company?'

'If he wants to,' I said.

'No chance,' Tom said. 'I'll let you do the tourist bit. I'm quite happy here, thank you very much.'

I smiled to myself as I stretched out on my bunk.

Raz and Reuben were sprawled over their bunks next to me. They looked up from the tattered paperbacks they were reading, as if glad of any diversion. 'You'll never be able to give those back to the mobile library,' I said.

Raz smiled. 'It's the same book, the only one we've got. We cut it in half and swop over when we've read our half.'

'Bit of a bugger if you get the second half of the book first.'

He shrugged. 'It doesn't matter. Sometimes it's more fun trying to guess what happened beforehand than what's going to happen in the end.' He yawned and stretched. 'So, your first night at the Bohara Hilton. What's it to be — baccarat, roulette, or just a gourmet dinner and a 200-dollar whore sent up to your room?'

I smiled. 'Which of those was it that tempted you up to this palace of delights, Raz?'

'Just the money, Jack. Just the money. Me and Reuben go back a long way together — we even enlisted in the army at the same time. We've got big plans for a business, haven't we, mate?'

Reuben raised his eyes from his book and nodded. 'Just don't go giving them away to every bloke you're talking to, that's all.'

'As if,' Raz said.

Reuben grunted and looked down again. I could see his lips moving slightly as he read.

'You need capital in business though,' Raz said, as if he were quoting from some government pamphlet. 'And we didn't have too much of that, so we signed up for a couple of years here — it's all tax free and there's a cash lump sum when we finish.'

'But why be a mercenary?' I said. 'There's plenty of work in bodyguarding, isn't there?'

He gave me a patient smile. 'Have you ever tried body-guarding work? If there's a more boring way to earn a living, I've yet to find it. It almost makes sentry duty at Aldershot look attractive. Ninety-nine per cent of the time you're hanging around waiting while the client has a tom-tit or a wank or a three-hour lunch. Sometimes you hang about freezing your nuts off all day and then get stood down again. And even worse is when you get sent to babysit the client's wife while she spends a few oil wells' worth in Harrods and Harvey Nicks. And the money isn't even that flash any more. Anyone who's ever held a rifle thinks he can bodyguard; there's too many of them and the rate's gone right down. No, bollocks to that. We've done that, haven't we, mate?'

Reuben nodded without even raising his eyes from the page.

'You might as well be dead,' Raz said. 'Give me something with a bit of action, a bit of juice and a decent wodge of cash at the end of it any day of the week.'

'Even when you're getting shot at as well?'

''Course.' He paused. 'You must feel the same way or you wouldn't be here, would you?'

'Erm, no,' I said. 'I suppose I wouldn't.'

I turned over and closed my eyes. I lay there replaying in my mind the shadow shape of Layla's body outlined against the blind, trying to hold off sleep as long as I could, knowing that the familiar nightmare would once more be lying in wait.

I got up as soon as the first grey light of dawn showed in the sky, but by the time I'd showered and grabbed some breakfast, Layla was already waiting for me. I started to walk towards the Huey.

'I don't know where you're going,' she said, 'but I'm heading for Boroyende. We drive part of the way and then walk the rest.' She climbed into the driving seat of one of the mine pick-ups.

'The mining companies do have some uses, then,' I said.

She gave me a sharp look. 'It's no special privilege. It's part of the deal with Medicaid International.'

We drove out of the gates of the inner and outer compounds and through the shanty town outside. Impassive faces glanced at the mine vehicle, but when they saw Layla at the wheel, there were smiles, waves and shouts of recognition.

'Quite a fan club,' I said.

'I try and help them, that's all.'

We drove up a steep track skirting the spoil heaps from the mine and climbing the bare rock wall of the valley towards the ridge. The narrow summit plateau bridged two vastly different worlds. Behind was bare rock, polluted water, the din of heavy machinery and ugly shanty towns shrouded in a pall of dust and smoke.

Ahead of us was an apparently unspoilt, lush valley, a patchwork of villages and small fields, surrounded by broad swathes of dense forest. Only as we began to descend the hillside did I start to see the scars of war on the land – smashed and burned buildings, splintered trees and abandoned fields slowly reverting to forest.

We drove on towards the distant mountains. The vegetation grew more sparse and patchy and the few tribespeople looked desperately poor and thin. Some men were dressed in rags, others wore no clothes at all. All carried pangas – bush knives.

'They subsist on slash-and-burn agriculture,' Layla said, as if reading my thoughts. 'In most of the last few years, the fighting has forced many of them to flee before they've even been able to harvest their crops.' She shrugged. 'Some say it's deliberate; the rebels and the government forces drive them out, then share the crops between themselves.'

Some villages had disappeared altogether, their sites only detectable from the overgrown orange and mango trees and the circles of burned, blackened earth, already colonised by seedlings, where huts had been torched.

Layla pulled up at another set of ruins and parked the pick-up.

'What now?' I said.

'We walk.'

'And the pick-up?'

'Will be all right here, unless the rebels come.'

'I'll just make sure.' I opened the bonnet, pulled off the plug leads and slipped them into my pocket. I picked up my rifle and a rucksack heavy with ammunition, and followed Layla through the ghost village and out along a well-worn path leading away into the forest. It was green and cool at first, after the heat of the sun, but before long our clothing was soaked with sweat.

We walked for an hour, Layla unhesitatingly choosing a branch as the path forked or merged with others. We crossed one straighter and broader than the others and beneath my feet through the leaf-mould I felt the roughness of gravel, I stooped and cleared away an area of leaf-mould and picked up a handful of grey ballast. Nearby was the rotting ghost of a baulk of timber like a railway sleeper.

Layla answered my unspoken question. 'It's the track of the old railway line,' she said. 'It was closed and abandoned twenty years ago, but they still use part of it as a track.'

We walked on and eventually the path we were following widened into a green track and small, cultivated fields began to appear, niches carved out of the enclosing wall of the forest. We passed women plodding along the side of the track with head-loads of firewood, and men carrying hoes and pangas striding out towards their fields.

All gazed warily at my rifle, but broke into broad welcoming smiles as they recognised Layla. Many of them embraced her and the women held up babies for her inspection, their faces glowing with pride. Layla was soon surrounded by them and she stopped to carry out her first impromptu treatment at the side of the track.

I walked the last few yards to the village alone. I had seen a brief flurry of movement through the screening branches as I walked along the track, but by the time I reached the heart of the village, it appeared to be deserted. The men were in the fields, and some of the women and children were gathering wood or fetching water from the river I could hear rippling through the trees, but the rest must simply have fled at the sound of a stranger's approach.

The path ended in a clearing of beaten earth. A breadfruit tree stood in the centre, casting a pool of shade. Around the edge of the clearing were ranged a dozen mud-walled huts, roofed with palm thatch.

I glanced inside the first hut; it was empty. The earth floor was swept clean, the cooking pots and bowls were stacked on a shelf nailed between two of the stout bush poles supporting the roof, and the sleeping mats were neatly rolled. I had been in far worse English houses.

The next hut must have belonged to the village carpenter. There were tools with the dull glint of age and the patina of constant use, and a handful of nails burnished where they had been hammered to straighten them. There were also scraps of wire, rope and string and a broken saw-blade refitted with an improvised handle. The furniture included a beautifully carved and jointed rocking chair that any English craftsman would have been proud to have made.

I stepped back outside and a moment later Layla joined me. 'That was quite a welcome you got back there.'

She gave a self-deprecating smile. 'I've known them a long time. I was actually based in Boroyende for three years when I first came out here and I've been doing clinics in the village ever since – eight years altogether. I've nursed them through a few illnesses and diseases, delivered their children, come to their weddings.' A shadow passed over her face. 'And the funerals of those I could do nothing for. They're good people. They deserve a lot better deal from life than they've had in recent years.'

She walked to the centre of the clearing and called out. Slowly the frightened people began to reappear from the forest. A grizzled, white-haired old man led the way. He embraced Layla and talked animatedly to her in one of the local languages.

She gave halting replies, pausing frequently as she searched for the right word, then she turned and gestured to me. Whatever she said must have been reassuring, for the old man gave a broad smile and shook my hand.

'This is Njama,' she said to me. 'He understands a little English, if you speak slowly.'

I introduced myself and made the ritual congratulations on the beauty of the village and the health of the crops. He smiled, bowing his head in acknowledgement, then clapped his hands and signalled for food to be brought. They had little enough but it was shared without a second thought.

As people moved around the village, I noticed that several of them had only one arm. 'What happened to them?' I said.

'The rebels,' Layla said. 'Anyone suspected of supporting the wrong side at the election had their arm severed in punishment. You get the idea: cut off the arm that voted for the government. Thousands of people were mutilated. You see them everywhere.'

Layla studied me for a moment. 'Other, even worse things are done every day here,' she said. 'The names of the rebel leaders tell you all you need to know about them: Jepeh-Gutu – "short talk under torture"; Darea-Gbo – "I will flog you until your body covers your feet"; and Kebalai – "one whose basket is never full" . . . because he kills so many.

'For every soldier that dies, nine civilians perish, and since Islam requires respect for the dead, their victims are mutilated and sometimes skinned while still alive. The government soldiers are little, if any, better. Villagers like these are caught in the middle, maltreated, and preyed upon by both sides. The miracle is that they keep their decency and their humanity in the face of such horrors.'

She looked past me and called out to a boy, loitering at the edge of the clearing. He hesitated, then made his way over to us. He stayed close to Layla, as he looked shyly up at me from her side. He seemed no more than nine years old, but when his gaze met mine, the sad, world-weary eyes of a far older man looked back at me.

'Kaba is from a different tribe,' Layla said. 'But Njama's people have taken him in. He has no family of his own.' She stroked his hair as she spoke. 'His tribe are traditional hunters. Their weapons were old and primitive but they rearmed themselves with those of their dead enemies . . . and if you can't find a Kalashnikov on the battlefield, you can buy one for the price of a chicken. At first, they fought to defend their villages against the army and the rebels alike, but then they were recruited by the government as mercenaries or forcibly conscripted by the rebels.

'When the rebels attack a village, they usually kill the adults and take the children. The boys are formed into "Small Boys Units", brutalised, drugged and sent into battle. They become so indoctrinated that children as young as eight speak only in military jargon. They talk of "rations" rather than food, and when they are happy – which is rare – they say they "have good morale". They're highly valued as soldiers because they're fearless and take no prisoners. They go into battle believing that they can disappear at will and that bullets cannot hurt them.'

'And has their belief in their own invulnerability survived the evidence of their friends dying around them?'

She shrugged. 'They are told that if one of them dies, it is because he has broken one of the myriad rules governing their way of fighting. They are not allowed to have sex with a woman before they fight. Kaba was too young anyway. He was especially valued because virgin boys have the strongest juju, the strongest magic to turn bullets into water.'

'And virgin girls?'

'They face an equally horrible fate. The older ones are used as camp prostitutes. They are discarded or killed when they become pregnant. There is also a belief among many Africans that the only cure for Aids is to have sex with a virgin. The result is that girls as young as two years old are raped and contaminated with the Aids virus.'

She paused, looking away from us towards two small girls playing in the dust. As I followed her gaze, I saw their sallow faces, and their skin tight-stretched over their bones and disfigured by open sores, over which flies crawled.

When Layla turned back towards me, I saw a tear glistening in the corner of her eye. 'Kaba speaks good English,' she said, at length. 'Let him tell you his story.' She gave the boy a gentle smile and held his hand as he began to speak.

'I was a captain in one of the Small Boys Units,' he said. 'I had six bodyguards of my own and many troops. Our job was to cut off people's hands, to kill and burn houses. I was promoted because I did it well. The rebels gave us tablets with our food. They gave us power; they made us brave.'

'They feed them a mixture of amphetamines, marijuana, alcohol and gunpowder,' Layla said.

'It made our hearts strong,' Kaba said. 'We were not afraid of anything. We killed many, many people. Sometimes we drank the blood of those we had killed. The men ate the hearts and livers, as well. We boys were not allowed to eat people, but we all drank the blood. We were told it gave us power.'

I shuddered to hear tales of such horror from the mouth of a nine-year-old child. 'What happened to your parents?'

'They are dead.' He hesitated, twisting his hands together. 'I killed them. The rebels captured me and told me, "Kill your mother and father, and your brothers and sisters, or we will kill you." I had to set fire to our own home. I saw them dying.'

He pulled his hand away from Layla's and walked back across the clearing. As we sat down to eat I felt his dark, brooding eyes upon me. As Layla talked to me about the village, I saw her eyes frequently stray towards Kaba, still sitting alone at the edge of the clearing. His story had left me with little appetite, but out of politeness I took a little of the dried, smoked fish and rice.

'As you can see, it's a limited but adequate and very healthy diet,' Layla said, 'provided they can harvest their rice undisturbed. They also eat fruit, potato leaf, cassava and okra, and catch fish in traps.'

She handed me a trap. It was beautifully made, a delicate cylinder of woven grass and reeds, the filaments so fine they were almost invisible.

A jug of palm oil was passed round and poured over the food. 'It makes it more palatable,' Layla said. 'They use palm oil for everything. They cook with it and preserve food in it; fish in oil keeps for months. It's also mixed with ashes and used as soap. It looks strange – it's black – but it's both medicated and medicinal. You'll find most things here have at least a dual purpose. They weave cloth not only for clothes and bedding but also as currency; you can barter almost anything for it. And white cloth is given as a symbol of peace.'

'Not much demand for white cloth these days, then?'

Njama had been listening intently to our conversation. He began to speak to me, partly in English and partly in his own language, pausing frequently to allow Layla to translate. 'We have lived here for many generations, our land is good, but we have lost too many people. The rebels come, or the government soldiers, it does not matter. Both sides steal or burn our crops. We try to hide in the bush, but they kill any men and women they find, and take our children away.'

He pointed towards the ruins of a building on the edge of the village. 'We worked for years to build a school for our children. My own children were babies when we began. Three times the rebels or the soldiers burned it or destroyed it and three times we rebuilt it.

'When the rebels returned and burned it again, we had no more heart to rebuild it once more. My children – those that are left – are now grown men. I don't believe the school will ever be built now, not even in their children's lifetimes.'

His expression had such sadness and yet such dignity that there was a lump in my throat as I waited for him to continue.

He gestured around him. 'In these times, we dare not even stray far from the village. We have to clear and cultivate where we can, when we can. Our fathers left the land fallow for twenty years after cropping. Now it is six, five, even four. And the monkeys, the baboons, the brush deer and the birds take as much of our crops as the rebels do. We've tried to dam the streams through the swamps to grow more rice, but they only become sandy and infertile. It's best to leave them and plant only where nature allows.'

As soon as we had finished eating, a queue of patients formed for Layla to examine. As she worked, Njama took my arm and led me away across the village towards his hut. He ushered me inside.

His sons, four beetle-browed men ranging in age from twenty to thirty, I guessed, followed us in. It was a few minutes before I realised that three of the four had had their right hands severed at the wrist. Njama's lips tightened as he intercepted my look, but he allowed no other emotion to show on his face.

The sons stared at me but did not speak as their father proudly showed me around. The internal walls were bare mud. The men's weapons – pangas, spears and a hunting rifle so old it qualified as an antique – hung from pegs and nails driven into the walls. The stock of the rifle was decorated with carvings, metal studs and scraps of plastic tape.

The family's few other possessions were perched on a rickety wooden shelf. The hut had largely been furnished with war surplus. A line of shell casings held water, rice, dried fish and palm oil, and metal from the doors and body panels of wrecked vehicles had been beaten into plates and bowls.

Njama pointed to the window openings in the hut, glazed with brittle plastic sheeting that rattled in the wind. The pieces were yellow with age, and scratched almost to opacity by wind-driven sand and grit, but they were the only windows in the village.

When I had finished admiring them, he raised his eyes to the ceiling, his face glowing with pride. I followed his gaze and found myself staring at a fly-specked electric light bulb dangling from the thatched roof.

Baffled, wondering if this was purely for decoration or some bizarre form of cargo cult, I turned to Njama for an explanation. He walked to the wall and pulled a switch. The light bulb lit with a feeble glow, casting a fitful light into the dark recesses of the hut.

I shook my head in disbelief. 'How?'

He laughed, unable to conceal his pleasure at dumbfounding me, then led me out and around the side of the hut. We walked down to the edge of the river, where he stood back with his hands on his hips, still beaming with pride. Stripped of its tyre, the rusting wheel of a truck had been set up on an axle fixed to the riverbank. Rough metal paddle blades, cut from the same truck's bodywork, had been fixed at intervals around the rim. They spun in the current, powering a dynamo.

I smiled and inclined my head in tribute to his ingenuity. 'You remind me of my father. When I was a small boy, he was always out in his shed in our garden, trying to find uses for bits of metal and wire or the motor from an old vacuum cleaner.'

I reached in my pocket and took out my Swiss Army penknife. I showed him the different tools and blades, then folded it up and pressed it into his hand. His eyes filled with tears. He shook my hand, then turned away to show the knife to his sons. They clustered around him, exclaiming at each new blade or tool that he produced from the handle, like a conjuror pulling rabbits from a hat.

When I made as if to leave, Njama detained me for a moment. He took my hand and stared hard into my eyes. 'You will not take Layla away from us?' he said.

I shrugged, embarrassed. 'I hardly know her. We work together, that's all.'

He smiled. 'But I have seen the way you look at her.' He studied me again. 'I think you will bring her happiness.' He spread his hands, encompassing the whole village. 'And if you do that, you will have many friends here.'

I was silent most of the way back from the village, mulling over what I had seen and heard. Layla glanced across at me frequently as we walked along the forest path away from the village and drove back over the ridge to Bohara. 'It's both better and worse than I imagined,' I said at last. 'They have nothing and yet they have everything they need. But when you hear Njama or Kaba talk . . .' I fell silent once more, seeing Kaba's young-old face in my mind as he recounted those unspeakable horrors in his flat, expressionless voice.

'I wish there was something I could do for them,' I said.

Layla gave me a sharp glance. 'There is. But you have to be willing to work for someone like Medicaid for the benefit of the villagers, not the mercenaries and the mining corporations. I'm not sure you'd be able to do that.'

It was more of a question than a statement. I didn't reply.

Chapter 4

We collected Grizz and Tom from Bohara and flew back to Freetown that afternoon. The flight had been uneventful and as I swung in towards the base, I was already thinking about a cold beer when there was a sudden silence. The whine of the turbines had disappeared. In its place there was just the rush of wind and the chopping noise of the rotors, slowing even as I became aware of it. Then there was the scream of a siren.

I shouted a warning. 'Engine failure. Prepare for auto-rotative landing. Get back in the cab, Layla. Hold on for your life.'

There was no time to think; autorotation needs instant reactions. Before my brain had fully processed the information, my hands were already making instinctive adjustments to the controls. A helicopter in free-fall drops at around 1,700 feet per minute. Already under 200 feet, I had less than six seconds to react to the power failure, move the collective and adjust the pitch angle, identify a clear area and land in it.

If we'd already been in the hover, I'd have held the collective steady until we were inches from the ground and then forced it up to cushion the landing, but in flight trim I had to ram the collective full down at once to neutralise the pitch angle of the rotors. If they remained at flying angle, the blades would slow and stop immediately. Rigid in flight because of the centrifugal force, the blades would fold up like a bird folding its wings, with similar results.

Once I'd neutralised the pitch angle and the rotor blades were flat, even though the Huey was still in free fall, the uprushing air as the heli dropped would continue to turn the rotors and provide enough uplift to cushion the impact with the ground. That was the theory, at least.

There was a clear, roughly level patch of land just inside the perimeter of the base. I aimed straight at it and fifty feet from the ground I hauled back on the cyclic to flare the heli and bleed off the forward airspeed down to zero. I kept the nose in the flare as we plummeted groundwards, then at the last minute I pulled enough pitch to level it.

We crashed down with a sickening thud. My teeth crunched together and my neck was whipped back into the headrest. The heli bottomed on its springs and gave an almost human groan as it bounced up again. We came to a rest, canted at a slight angle.

The rotors wound down and stopped and there was a sudden silence. I was already tearing at my straps and twisting to look back into the cab, as I called Layla's name. The cockpit was cushioned from the worst of the impact by the powerful shock absorbers, but the cab had almost no protection. People in the back often suffered crushed vertebrae after an autorotative landing.

'Layla.' I struggled through the narrow gap between the seats and into the cab. She was still strapped into her seat, her eyes closed, her face deathly white. 'Layla!'

Her eyes flickered open. 'I'm all right. I was just scared to death, that's all.' She started to unbuckle her harness.

'Don't move until you're sure your back's all right.'

She made some cautious exploratory movements of her neck and shoulders, then eased herself away from her seat. 'I'm okay I think, a bit bruised, nothing broken.'

'Thank God for that.' I began to help her towards the door.

'Well, don't worry about me, will you?' Grizz said. 'I'll just sort myself out, shall I?'

'Sorry, Grizz. Are you all right?'

'As a matter of fact I am, yes, but thanks for asking anyway.'

Tom began to giggle and within seconds we were all creased with laughter. There was nothing particularly funny about it, but the release of tension coupled with the adrenalin rush of survival made it seem the greatest joke we'd ever heard.

We clambered down from the heli, wiping our eyes, and began looking the heli over.

'Nothing broken as far as I can see,' I said, 'but if it's all the same to you, Grizz, I'd just as soon not take that up again until we know why the engines cut out like that.'

'I'm with you on that,' he said. 'I'll get a few of the guys here to give me a hand to haul it back to the hangar – they might as well do something for a change in return for all the money we pay them. I'll strip it down and put it back together again.'

'What about us?'

'I'll need one of you to give me a hand. The other one can take Layla back to Freetown and come back out here tomorrow.'

I turned to look at Tom.

He stared at me for a moment. 'All right, all right, you win. I'll stay here.'

'I never said anything.'

'You didn't have to.'

I tried hard not to look too pleased.

Grizz handed me a rifle and some spare clips. 'You shouldn't need them,' he said, 'but it never hurts to be prepared.'

'You must have been a Boy Scout in an earlier life.'

He smiled. 'And take this radio. Just so we can stay in touch.'

'All right, but I don't want you bothering me all the time when I'm trying to relax.'

Grizz gave an enigmatic smile.

'What?' I said.

'Nothing. Just have a nice night, that's all.'

Layla studied him, arms folded, head on one side. Then she looked around the dusty, fly-blown base and laughed. 'I tell you what, Grizz. We'll be hard pushed to have a worse night than you.'

We drove back to Freetown, pausing to dispense a few more packs of cigarettes at the roadblock we encountered on the way. It may have been my jumpy imagination, or the memory of my conversation in Boroyende, but the ragged groups of armed men manning the barrier seemed more hostile and threatening than they had on the previous day. Nonetheless, they let us pass without hindrance and we reached the city in the late afternoon.

The sky was pale, almost white, and the low sun was a faint ghost of itself, obscured by dust. The months of humidity and torrential rain had at last given way to the dry, dusty harmattan wind, laden with fine sand carried from the Sahara. As we drove back down the hill to the city centre, it hung like fog in the wind.

Before I got out of the pick-up, I wrapped a piece of rag

around my face like a mask, but almost at once I could feel the dust in my nose and taste it in my mouth. The air was full of creaking sounds as the wooden buildings dried in the wind.

When I reached my hotel room, I found that the dust had seeped in around the edge of the windows and suffused my books, magazines and clothes. It was so fine that it even passed through the mesh of the mosquito net and settled like talc on my bedding.

I took a quick, brackish shower and met Layla, as arranged, for dinner. The owner of the hotel fussed around us as if we were visiting royalty, but the menu was a less than regal choice of smoked fish, rice and okra – or an otherwise unidentified stew.

We chose fish and, more in hope than expectation, I ordered a bottle of wine. I took a dubious sip, then another. 'It's delicious,' I said, 'full-bodied and Lebanese – just like the hotel owner.'

She smiled, and the stress lines etched into her face disappeared.

'That's better,' I said. 'Leave your problems outside the door and relax for a while.'

'And yet I get the feeling that's not something you're very good at doing.'

I bowed my head. 'Guilty,' I said.

She studied me. 'So why are you here? I'll grant you this, you don't seem like the other mercenaries. Yet what are you? Twenty-eight? Twenty-nine?'

I nodded. 'Right first time.'

'The other guys are all pushing forty. You could have had another ten years in the RAF, couldn't you? So why leave? And why come here?'

'I guess I needed a change.' It sounded lame even to me.

'Is that it?' She waited in silence for me to continue.

'I'm a pretty rootless person all round,' I said. 'The air force life doesn't exactly do much to change that. We're always on the move; we're posted every three years and in between that we're away on exercise or deployment most of the time. And very few of us, even the married ones with kids, have any real contact with the people in the countries we're sent to.

'In fact in some ways the married ones are the worst. The single blokes at least have some contact, even if it's only hanging out in the bars and trying to chat up the local women, but the married ones just tend to set up isolated little enclaves of Englishness where they are – like Virginia Waters in the Congo. The gardens are arranged in neat rows so that even the plants are saluting, and while they like ordering the locals around, they don't like them as people – they're not British, after all.

'Everyone calls Britain "home", but it isn't really that any more for most of them. They don't have many friends back there or any recognisable home to go back to. And if they do go back, most of them find that the image they have of the country is years out of date with the reality. Lots of them don't stay long before they go back abroad again. They'd rather be expatriates sitting round a pool somewhere and talking nostalgically of Britain, than go back and face the real thing.'

'They?' Layla said, a smile playing around her lips.

I gave a rueful grin in reply. 'All right, "we" then.'

'So when were you last back in the UK?'

'Last Christmas. I flew in on Christmas Eve and left again on Boxing Day.'

She shook her head. 'That doesn't sound like the perfect family Christmas to me.'

'It isn't, but then I don't really come from the perfect family background. My mum and my father divorced when I was young. I lived with my mum until I was fourteen, then I insisted on going to live with my father.' I paused. 'It broke my mum's heart, but you know what you're like when you're in your teens. I—' I groped for the right words. 'It's not that you're deliberately selfish, but no one and nothing else but yourself exists in your world at that age. When you grow up you look back and can't believe how selfish and insensitive you were.'

She nodded. 'We're all the same, Jack. It's just part of growing up.'

'Anyway, my father had his own life by then and I was never sure if he really wanted me with him. I stayed two years, even though I was miserable most of the time. I ran away twice, but I was brought back each time by the police.'

'Why didn't you go back to your mother's?'

'I didn't feel I could. Anyway, I'd made my choice and I had to live with it. I left my father's for the last time on my sixteenth birthday. I joined the air force the same day.'

'Are you in touch with your parents now?'

I shook my head. 'Not my father, and I only see my mum at Christmas.'

'For about twenty-four hours,' she said.

'I should do more, I know, but . . .'

She laid a hand on my arm. 'You're lucky, you still have time to put it right. It's not too late.'

'Maybe.'

We sat in silence for a while. 'You still haven't told me why you chose to come here to Sierra Leone,' Layla said.

'I – I just wanted a steady job, I suppose; no excitement—'.

'And no responsibilities?'

'That too – just drop off the men and supplies and get back to base.'

She gave a wry smile. 'Sierra Leone isn't exactly noted for its quietness, and when things go wrong here, even those on the sidelines find themselves involved whether they like it or not.'

'But the last trouble with the rebels was some time ago. Things are quieter now. Aren't they?'

She touched the tips of her fingers together, staring at them as she spoke. 'They seem quieter, but Njama has heard rumours that the rebels are on the move again. There's something in the wind. You can sense it everywhere around you; nothing you can put your finger on, but people are uneasy, spooked. And if the rebels come back, the government soldiers are as likely to join them in the killing, raping and looting as they are to fight them.' She forced a smile. 'I hope you get your steady job, for all our sakes.' She squeezed my hand then released it. 'I'm sorry. I'm probably just projecting my stupid, irrational fears onto everyone else.' She fell silent.

I poured us each another glass of wine. 'So what about you?' I said. 'Why are you here?'

She shrugged. 'Partly through choice, partly as a punishment, I suppose. I wasn't born to be a diplomat and I'm sometimes a little too political, even for Medicaid International. I got into big trouble at my last posting. I expressed my opinions a bit too forcefully to one of the local politicians. It took some hasty diplomacy to prevent the entire medical team being expelled. 'I suppose I was lucky not to be sacked, but this was the worst posting they could think of to give me.' She smiled. 'Funnily enough, despite all the deprivation and violence, I love it here. I feel as if I belong.'

The hotel owner cleared away our plates and brought tiny cups of thick, black Lebanese coffee with powdered milk and gritty, discoloured sugar. We sat talking late into the evening, long after the other diners had left. As we said goodnight outside my room, I leaned forward to kiss her.

She let my lips brush against hers, but when I tried to prolong the embrace, she pushed me away. 'Let's just keep it friendly,

Jack,' she said. 'I'd need to know an awful lot more about you before I'd even consider being the next notch on your bedpost.'

'I know that,' I said. 'I didn't—' But she was already walking away down the corridor, leaving the trace of her perfume hanging in the air.

When I got into bed, I lay staring into the darkness for a long time but, like almost every night since Kosovo, it was the familiar nightmare that was waiting for me when I at last fell asleep. This time there was a difference, however, a hand began beckoning from the flames and a man's voice shouted over and over, 'Come in. Come in.'

I awoke. The voice continued. 'Jack, come in. Jack, come in.'

I lay there trying to make sense of it, as the cold sweat trickled down my forehead. Then I sat upright, clambered out of bed and began to rummage through the pitch-dark room for the radio Grizz had given me. I found it at last, buried under my discarded clothes on the seat of the chair.

'This is Jack. What's happening, Grizz?'

'There's shit flying at Bohara. A big rebel assault. The guys have taken casualties. Get Layla, and get out here as fast as you can.'

I was filled with a feeling of dread. 'What about the heli?' I said, clutching at straws. 'It's not fit to fly until it's been fixed.'

'We've sorted it,' he said. 'Now get out here pronto.'

I tossed the radio onto the bed, groped my way to the bathroom and splashed the trickle of water on my face and then dragged on my clothes. I ran down the corridor and pounded on Layla's door.

A sleepy voice answered at once and she came to the door wrapped in a towel. Even half asleep she looked heart-stoppingly beautiful.

'Grizz has been on the radio,' I said. 'There's trouble at Bohara. We've got to get going at once.'

She stared at me for a moment. 'What sort of trouble?'

'The rebels.'

The blood drained from her face, but she didn't hesitate for a second, already turning back into the room. Through the half-open door, I saw the sheen of starlight on her skin as she dropped the towel and pulled on a T-shirt and jeans. A moment later she was hurrying out of the door, holding her medical bags. We ran downstairs, through the deserted hotel lobby and out into the darkness. It was a still, beautiful night. The stars misted the sky above us and only the faint whine of the mosquitoes broke the silence.

I revved up the engine of the pick-up and we drove off fast through the dark, deserted streets. The few people we did see as we drove across the city melted into the shadows and the sidestreets at our approach. There was one exception, a power-fully built figure who stepped into the road and held up his hand to signal us to stop. He kept his other hand out of sight behind his back as we approached, but I caught the glint of metal reflected in the headlights.

I slowed a fraction as if I was going to stop, then floored the accelerator and aimed the pick-up directly at the man. I swerved aside at the last moment as he flung himself into the gutter.

'Can't be too careful,' I said as we sped away.

Layla did not reply. She sat silent in the passenger seat staring out through the windscreen, her lip caught between her teeth.

'Are you all right?' I said.

'What? Yes, sorry, I was just thinking about Njama's people, wondering if they're safe.'

'As far as I know, the rebels are only attacking Bohara, not Boroyende.'

'Maybe, but Njama was worried. There had been rumours of a rebel advance and anyway, he's learned to trust his instincts over the years. It's what's kept him and his family alive while so many others have died.'

'So do you think the fighting will spread?'

She shivered. 'I don't know. The country's tense, no doubt about it, and it wouldn't be the first time a rebel advance in the east had triggered violence here as well.'

We left the city behind and began the climb through open country towards the mountains. As we approached the bend where we'd encountered the roadblock on the way into Freetown, I slipped the radio and my pistol into the mess of litter under the seat. Then I remembered the rifle that Grizz had given me. It was still sitting in the hotel room, propped against the side of the wardrobe. I cursed under my breath, but it was too late to go back for it now.

I was only half expecting the barrier to be manned, for I could not imagine there had been any other traffic on this lonely road that night, but as we rounded the corner, I brought the pick-up to a juddering halt. A dozen heavily armed men stood guard on the barrier. They levelled their rifles at us as soon as we came into view, as if they had been lying in wait for us.

'Shit,' I said, reaching for a carton of American cigarettes. 'This doesn't look too clever.'

'Just keep calm,' Layla said. 'Give them the cigarettes, keep smiling and we should be all right.'

I wound down the window and held out the carton as we came to a halt in front of the barrier. For once there was no rush to grab it from me. The soldiers looked wired and edgy, their eyes never still. I shot a worried look at Layla and reached under my seat, easing the pistol out to where I could reach it.

Layla saw the movement out of the corner of her eye and at once laid a warning hand on my arm. 'Don't overreact,' she said. 'We're heavily outnumbered. Don't provoke them, just keep it light and pleasant.'

One of the soldiers – the leader of the group from his girth and the mirrored sunglasses he wore like a badge of office – walked to the door of the pick-up. He took the cigarettes from me, then jerked his head. 'Get out of the car.'

I shot a sideways glance at Layla. She gave an almost imperceptible nod as she felt my eyes on her. 'Do as he says. What else can we do?' The shake in her voice betrayed her own fear.

We got out, but stood close to the pick-up as the soldier searched us in turn. He lingered over the search of Layla and I saw her flinch as he handled her breasts while pretending to search for concealed weapons. Then he stepped back and signalled to two of the others to search the vehicle.

They handed him Layla's medical bag, then one of them found the radio and pistol under the seat. The find ratcheted up the tension several more notches. I could see a vein pulsing in the leader's temple as he turned the radio and the pistol over in his hands, and when he looked up, his eyes were hooded and angry.

'What is this?' he said. 'Who are you? What are you doing here?'

'As you can see from our medical bag, we're doctors with Medicaid International,' I said before Layla could speak. 'We're on our way to treat a very ill patient, please let us pass.'

'Since when do doctors carry guns?'

I spread my hands. 'These are dangerous times. I carry it only for protection from robbers and bandits.'

He studied me for a moment, weighing my words. 'Where is this patient of yours?'

'At the army camp at the top of the hill.'

He stiffened. 'He is a soldier, then.'

'No,' I said. 'She is a civilian. The soldiers took her to the camp because she was so ill.'

'What is wrong with her?'

Layla jumped in before I could reply. 'She is with child. She has been in labour for almost two days. If we do not get to her soon, both she and her baby will die.' She paused, holding his gaze. 'Please,' she said. 'Imagine if this was your wife and your baby. One day it might be.'

He hesitated, then gave a curt nod. With some show of reluctance, his men began moving aside the barricade.

'My pistol and my radio?' I said.

After examining them for another minute, he shook his head. 'Radios are the tools of spies, not doctors,' he said.

I thought about arguing, then let it go. 'And my pistol?'

He slipped it into his pocket. 'You will have no need of this. I and my men control this road. We permit no thieves or bandits.' He smiled as he said it, his look challenging me to argue with him, if I dared.

I bowed my head and we got back into the pick-up. I drove through the gap in the barricade and then accelerated away up the hill. In the rear-view mirror I could see some of the soldiers raising their weapons and firing volleys of shots into the sky. I could only hope it was in celebration of the booty they had plundered, not a signal to others lying in wait farther up the road.

'Quick thinking, Layla,' I said as we passed out of sight of them. 'I thought we were in deep shit there for a moment.'

'We were,' she said. 'And we still might be.'

'What do you—'? I fell silent as I heard the sound that had alerted her, gunfire coming not from behind us but from somewhere in the darkness ahead.

I had braked to a halt without even realising I had done so. We exchanged a glance, but neither of us spoke. I switched off the lights, then put the pick-up in gear and began creeping forward again, steering only by the faint glow of the starlight reflected from the surface of the road.

The sound of firing continued and strengthened as we climbed the hill. When we crested the brow, I saw a glow of reddish light away to our left. It pulsed and flickered, sending sparks spiralling upwards from it.

'The base?' Layla said.

I nodded.

'What do we do?'

For answer I pulled the pick-up off the road into a small clearing at the edge of the forest. 'We'll go forward on foot,' I said, 'and see what's going on. We'll cut through the forest parallel to the road until we pick up the track to the base.'

We climbed out and began to inch our way forward through the trees, stumbling over roots and deadfall branches. Even though the sound of gunfire drowned the noise we were making, my heart thumped wildly at every twig snapping underfoot as we crept on through the forest.

I was soaked with sweat, as much from tension as the exertion in the heat of the night. Pumped up on adrenalin, I was on hyper-alert, straining my eyes into the darkness ahead, imagining rebel soldiers hiding behind every bush.

We struggled on up the hillside and in the distance ahead I saw a faint grey line where the track to the base cut off to the left. I wiped the sweat from my eyes then drank a little water from my canteen. 'Almost there,' I said.

As I spoke I heard the rattle of a heavy machine gun from the direction of the base and the crack of rifle fire. I felt the strength drain from me. I stood helpless for a moment, unable to move. I was banking on being able to reach Grizz and the helicopter, but if the base was already overrun by the rebels, I could think of nowhere else to turn, and nothing else to do.

Layla read the look in my face. 'We have to get closer,' she said, 'and see what's happening. They're fighting, so at least the base is still holding out.'

I nodded, ashamed of my momentary weakness. Layla was probably even more scared than me, yet she had stuck with me without complaint, putting her trust in me to see us through. I squared my shoulders. 'We'll work our way through the forest close to the gates of the base. We should at least be able to see what's going on from there.'

The rattle of gunfire grew louder as we approached. I could smell smoke and cordite on the breeze drifting through the forest. We slowed our pace and inched forward, crawling the last few yards through the undergrowth at the edge of the track. I raised my head a little and parted the branches in front of me, then flattened myself at once.

Not more than thirty yards in front of us was a rebel position. Their commander was directing fire, shouting orders into the radios he held in either hand. Other groups of rebels were scattered around the perimeter of the base and the heavy machine gun I had heard earlier was set up a hundred yards to his right. The belt kept jamming, but each time the crew managed to free it a terrifying torrent of fire was unleashed on the hard-pressed defenders inside the base.

The barracks huts nearest to us were ablaze, but through the smoke I could glimpse the hangar where the heli was stored. It looked to be relatively intact so far and was still protected by a cordon of defenders. As I stared into the swirling smoke, I saw a figure run from one patch of cover to another. His face was streaked with mud or cam cream, but I caught a glimpse of a white face and felt a surge of relief that Grizz was still alive and still directing the defenders.

Even so the position seemed hopeless. There were no more than a couple of dozen soldiers at his disposal and at least ten times that number of rebels were grouped around the base. I could see perhaps fifty bodies, mostly rebels from their dress, scattered around the perimeter fence either side of the wire. Rebel attempts at a frontal assault had obviously failed, but they had only to hold their position to slowly draw the noose tighter around Grizz and his men.

I wormed my way back into the undergrowth and whispered to Layla, my mouth close to her ear. 'It doesn't look good. There are a hell of a lot of rebel soldiers.'

She took my hand in hers and held my gaze. 'Don't try any schoolboy heroics. That'll just get us both killed to no purpose.'

The longer we watched, the more hopeless the defenders' position seemed. Each time groups of rebels tried to rush the base, they were cut apart by concentrated fire. The dead and dying lay where they fell as the others retreated with the wounded. But the defenders were losing men too and a war of attrition could only have one end.

Grizz was still moving among his men, shouting orders and directing fire, but I could see no sign of Tom. Much of the rebel fire was wild and many rounds went wide and high as they emptied magazines on full automatic, but the sheer volume of fire from all sides kept the defenders pinned down and exacted a steady toll on casualties. I saw three men fall and not rise again and a fourth was blown apart by a round from the heavy machine gun. It caught him in his chest and he seemed to disintegrate before my eyes.

The thunder of fire intensified again, but then above it there was another noise. I strained my ears trying to make sense of it. Then I heard the rumble of an engine and a dark shadow appeared on the track in front of us. A truck pulled up, disgorging another group of rebel soldiers.

Their numbers seemed to make a crucial difference. They were now steadily moving closer, pinning the defenders down under a hail of fire while groups tried to penetrate the perimeter fence, using the ruins of the barracks as cover.

The rebels seemed absolutely without fear. Again and again waves of attackers jumped from cover. Protected by nothing more than the juju emblems they wore, they ran straight into the guns of the defenders, firing from the hip until they fell and each time, more sprang up to replace them.

I felt impotent and ashamed not to be shoulder to shoulder with Grizz and the others, rather than a spectator cowering in the shadows, watching a fight that looked sure to end with the death of many of the participants.

'We have to get into the base,' I said. 'If I can get the Huey airborne we've a chance of driving these bastards off.'

'We can't,' she said. 'They've got it completely surrounded. If we try, we'll be killed.'

'We've got to do something. If we just sit here, Grizz, Tom and everybody else are going to be slaughtered. We've got to create a diversion somehow. Come on.'

'Where are we going?'

'Back to the pick-up.'

Chapter 5

We tried to retrace our steps through the forest, but in the darkness I missed the clearing where we had left the pick-up, and we had to work our way first down and then back up the road, with the crash of gunfire continually reverberating in our ears. I was in a frenzy of worry and impatience by the time we finally found the place.

Before I drove away, I ripped my shirtsleeve off, then unscrewed the cap from the fuel tank and dowsed the cloth in petrol. I left half of it protruding from the neck of the tank, then drove slowly up the hill, without lights, and turned down the track to the base.

The thunder of gunfire grew louder again and as we rounded a bend, I saw the muzzle-flashes of scores of weapons and the baleful glare of the burning buildings. I stopped the pick-up in the deeper darkness beneath a clump of trees overhanging the track.

Even though my heart was pounding with fright and the urge to do something, anything, rather than remain motionless – a sitting target – a moment longer, I made myself wait. The commander's position was directly ahead of me down the track, just beyond the truck we had seen arrive. I turned my head and let my gaze travel slowly along the perimeter of the base, picking out the other groups of rebels.

I touched Layla's arm and pointed to a section of the fence almost midway between two groups of rebels. A tree grew close to the wire and the ground dipped down towards the fence, giving a little cover. 'That's the best place,' I said. I stripped off my flying jacket. 'Take that and sprint down to the fence. Wait in the shadow of the tree until the balloon goes up, then throw the jacket onto the barbed wire and climb over it. Then don't stop until you get to Grizz, but keep bobbing and weaving, and keep yelling to let him know you're a friend not a foe.'

'And where will you be?'

'Right on your heels all the way.'

She shook her head. 'It's too dangerous, Jack. Even if the rebels don't shoot us, when Grizz's men see us climbing over the wire, they're not going to wait for us to identify ourselves, they're just going to kill us. They'll shoot first and ask questions afterwards.'

'That's the chance we have to take. It's the only way. They've taken casualties already, but if we don't get into the base and get that heli airborne, they'll all be killed.'

I leaned across the seat and kissed her. She stared at me, then took my flying jacket and slipped out of the pick-up. I watched her for a moment, running down the slope to the tree, moving as fast and silent as a cloud shadow over the ground, then I reversed along the track a hundred yards.

I got out of the pick-up and began searching in the dirt at the side of the track. I found a good-sized rock and slipped it into the footwell of the pick-up, then walked back to the tailgate. I took a few deep breaths, filling my lungs with oxygen. I struck a light, ignited the cloth trailing from the neck of the petrol tank and sprinted for the cab. I put it in gear and accelerated through first and second gears. Then I lined up the pick-up on its target, and rolled the rock onto the accelerator pedal, jamming it to the boards. I held the door open, flicked on the mainbeam lights and then dived out of the side.

The impact as I hit the ground drove the air from my lungs. As I rolled over and over in the dirt, I heard the scream of the engine being answered by a storm of gunfire as the rebels began to bring their weapons to bear on the unexpected threat bearing down on them.

Still accelerating, the pick-up bucketed along the track, then lurched off it, bumping over the rough ground until it hit a rock and overturned. It slid on its side the last twenty metres and came to a juddering halt with a terrible grinding of metal as it hit the rear corner of the truck.

There was a beat of silence then a blast as the petrol tank exploded and a column of fire erupted into the air, freezing every combatant for a moment like the strobe of a flashgun. Even before the glare had faded, I was sprinting down the slope, running bent double towards the wire.

I saw a dark shape outlined against the fence as Layla threw the jacket onto the coiled barbed wire and began to climb. I reached the bottom as she struggled over it, and heard her stifle a cry of pain as a barb protruding through the jacket spiked her hand. Then she was over and dropping to the ground.

I was almost at the top when I heard a shout from inside the base and a burst of gunfire was directed at me. A moment later I was also spotted by the rebels and they too, began to fire. Caught in a lethal crossfire from both sides in the conflict, I threw myself forward. I felt the barbs ripping and tearing at me, then I was falling to the ground.

I landed heavily on my side, but staggered to my feet and was off, stumbling after Layla, running and diving for cover as bullets cracked and whined around me. We rolled over and lay still as we drew breath, then we were up and off again, running towards the burning buildings. Even though we were dodging and weaving, we were sharply outlined against the flames for a few seconds, long enough for the rebels to sight on the clear target. A fresh burst of gunfire rattled around us, throwing up dirt and fragments of rock, and one round passed so close to my ear that I cried out in shock and terror as it howled past me.

Then we were through the outlying buildings and diving for cover again as the defenders opened up with renewed venom. We flung ourselves into a hollow and lay still as bullets chewed at the earth above our heads.

We were in dead ground between the sides, shielded from the rebels by the lip of the hollow behind us, but barely protected from the defenders ahead of us. I waited for a lull in the firing then, still in cover, I cupped my hands around my mouth and shouted, 'Grizz!'

I shouted again, 'Grizz!' Then I lifted my head a fraction and raised my arms above me. I waited. There was an isolated shot, then silence. I straightened a little more, and advanced a couple of feet out of cover. Four black soldiers had their guns levelled at my guts. I could see puzzlement on their faces at my white skin. It was probably all that was keeping me alive.

Beyond them I saw Grizz with his back to me, crouching behind an earth mound and directing fire towards the far side of the airfield. I heard Layla start to follow me. 'Not yet,' I said. 'Wait there.'

She ignored me and crouched alongside me, her arms also raised. I shouted again at the top of my voice. 'GRIZZ!'

I saw him turn, stare towards us, then shout at the soldiers. They kept us covered, a semi-circle of guns pointing at us as we moved slowly forward, crouching to keep in cover from the rebels. A moment later Grizz shouted again and came sprinting towards us. He pushed past the soldiers, dragged us down into the cover of the earth mound and then grabbed us both in a bear hug. 'Thank Christ,' he said. 'I'd written you off. Can you get airborne and give us some help here?'

'Just watch me. Get your boys to give me some cover while we get the heli out. It will fly, won't it?'

'Let's hope so,' he said. 'We fixed it, but obviously we've had no time to test it.'

'Guns?'

'Fully loaded. No time for the rocket pod, though.'

'Right.' I turned and ran at a crouch towards the hangar. 'Where's Tom?' I called over my shoulder.

'You'll have to manage without him. He's been hit.'

I checked. 'Shit. Is he badly hurt?'

'It's not fatal. A leg wound.'

There was no time for more questions, the lull in the rebel fire had ended and it was picking up in intensity as we dragged open the hangar doors. I put on the night vision goggles and fired up the engines while the heli was still inside the building, preferring the risk of setting the hangar alight with the back-blast of the exhausts to the danger of sitting exposed on the concrete while the engines warmed up.

I kept a wary eye on the gauges as I revved and slowed the engines, listening for any abnormalities, but whatever Grizz had done to them in the stripping down after the autorotative landing seemed to have cured the problem. The throaty rasp of power as I raised the collective sounded sweet as a nightingale to my ears.

The defenders laid down a barrage of fire until Grizz gave them the signal, when a dozen of them dropped their weapons and ran to help push the Huey out of the hangar into the open.

As soon as the nose of the heli began to appear the rebels redoubled their fire, raining down everything they had in a massive barrage to try to stop the Huey getting airborne. Even though an earth embankment partly shielded it from the rebel fire, rounds were cracking and rattling on the heli's metal skin and I felt as exposed as a fly on a window pane. I tried to force myself to concentrate only on the controls in my hands.

It seemed an eternity until the tips of the rotor arms cleared the framework of the hangar door. As soon as they were out, I crashed the control into flight idle and gunned the engines. The rotors turned, blurred and accelerated into an unbroken disc overhead. At once I jammed the collective to the stops, and eased the cyclic forward.

Grizz threw himself into the cab as the Huey lifted on its springs and then we were airborne. I banked hard away from the main concentration of rebels, climbing rapidly to two hundred feet, then I swung it around and came in low and fast at my first target, the rebel command position.

I heard the chatter of the mini-gun as Grizz opened up from the door of the cab, laying down a barrage of fire, but I held off with the nose gun until the cross-hairs intersected on the left-hand man in the rebel group. Then I squeezed the trigger, easing the right rudder down to walk the line of fire right across the cluster of rebel troops. The nose guns thundered and I heard the heavy rattle of ejected cartridges and smelt smoke and the tang of cordite.

I was already banking to bring the next group of rebels into my sights, the men manning the heavy machine gun. I squeezed the trigger again, swinging the heli around to move the line of fire through the target. As we flashed overhead, the ground below me shook and erupted. Clods of earth were flung high into the air and clouds of dust mingled with the smoke. As it cleared, I saw that the troops around the gun had disappeared.

A few rebels returned fire, but it was ragged stuff. I'd seen even hardened troops lose all semblance of discipline under an aerial assault and, brave as they were individually, these half-trained soldiers quickly disintegrated into a panic-stricken rabble. They began running, scattering in all directions. I saw the commander jump into the truck and begin urging the driver back, but its way was blocked by the twisted, blackened hulk of the burned out pick-up. I lined up the guns and riddled the truck from bumper to bumper. It disappeared in a cloud of smoke and flame.

I stared through the dust and smoke, banked and returned once more to the attack, pursuing the rebels as they fled down the road. I fired again and again, and Grizz shot up anything that came within his own field of fire. There were more explosions and another vehicle blew up in a column of red flames.

I pursued them until I had emptied the guns, then left them to their headlong flight and banked around, back to the base. By the time we landed, the small-arms fire had ceased. I climbed down from the cockpit and looked out on a scene of complete stillness and silence. Slowly the defenders began to emerge from behind the barricades.

Grizz slapped me on the back, 'Great shooting, ace.' Then he moved among his men, talking to each one. They began to fan out across the base, pausing to examine each fallen rebel. There was a drum roll of single shots as the injured were finished off with a bullet in the head. I turned away, uncertain of my response to what I was seeing.

Grizz caught my eye. 'That's war here for all sides,' he said. 'The Geneva Convention didn't make it this far. There's not enough medicine, food or anything else to supply your own side, let alone prisoners of war. So . . .' He put his forefinger against his temple and mimed pulling a trigger.

One of the soldiers shouted to Grizz. He ran across the base and out through the gates, towards what had been the rebel command position. I saw him stoop to examine one of the bodies. He searched through the dead man's clothing, stood in thought for a moment, then whistled and beckoned to me.

When I reached him, he pointed to the corpse. 'That explains the rebel attack.'

The body was at the rear of the command position. From his posture, the dead man had been crouching behind a rock, safe from ground fire, but still fatally exposed to the guns of a helicopter overhead. The round that had killed him had punched a football size hole in his chest. Enough of his blood-soaked clothing remained intact to show that he had been wearing a faded flying suit. Even more surprising, he was white, with the broad face, heavy brows and narrowed eyes of a Slav.

'Must be a Russian or a Ukrainian,' I said. 'Some of those guys'll work for anyone for a few dollars. They must have had Intelligence that we were keeping the heli here.'

Grizz nodded. 'No wonder they were throwing so much at us. If they'd managed to take the Huey, they'd have wiped out Bohara in a couple of days.'

'Could it be part of a push on Freetown?'

'I don't think so. There've been no reports of any other activity this side of Bohara. It may come, but not just yet. Their first priority will be the diamond mines. If they can take and hold those, they can buy all the weapons they want – even helicopters.'

We walked back onto the base as Layla emerged from a

bunker. She looked drawn and deathly pale. The three of us looked each other over. Grizz's face was a mass of cuts and grazes and there was an ugly looking wound on his left forearm. From his expression, we didn't paint too pretty a picture either.

'Where's Tom?' I said, suppressing a guilty twinge that I had only just thought about him.

He gestured towards another low building alongside the hangar. 'He's in the hut there. Like I said, he's wounded, but he's okay, I think. He caught a bullet in the leg, a flesh wound, but he made a lot of fuss about it – you know what pilots are like – so we dosed him up with morphine.' He switched his gaze to Layla. 'Now the heat's off, you can look him and the rest of the casualties over. Come to think of it, you look like you could use some treatment yourself.'

'You and me both,' she said, staring at the wound on his arm.

He led us over to the hut. The casualties lay on the floor or were propped against the inside wall. Tom was slumped just inside the door. He stared up at us and smiled and waved in recognition, but his speech was a blurred, morphine-fuelled stream of incoherence.

I glanced at Grizz. 'I think I'll make the next flight solo as well.'

The water canteen Tom had been carrying on his hip had been shattered by a round but it had saved his leg, and maybe his life. There were messy flesh wounds where the shards of the shattered metal had been forced into the flesh of his thigh and Layla had to dig them out with the point of a knife before she could bandage the wound, but the bones were not broken and the shrapnel had missed his arteries.

Some of the other casualties had horrific wounds, but Layla moved among them, fast but purposeful, showing no trace of panic as she assessed them. 'This one will wait. This one now.'

She could do nothing for three men near death, 'expectant' in the medical euphemism, and they were moved out of the hangar away from the others. She sent an uninjured friend or comrade to sit with each of them. I heard the low murmur of voices offering consolation, prayers, promises to look after wives and children, and then the growing silence as, in turn, the life of each mortally wounded man ebbed away.

I forced my thoughts away, on to our own predicament. 'What's our next move?' I said to Grizz, who had been talking on the satcoms while Layla had been working.

'We must get the heli to the airport at once,' he said. 'The rebels could return to the attack and I can't count on you to bail us out a second time.'

'And when we get there?'

'We load up as much ammo as we can carry and get out to Bohara fast. It's still under attack, but the guys are holding them off – for the moment at least.'

Grizz posted guards to warn of any return to the attack from the rebels and then we checked over the heli while Layla finished treating the wounded. The Huey had a few new bullet holes, but the only serious damage we could find from the fighting was a hydraulic line part-severed by a stray round.

I fixed it with a length of plastic tube and a couple of jubilee clips. Grizz looked it over. 'Not bad, not bad,' he said. 'You might make a flight engineer yet, but I'll have to see what you can do with a roll of speed tape before I can decide.'

'What about the fault that caused the engine failure?' I said. 'Could it recur?'

'I told you, we fixed it last night, before the fun started.'

'That doesn't entirely answer my question.'

He shrugged. 'Can I give you a written guarantee that it won't happen again? No. Have you ever met a flight engineer who would? No. It was broke; we fixed it. End of story.'

We loaded Tom and the worst of the wounded into the back of the Huey. Grizz once more manned the door gun.

'You can sit in the front,' I said to Layla. 'The co-pilot won't be needing the seat and you're as safe there as anywhere.' I checked to make sure the sliding armoured panel beneath her seat was all the way forward, then handed her a couple of flak vests.

'Two?' she said.

'Wear one and sit on the other. The seat's armoured but it always gives me an extra feeling of security to know that my genitals are well protected.'

She smiled. 'Women don't have the same psychological problems as men. But I'll sit on it anyway if it makes you happy.'

'Deliriously,' I said.

I called the tower at the airport before we even took off, making very sure they were aware that the incoming helicopter was friendly. 'This is Decisive Measures helicopter Grizzly One, flying from Defence Force Base Seventeen, seeking clearance to land.'

I received an almost immediate reply. 'Come on in, Grizzly One,' a laconic voice replied. 'You've got the place to yourself.'

'What's your situation there?'

'The airfield's secure. No problems at the moment.'

We lifted off, not without a few reproachful looks from the remainder of the garrison we were leaving behind. We were heavy-laden, an easy target as we lumbered skywards, and my heart was in my mouth as we made our ascent, rising in tight spirals over the base. As far as we knew, the rebels had no SAMs, but just the same I was on hyper-alert, my hands tensed on the controls, ready to throw the Huey into evasion at the first sign of ground fire.

I glanced across at Layla. 'Keep alert,' I said. 'The rebels could have regrouped and if they see us flying out of here, they're certainly going to give us a send-off. If you spot any ground fire, give me the warning and the direction it's comi—'

As I spoke I caught a flash of fire and a blur of grey smoke from the edge of the track leading away from the base. 'Missile launch!' I shouted, wrenching the collective up to full power and kicking the Huey into a savage break away from the threat. At the same moment I heard the bark of the door gun as Grizz fired back at the target.

There was the familiar feeling of ice in the stomach as the missile trace disappeared from sight below me. I twisted my head around to catch a glimpse of it, whipping my gaze right and left, trying to pick it up. Then below and behind us, I caught sight of a grey plume of smoke and the flash of an explosion.

I eased back on the collective a little and set the Huey back on a level course, then jabbed the intercom. 'What the hell was that? I thought you said they didn't have any SAMs.'

'They don't, as far as we know.' Grizz sounded his usual imperturbable self. 'That was an RPG. They're not very accurate with them but they're quite innovative in their use. They replace the impact fuse with a time fuse to improve their chances against helis; they don't have to hit them then, just get a grenade in the general area.'

'Thanks,' I said. 'It's always nice to know these things. Any chance you could mention them at the briefing next time, rather than when one's just been fired?'

'Yeah, sorry about that. I never said I was perfect.'

I saw a few muzzle flashes from sporadic rifle fire as we maintained our climb, but we were at extreme range and there was no telltale rattle of rounds against the fuselage. I kept the

Huey climbing to well above 5,000 feet, then banked in a long turn west towards the airport.

I glanced at Layla. She was deathly pale. 'You're not doing badly for a first flight as co-pilot. Want the job permanently?'

She shook her head. 'It was horrible when that thing was fired at us. I felt so exposed, so helpless. It was even worse than being shot at.'

I nodded. 'But the end result's the same if you get hit.'

It was a relief to see the apparent normality of the scene below us as we approached the outskirts of Freetown. A few vehicles moved to and fro along the roads, a tramp steamer was nosing its way into the mouth of the Sierra Leone river, and as we banked to come in over the airport, I could see a transport aircraft with Nigerian markings unloading near the end of the runway.

As we hovered over the airfield, I switched on the landing light and moved the lever to swing the fierce beam in a broad arc around the landing site. The heli flared out and settled on to the dusty concrete in an untroubled landing.

I helped Grizz and Layla to unload the casualties. The most seriously injured were taken away in a rattletrap ambulance emblazoned with the Medicaid International logo, the less seriously wounded, Tom included, were seated in the shade and given a cool drink.

Tom still looked spaced out. 'Will he be fit to fly when we get there?' I said.

Layla frowned. 'His leg is no problem; it's only a flesh wound. But he needs time to get the morphine out of his system.'

'How long?'

'Tomorrow morning ideally.'

'But he could do it sooner?'

'It depends. What's he going to be doing?' she said.

'Sitting in the passenger seat watching the scenery, unless something goes wrong.'

She turned back to him and checked his pupils and his reactions again. 'Four hours, absolute minimum. Okay?'

I nodded. 'Okay.'

I turned to Grizz. 'So what's the first job?'

'Resupply to Bohara — ammunition, grenades, everything we've got.'

Grizz unlocked one of the bunkers and we began loading boxes of 7.62 mm ammunition, grenades and RPG rounds into the cab of the heli, stacking them roof high and lashing them to the sides with webbing.

'What about Layla?' I said, as we worked.

'What about her? She comes with us.'

'It's too dangerous,' I said.

'It's too bloody dangerous everywhere these days. Besides, she's needed; they've taken wounded.'

Chapter 6

We waited for dusk before taking off. Soon, it was a dark, moonless night. The mountains rising to the north of us were blacker even than the night sky and the distant river winding beneath the canopy of the forest gleamed like dull pewter.

The airfield was blacked out and the only light was the faint glow of the instruments, but the darkness would give us some protection from rebel ground fire, and with night vision goggles I could have flown the Huey down a coal mine at midnight.

Tom limped over to the Huey and climbed into the cockpit. As he settled himself into his seat, he winced and gave a sharp intake of breath.

'That's a good sign,' I said. 'Shows the morphine's wearing off.'

'Just fly the heli,' he said, 'and spare me the wisecracks.'

I glanced behind into the cab. Grizz was stationed by the open door squatting behind the mini gun. Layla was invisible in her precarious perch among the ammunition boxes. If we encountered ground fire and rounds went through the cab . . . I shook that thought off at once and forced myself to the safe, familiar discipline of pre-flight checks.

I punched the coordinates of our course of the terrain into the computer, following radar. Just before I started the engines I shot a sideways glance at Tom. 'Are you really all right to take over control if you have to?' I said.

'No problem.'

'Are you sure?'

'I'm sure. Get on with it.' The waspish note in his voice gave me more reassurance than his words.

I flicked the ignition switch and pushed the starter. There was a high-pitched whine and a grumbling rumble as the right engine turned over. I watched the rev counter rise and then pushed the fuel switch. The engine noise thundered, then settled into a steady roar.

I fired the left engine, redoubling the noise. As the temperature needle climbed I grabbed the rotor brake and pushed the lever forward into flight idle. The drooping rotors creaked into life. The whock-whock-whock as they began to turn, accelerated into a blur of noise and motion. The blades seemed to lengthen as they straightened under the centrifugal force and the downwash tore at the concrete and dry earth, sending clouds of dust rising around us.

I felt the Huey lift slightly, straining to be airborne, its weight now carried by the rotors not the ground. I scanned the gauges once more, then I pulled the night vision goggles down over my eyes and switched them on. There was a faint electronic whine and the dark night landscape turned green before my eyes, sparkling into life. The course of the river shone like a ribbon of light and the starlight flickered from the rotors like sparks of green fire.

I pressed the intercom. 'Here we go. Hold on, it's going to be a bumpy ride.'

I released the parking brake. As I raised the collective, I paddled the right rudder to turn us around. The engines thundered and the Huey rose into the air, ponderous under the weight of its load. I pushed the cyclic away from me a notch but still trod the rudders to keep us in a tight turn over the airfield as we rose clear of the ground effect and the downdraft blew away the dust cloud.

I held it in the hover at a hundred feet as I got clearance from the tower and radioed ahead to Bohara. 'We're on our way. ETA 20.15 hours. Over.'

The reply was masked by static. 'The sooner the better.' I could hear the sounds of gunfire punctuating his words.

I raised the collective and pushed the cyclic forward, putting the Huey into a gradual descent. I watched the air speed rise as it continued to coast downwards. The changing air pressure in my ears and the easing whine of the turbines told me we were descending without even having to look at the gauges or out through the canopy.

I waited until the altimeter hit fifty feet, then levelled with a stomach-churning jolt. Still accelerating, we thundered eastwards into the night, rising and falling in response to my green-tinged vision of the terrain unfolding ahead of us.

I pushed us up to clear a ridge, then down again in a gut-loosening plummet to a valley floor, and rising once more to the next ridge. As I moved the controls, I gave a running commentary to Grizz and Layla in the back to help them brace themselves for the next lurch as the Huey swooped and soared, twisted and turned.

There had been no ground fire so far. I tried to imagine the unseen groups of rebel soldiers in the darkness ahead. They would have little warning of our approach, only a distant rumble of engines, swelling rapidly to a deafening clamour. There would be a storm of wind from the rotors and an unlit shape, black as a bat, flashing overhead. By the time they had brought their weapons to bear, the thunder of the Huey's engines would already be fading back into the night.

I kept my gaze moving over the landscape, not staring in any one direction but using my peripheral vision to pick out detail. Rock outcrops showed as solid green bars in my goggles with the feathery outlines of trees rising above them.

In the past I'd spent tens of hours in training learning to night-fly, making landings at sites I never saw. I returned to base exhausted but exhilarated from pushing myself and my machine to the limits.

Despite that long experience, I could never completely rid myself of the feeling of impotence at entrusting the lives of myself and my crew to the night vision goggles, no matter how sophisticated they were.

We had been climbing steadily for some time to clear the last major ridge separating us from Bohara. As we neared the summit, the first starfires of shots pierced the darkness below us and I heard the tick and rattle of rounds against the armoured skin of the Huey.

I felt sweat start to my brow and gripped the controls even tighter. We cleared the ridge and lurched downwards again in a sickening fall. I thumbed the radio. 'Bohara, this is Grizzly One. We are on approach now, taking incoming fire.'

I switched my gaze forward, straining my vision into the green-tinted darkness, looking for the signal from the unlit base, invisible in the darkness. I tracked the intermittent silvery glint of the river, appearing and disappearing beneath the canopy of the forest, then in the distance I saw a single square of beads of light begin to glow in the enveloping velvet blackness, pinpricks of light in the immensity of the night.

The groundfire was increasing in intensity now and I pushed down even further towards the forest floor. We were flying at over 100 knots and so low that the rotors were skimming the tops of the trees and the fuselage was hidden between them as we flew. There was nothing but a blur around us and the impression of speed was quadrupled by the proximity of those rushing green walls. Then we were out of the forest, and I pressed down still lower over the rocky moonscape created by the mines.

The air speed indicator was twenty kilometres higher than the ground speed, showing that we were battling a strong headwind, and the speed bled off further as the Huey dropped nearer to the ground.

As we approached the base and began to slow still further, preparing for landing, the fire intensified. A blizzard of rounds filled the air around us and arcs of tracer seared upwards. Tracer rounds always look brighter, larger and closer at night, but these seemed big as footballs. Fired from a heavy calibre gun, they could cut through the heli's armoured skin like paper. I suppressed my fear as well as I could, trying to ignore the stabbing streaks of red and orange light reaching up towards us.

The dotted arcs of fire looked widely spaced from a distance, then coalesced into what seemed a continuous stream of light as they sliced directly towards us. I knew that between each tracer round there were four other shells. It seemed impossible that anything could fly through that inferno and not be carved into pieces.

I jerked the heli left and right and sent it rising and falling, trying to unsettle the rebels' aim, but each time the lines of tracer cut back through the sky towards us.

Away in the darkness, I could see the fainter flames of cooking fires speckling the hillside. Here we were fighting for our lives and a short distance away the age-old routine of village life was continuing as if all they were witnessing was a tropical storm. I forced myself to concentrate only on the pressure of the collective and cyclic in my hands and the mushy feel of the rudder pedals beneath my feet.

Another line of tracer walked across the sky towards us. I swerved left and right, climbed and dropped, then put the heli into an almost vertical bank. The G-force pinned me to my seat and dragged at my arms as I fought to move the controls, but still the tracer worked its way closer and closer towards us, thrown off for no more than a fraction of a second by each manoeuvre.

I felt I could have reached out of the cockpit and picked off one of those blazing rounds as it hung suspended from the sky. My thoughts were stupid, trivial, not: Will I live through this? but about the tax return I hadn't filled in before I left England and the fridge I'd forgotten to defrost.

I looked ahead. A line of fierce red tracer slashed through the sky ahead of us. Like a gun on a grouse shoot, the unseen gunman was aiming ahead of his target. If we held course, flying straight into a curtain of fire, we would be shot down.

I pulled an abrupt, pedal turn, swinging through 360 degrees in barely more than the Huey's own length. I heard a cry of surprise from Grizz in the back and a rattle as an ammunition box broke loose from its ties.

I held my breath, then saw the tracer exploding harmlessly behind us. It snapped off for a few moments, then reappeared, again slicing though the sky to overhaul us. I gave it another second, then pulled the same manoeuvre. Once more the tracer whipped past us and disappeared in our wake.

The mini-guns again chattered as Grizz opened up from the back, trying to suppress the fire, but I could hear the smack of more and more rounds puncturing the Huey's armoured skin, and the whine of ricochets was audible even above the clamour of the rotors.

The compound lights had been extinguished after that one brief showing but one of the mercenaries was guiding me in using a torch with tape across the glass to leave only a thin, faint lozenge of light glowing in the darkness. It was a risk – if I could see it, so could any of the rebels – but without it I would not find them at all.

With no other fixed points in the ocean of darkness, it was hard to orient to a single pinprick of light even wearing NVGs. I knew it was motionless, but the light appeared to move around in the darkness. I avoided looking directly at it and kept my gaze moving, using my peripheral vision to orient myself and bring in the Huey.

I pulled back the cyclic, banking into the wind ready to land. 'Ground speed fifty, altitude one hundred feet,' Tom said.

I stamped alternately on the right and left rudder pedals as we came in, twitching the tail from side to side in the hope of throwing off the aim of the rebel gunners, but as I prepared to flare for landing, the torrents of ground fire increased still further. An RPG round exploded with a blinding flash in the darkness ahead of us and a moment later a string of flares ignited. As they drifted slowly down, they lit up the compound and the light glinted from the fuselage of the heli.

'We can't land,' Tom said. 'Just ditch the ammo and let's get the hell out of here.'

I began to argue, but I knew he was right. I pushed the

intercom. 'We're going for a rolling drop. Get ready and I'll count you in.'

I saw the dull glint of the wire fencing surrounding the compound just ahead of us in the darkness. I tried to hold the Huey steady, steeling myself to ignore the gunfire ripping up the night around us.

The garrison was pouring out a torrent of fire from inside the compound but it seemed to have no impact on the volume of rounds being directed at us. The seconds crawled by as we at last cleared the fenceline and reached the drop zone. 'Five . . . four . . . three . . . two . . . one . . . Begin drop!'

Grizz and Layla started pushing and kicking out the cases of ammunition as I kept the Huey creeping forward over the floor of the compound. We were dropping the ammunition cases from thirty feet and I saw one split open as it hit the ground, spilling rounds onto the dirt like a fruit machine paying out a jackpot, but Grizz was already shouting, 'Load clear. Go! Go! Go!'

I rammed up the collective and, free of the heavy load, we bucked into the air. I nosed the Huey over hard as soon as we were clear of radio antennae and satellite dishes on the super-structure of the accommodation block. I kept us climbing fast towards safety, away from the muzzle flashes and the metallic ticking like a cooling engine as rounds spat into the armoured underside of the heli.

The firing from within the compound ceased as soon as we were clear. The rebels outside kept blazing away both at the base and at us, but we were now moving out of range, disappearing back into the blackness of the night.

I grabbed the intercom. 'Everyone okay back there?'

'A few more holes in the cab,' Grizz said, 'but none in us as far as we can tell. Any chance of taking the high level route back?'

'Sure,' I said. 'I'll give the night vision goggles the rest of the night off.'

We flew back to the airport, but returned to Bohara twice more during the night, each time dumping more ammunition into the compound and then disappearing into the night as rounds buzzed around the cockpit like angry hornets. Even when we reached 5,000 feet – extreme range – the rebels still blazed away at us as if ammunition was no problem.

Dawn was breaking as we flew back to the airport again. We reached the airfield unscathed and I began to spiral down in tight, winding turns, keeping within the perimeter as we dropped. As I flared for landing, I saw a giant Hercules transport drawn up on the hard standing near the Decisive Measures compound.

As soon as we'd landed, we clambered down and began checking over the Huey. There were a few more perforations in its metal skin and some nicks in the edges of the rotors where rounds had clipped them, but there was no significant damage. We finished the check and turned away from the Huey in time to see a field gun being unloaded from the Herc.

'That's ours,' Grizz said. 'Let's grab some breakfast and then get that gun up to Bohara.'

'Jesus,' Tom said. 'We're a sitting target already without a two-ton pendulum hanging underneath us. Do they really need it?'

'Those weren't fireworks the rebels were throwing at them, Tom,' I said. 'Of course they fucking need it.'

I studied him for a moment. I'd been trained by him at Finnington when I was beginning my air force career in helis, but that was just about all I knew of him. When I discovered we'd be flying together again, I asked the air force rumour mill for information about him.

It appeared that he was a moderate pilot with an unexceptional career. There were no black marks on his record, but there was a whisper about him. The guy had served for twenty years in the air force — a period including the Falklands War, the Gulf War and a host of policing actions over Iraq, Bosnia and Kosovo — and yet somehow he had never been in combat. It might be that it had just been one of those unaccountable flukes — always in the wrong place at the wrong time — but my informants tapped their noses and hinted instead at a lack of bottle as the cause. At the time I had dismissed it as no more than gossip, but it stayed in the back of my mind.

The noise, the vibrations, the mental fatigue of holding concentration and the stress and tension of combat missions were also getting to me, but even allowing for his leg wound, Tom's state of mind was already beginning to worry me.

On the back of thirty hours with virtually no sleep, we had now been flying for twelve hours non-stop, and I'd almost lost track of the landings, take-offs and refuellings we'd made. Close to exhaustion, I was flying as if on automatic pilot, but there was no question of refusing to fly the mission, least of all when the guys at Bohara were taking incoming fire. I sensed a difference in Tom's attitude, however.

'That's the job, Tom,' I said. 'They need it, we deliver it.'

'In broad daylight?'

'If those are the orders, yes.'

'Even if it gets us killed?'

'That's why they pay us the money.'

Grizz looked up. 'Listen, Tom, I don't see any other helicopters or crews around here, so either we do it or the job doesn't get done at all. All right, you've got a hard job to do, but it's nowhere near as tough as the one the guys at Bohara are doing.' He paused. 'You're scared. I'm scared. The only difference between a loser and a winner is what you do while you are shitting yourself with fright. You can either lie face down in a foxhole crying for your mummy until some guy slices you up with a bush knife or you can pick up your gun and fight for your life. I know which I'd rather do.' He waited in vain for Tom to reply, then gave him a look that contained very little sympathy, and walked away, out of earshot.

Tom watched him go, then turned to face me. He held my gaze, his voice quavering with barely suppressed emotion. 'I didn't come here to die, Jack. I came to get my life back on track and give myself a breathing space, time to think and plan, not get shot to pieces over some stinking jungle thousands of miles from home.' He paused and softened his tone. 'You're a lot younger than me. Things look simpler, more clear-cut to you: there's right and wrong and not much room for anything else in between. And you fly – like all the young guys – as if the crashes and the shoot-downs only happen to other people.'

He gripped my arm tightly, as if trying to impress his words into me through my skin. 'Well, they don't, Jack. They happen to people just like you and me. One minute you're cruising along, cracking jokes and thinking about what you'll be doing on your next home leave, the next minute you're lying on your back in a tangle of broken metal, watching your life ebb away through a hole in your guts.'

He fell silent and when he spoke again, his voice was so low I had to strain to hear his words. 'My luck's run out, Jack. I've been hit already. The next one'll kill me.'

As gently as I could, I disengaged his hand from my arm. 'That's bullshit, Tom. You copped a flesh wound in your leg, that's all. If your luck had run out it would have killed you.'

I paused, struggling to find words to rally him. 'We're both knackered and by the book we've flown too many hours already, but we're going to do a few more to get the job done. We're going to fly in there with the twenty-five-pounder now and we'll do any other drops they need as well, and then we'll get the hell out again. In a few hours' time we'll be sitting with our feet up and a cold beer in our hands, laughing about this conversation. Now let's get some food and water and then get airborne.'

He hesitated, looking as if he wanted to go on with the argument, but then he shrugged and turned away. I watched him limp off towards a street vendor who had set up shop on the edge of the airfield. He was selling bean soup, smoked fish and rice. The price had gone up fivefold since the news of the rebel attacks had broken and he would take payment only in dollars, but there was little choice: it was that or K-rations.

While we ate, Grizz shouted and cajoled his private army into preparing the field gun. It was an ancient 25-pounder.

'I didn't know you were an antiques collector, Grizz,' I said.

He grinned. 'We use what we can get, smart arse. It's British Army surplus, but it came via Oman — one of the leftovers from Operation Storm twenty-odd years ago. It still works all right though and if the spotter's doing his job it'll land a round on a target just as well as a modern artillery piece — maybe even better.'

As we talked, the others sweated to loop two thick wire cables beneath the gun and stack the boxes of shells into the body of the heli. When all was ready, we refuelled the Huey and I fired up the engines to begin the pick-up of the 25-pounder. I flew forward a yard at a time, hovering over the unseen load as the guy in front hand-signalled me left, right, forward, lower. Grizz hung out of the side adding his own commentary over the intercom. A guy crouching near the gun reached up and hooked four cables over the hook as I held the heli in the hover. Then I heard Grizz shout, 'Got it. Let's go.'

I eased up the collective, slowly taking up the slack and allowing the heli to be pulled to the point of equilibrium of the cables. Then I raised the collective again. I could feel the air pressure building up under the rotors as they struggled to haul the overloaded Huey off the ground.

Finally, engines groaning under the weight, we began to climb. The controls felt stiff and sluggish under the added load and the drag of the gun – as aerodynamic as a lead brick – bled off some of our forward air speed.

Tom disarmed the circuit breaker for the hook release, ensuring we did not have an unintended drop. I had once seen a jeep that had been released from a thousand feet become embedded five feet deep in the ground and looked like it had been through a car crusher.

I adjusted the controls with small, almost imperceptible movements, knowing the danger of beginning a pendulum swing in the load that would increase until it threw the heli out of flying trim. Inexperienced pilots had been known to drive nose-first into the ground or to stall under the unexpected effects of the dead weight hanging below them, which could nullify or double the heli's own momentum.

The flight to Bohara seemed to take forever. The weight of the 25-pounder dangling below the Huey made every manoeuvre slow and ponderous, and I knew that when we came under heavy fire it would be impossible to fly the normal patterns of evasion. Any attempt to jink, climb or descend too steeply would simply throw us out of flying trim and send us crashing to the earth.

The one trick I could employ was to approach from an unexpected direction. It was one of the first things we were taught in combat training: never use the same approach path twice or the enemy will set up guns under it and cut you to pieces the next time you fly in.

Instead of the direct approach to Bohara from the west, I therefore circled south and east of the compound, coming in from the opposite direction to the one the rebels would be expecting.

The drop-off was still fraught with danger, however. With the field gun trailing below us we could not even approach at low level. Instead, I came in high and then dropped towards the compound in a dive that, because of the destabilising weight of the 25-pounder, was neither as tight nor as rapid as I would have wished.

The rebel gunners were not thrown for long by our flight path. They opened up with everything they had almost as soon as we came in sight of the compound. I could see scores of muzzle flashes and moments later rounds began to clip the fuselage. One whined away from the rotors above our head and I froze for a moment fearing they might shatter under the impact. More bullets struck sparks from the field gun below us and then ricocheted away, smacking against the underside of the Huey.

The fire intensified as the Huey dropped out of forward flight and into the hover, and the strain the massive load was imposing on the helicopter became even more obvious. The instruments showed that I was using maximum power just to hold it in the hover. We drifted forward a few feet and then eased down, dropping slowly towards the ground. Tom rearmed the hook release and I itched to give the signal to let go of the load, but I knew that if it was dropped from more than a few feet the 25-pounder would land with such an impact that it would be wrecked.

Grizz and Tom combined to talk me down as a hail of rounds rattled from the armoured underside of the Huey. One whined away from the metal frame of the Perspex canopy. The next one pierced it, punching twin holes in either side of the cockpit a few inches from our heads and showering us with fragments of

Perspex that rattled against my visor. Tom's voice cracked as he tried to give me instructions, but Grizz remained imperturbable, his words interspersed with bursts from the mini-gun. The rebels' brightly coloured T-shirts and looted clothes made them highly visible targets. While he fired small bursts of a dozen rounds, the rebels emptied their magazines in wild volleys.

'Left ten metres,' Grizz said. 'Forward five. Hold it there and descend.'

The low rpm warning began to sound. I shot a glance at the dial. The needle was still falling. We couldn't climb and could only build revs by descending. If we didn't drop the gun fast, we'd be going down with it. The vibrations through the fuselage were rattling the teeth in my head. I jabbed the intercom button. 'Prepare to release.'

'No!' Grizz yelled back. 'We're right over the heads of the garrison. Go forward ten.'

I tried to ease it forward but the Huey was now shuddering violently and the warning siren was screaming non-stop. I trod the right pedal, gaining a fractional power bonus from turning with the torque. I watched the rev needle hover and then rise again a touch. I let the Huey come round the full 360 degrees, then pushed the cyclic again. This time the heli moved, creeping forward over the ground.

I had ceased to be aware of the enemy fire around us, hearing only the bass groaning of the engines and the intermittent, strident shriek of the low rpm warning, and I saw only the patch of reddish-brown earth beneath us.

At last, Grizz gave the command. 'That's it. Hold it there. Release!'

'Release,' Tom said, the relief evident in his voice. The heli lurched upwards as he hit the button and the dead weight dropped away the last couple of feet to the ground.

We had hovered for no more than a minute, but in that time we were riddled with fire. More rounds struck the rotors and ripped through the cab walls. As we returned fire, spent casings from the mini-guns cascaded down on the tin roofs in the compound like tropical rain.

Grizz and Layla already had the cases of shells poised at the edge of the deck. I nosed the heli forward another twenty yards, clear of the 25-pounder, and they began kicking them out. The seconds crept by as I listened to the scraping sound the boxes made against the steel floor and the grunts of the two as they chained to push them out. More and more rounds struck the fuselage of the Huey. It seemed impossible that none had yet pierced a vital area. At last I heard Grizz's voice on the intercom. 'Last one clear. Go! Go! Go!'

I was already piling on the power. Free at last of the massive load, the Huey shot upwards like a cork held beneath the surface of the water then suddenly released. We hurtled away, clear of the perils from the ground and up into the sanctuary of the skies.

Chapter 7

We returned safely to the airfield but my thoughts of rest proved optimistic. We were back in action at once. As well as the field gun, fresh reinforcements had also arrived in the Herc. There was a group of black South African troops and their white NCOs, and a ragged looking bunch of white mercenaries – German, Russian, French and South African – all with the hard-eyed look of men who had killed before and would do so again.

'Decisive Measures seem to be getting a lot less choosy about where their recruits come from,' I said.

Grizz shrugged. 'Needs must. Let's get moving.'

By now, the run to the compound had become almost routine, a high-level approach, followed by a breakneck, low-level dash over the last few miles, dodging and weaving past the streams of ground fire. Each run added a few more ventilation holes to the Huey's skin, but I'd begun to feel almost invulnerable. I was at one with the machine, sure of its responses as I pushed it to the limits, weaving through the canopy of the forest, the rotors skimming the treetops. I was so confident in the Huey that, to squeeze through a gap between two giant trees rising above the level of the forest canopy, I could bank it over so far it would be almost standing on the edge of its whirling rotor disc.

We flared and landed or went into the hover over the compound only for the few seconds it took to drop the load we were carrying before we were airborne again in a fog of dust.

The pattern repeated itself this time. As we flashed in, Grizz raked the edge of the treeline and the scrub, firing at an unseen target, aiming anywhere that a rebel group might be hiding. There was little return fire. He stopped firing as we flared to land to prevent us being hit by ricochets from our own rounds.

We landed, keeping the rotors turning fast as the mercenaries dumped out their weapons and kit and jumped down. As they did so the landing zone erupted with hostile fire. Two groups of rebels were directing a withering crossfire from dead ground on either side of the compound. I heard the crack and tick of rounds piercing the helicopter's steel skin and ripping through the Perspex canopy above my head.

The seconds crawled by as the soldiers dragged out their equipment. 'Come on,' Tom shouted. 'Come on, let's go.'

'We're waiting for Layla,' Grizz said.

She had been treating some wounded at the compound, but was now returning to Freetown. I glanced towards the entrance to the bunker and saw Layla come sprinting from it, ducking and weaving as she ran across the compound and dived into the cab.

It seemed an age before Grizz called, 'She's in. Go. Go. Go.'

Before he had finished speaking, I was pulling the collective up to the stops and climbing and banking away from the rebel fire, swinging away over the end of the clearing as dust and smoke obscured the battlefield behind us.

We were airborne again in a tight spiral climb towards the safety of the skies. It was another run safely completed – until suddenly safety gave way to danger. Among the lines of ineffectual small-arms fire, I saw a series of huge, vivid red starbursts ripping upwards, outlined for a fraction of a second against the backdrop of bare rock and forest and then soaring up across the blue sky towards us. For a moment I refused to believe the evidence of my eyes.

'That's anti-aircraft fire,' Tom said. 'That ZFU they told—' His voice trailed away.

Sweat poured from my brow as I jerked and twisted the Huey around in a frantic pattern of evasion, fighting for my life as the unseen gunner tracked us, responding to each course shift. The red fireballs drifted closer to us. I pulled a maximum break, almost turning the Huey inside out, and the red fires blasted the empty sky where we had been heading only a few seconds before.

I pulled another gut-wrenching turn, then froze. Red fire burned a line through the sky towards us like an oxyacetylene torch cutting metal. It disappeared in the blinding glare of the sun, then reappeared as a red flash igniting directly ahead of us. I wrenched at the controls again, stamping down on the rudder pedals. It was too late.

Time seemed to stop, the red fire frozen in motion. Then there was a blast and a crash, and time accelerated again in a blurring frenzy of light, noise and heat. The red flares were on the inside of the cab, punching up through the armoured floor and out through the roof. The line burned its way across the floor, up through Tom's seat and out through the back of the cab.

There was the stench of burning, and a snowstorm of metal

fragments, plastic, rubber and fabric flew around me. Tom barely moved. He twitched a little, and then settled into his seat as if dropping off to sleep, but from the corner of my eye, I saw a rich, red stain spreading over his flying suit.

For a second every screen was blank. Then there was a blizzard of flashing lights and a rising cadence of alarms shrieking in my ears. The Huey gave a savage lurch and went into an accelerating spin. The tracer rounds, the red earth, dark green vegetation and vivid blue sky blurred into a continuous multi-coloured stream flashing past the cockpit.

Agonisingly slowly, each movement a huge effort, I pulled the levers, throttling back, cutting the power and the torque in an effort to hold it level. The blurring landscape slowed and came back into focus. I glanced around. The forest stretched away unbroken as far as the eye could see. There was nowhere to land.

I forced down a fresh wave of panic as I heard the clanking of the engines and saw the oil pressure dropping like a stone. I scoured the landscape below me again. The only gap I could see was a narrow channel torn through the trees where some forest giant had collapsed, up-rooted by a storm or crushed and throttled in the choking embrace of a strangler fig. On either side of the gap the wall of trees rose to a height of a hundred feet.

I nursed the failing helicopter towards the gash in the forest. It was strictly too narrow for the rotors but we had zero options. I lined up the heli, setting the tail rotor directly along the length of the gap. If it touched a tree on the way down, the tail would snap and the heli would spiral out of control.

I took a deep breath. Modern craft were lighter, constructed from materials unknown when the Huey was built, but the sheer solidity of the old helicopter had some advantages. The main rotors were almost fifty feet from tip to tip and the ballast weights at the ends gave the heavy blades such inertia that they could slice through brush and small branches without damage. It was a ten-to-one shot, but there was no alternative. More soberingly if the engines failed, we would drop like a falling brick.

The cockpit's powerful shock absorbers would give me some protection; they could soak up some of the impact of a dead-fall landing as long as the heli landed upright and level, but there were no shock absorbers under the cab. Even from a hundred feet the impact would be enough to shatter the spines of those in the back.

I began to lower the collective, inching us down. The body of the heli dropped below the tree tops. I held it there in the hover for a second, then moved the controls again. As the Huey sank lower there was a noise like gunfire and a snowstorm of wood fragments flew through the air.

The thick trunks of the trees would have snapped the rotors like toothpicks, but the outer branches were no thicker than my wrist and the velocity of the rotors cut through them like a chainsaw.

The noise and the blizzard of splinters increased as we dropped. The rotors made harder work of cutting their way through the thicker lower branches and we were still fifty or sixty feet above ground when they hit an immovable object – the jagged spike of a broken branch as thick as my thigh. The blurring rotors froze in front of my eyes and then shattered, sending silver shards knifing through the air.

The Perspex scarred and cracked, and a fragment of rotor blade smashed through it like a machete. Its leading edge sliced through my harness and into my chest as the Huey dropped towards the earth. As we crashed down through the trees I jerked the nose up at the last minute to level out. That way we might survive; if it went down nose- or tail-first, we would all die.

We hit the ground with a crash that drowned out even the screaming of the warning siren, and I blacked out.

When I opened my eyes, fragments of leaf were fluttering down onto the crumpled cockpit and a fog of orange-brown dust hung around it. My head was pounding and there was a stabbing pain in my chest. I could hear the hiss of fluid dropping on hot metal and the clicking of the engine as it began to cool. There was no sound from the surrounding jungle; every bird and animal had been put to flight by the crash of the helicopter.

I shook off my flying glove and touched my chest. My hand came away dark and sticky with blood. Then I looked to my right. Tom lay motionless in the co-pilot's seat. His flying suit from chest to ankles was a sodden mass of blood, his face as grey as if it had been cast from clay. I shuddered and looked away.

I called to Layla and Grizz. There was silence. Panic rose inside me. I called again, twisting my head to look behind me, then winced as the knife-sharp fragment of rotor blade sliced deeper into my flesh. It had been stopped by the breastbone. Had it penetrated a couple of inches farther, I would have been dead.

I heard Grizz mutter something and then Layla's hesitant reply. I almost cried with relief. 'Don't try and move for a moment. I'll get myself free and then help you.'

I undid my harness, then pulled myself as far back into my seat as I could. The broken rotor blade had a barbed edge and the skin on my chest caught and pulled. I stifled a cry of pain as it tore free, leaving a small gobbet of flesh impaled on the hook like fishing bait.

As I squeezed through the gap into the cab I heard the crack of gunfire and the tick of rounds against the metal skin of the heli. Grizz was already out of his seat, wrenching the mini-gun from its mounting.

'Get Layla out and make a break for it,' he said. 'I'll give you cover.' He handed me a grenade. 'Blow the tanks with this when you're ready to go. The diversion'll give us all a better chance.'

'Where do we wait for you?'

'You don't. We'll RV back at Bohara.'

'But Grizz—'

'Don't argue. Get going.' He loosed off a burst into the forest, then jumped out of the cab and sprinted for cover on the far side of the clearing.

I turned to Layla. 'Okay?'

She nodded. 'What about Tom?' She read the answer in my face.

I grabbed a rifle and as many clips as I could stuff into the pockets of the combat vest. Then I slid open the door on the far side of the cab, waited for a fresh burst of gunfire from Grizz, and waved her away towards the undergrowth at the edge of the clearing. She ran fast, low to the ground, dodging and weaving. As she dropped into cover behind a rotting tree-trunk, I swung out of the door. I stuck the grenade into the neck of the fuel tank, pulled the pin and sprinted away from the Huey, throwing myself into cover alongside Layla.

There was a deafening clamour and clouds of splinters and wood fragments flew through the air as rounds ripped into the tree-trunk like a buzz saw. I burrowed down into the earth like some frightened animal.

The grenade exploded, followed at once by an echoing, even more massive blast as the fuel tank detonated. A pillar of flame shot fifty metres into the air and debris whistled over our heads and scythed through the undergrowth behind us.

As the echo of the blast faded, I was on my feet, grabbing Layla's arm. 'Come on.'

We turned and ran deeper into the forest. The firing began

again almost at once, but though I could hear rounds smacking into the rotten log behind us, no shots followed us as we crashed through the undergrowth, stumbling over roots and vines that snared our ankles. We ran on until the gunfire was only the faintest of echoes, then slowed to a walk, gasping for breath, our chests heaving. It was hard to navigate through the dense forest, but I tried to keep us on a steady north-westerly bearing.

'What do we do?' she said.

'I don't want to make directly for Bohara. If the rebels are pursuing us, that's the direction they'll assume we're taking. We'll aim to pass well to the north of the compound and then approach from the east.' It was the safest direction — if there was any such thing.

The sound of gunfire had now ceased altogether. We moved on as fast as we dared, scared by the dangers that might lie ahead, but even more terrified of the rebel force behind us.

The trees had begun to thin now, with patches of cleared land hacked and burned out of the forest. Some were overgrown and beginning to revert to jungle. Others were planted with crops, showing that a village was not far away.

We reached the edge of the forest and looked out over a broad valley. A river wound through it and the floor and lower slopes were covered with savannah grassland, studded with clumps of trees. On the upper slopes the forest began again, cloaking the ridges and the head of the valley.

I could see a village set in the sea of elephant grass, a cluster of huts made of crude wattle-and-daub walls and palm thatched roofs supported on bush pole rafters. Many of the huts were dilapidated, with collapsing roofs and mud oozing out of the walls, like chocolate melting in the heat.

We moved through the chest-high grass and crept up a low ridge to peer down at the village. Despite the dereliction of the houses, it seemed a picture of tranquillity and normality. Women sat in the doorways of their huts as children played around them. A couple of scrawny hens scratched at the dust. The younger women were returning from the riverbank carrying head-loads of water and clean washing.

We lay resting and watching them for some time. 'What do you think?' I said.

'I know these people,' Layla said. 'I think we're safe here.'

As I began to get to my feet, I heard a faint noise behind me and then a blow exploded against my temple. I staggered and collapsed to my knees. When I raised my head, shaking it to clear my blurred vision, I found myself facing a group of at least twenty men. I closed my eyes, cursing myself for my stupidity. Our headlong flight through the forest must have left a trail that even a blind man could have followed. We should have kept moving fast through the grasslands, rather than pausing here, allowing the rebels to overtake us with ease.

Their hair was tangled into rough dreadlocks plaited with scraps of ribbon, thread and shards of broken mirror. Their eyes were bloodshot and their pupils like pinpricks. Most of them were little more than boys, but there was no mistaking the cold, murderous look in their eyes; if the spear pressed against my stomach was not enough to get my attention the circle of AK47s pointing at me certainly was.

Their leader, a bloated, brutish-looking veteran at least eighteen years old, stood watching as we were searched. My combat vest was ripped from my back and handed to him. He emptied my wallet, tucking my money into his pocket, and put my pistol into his waistband. My survival equipment was picked over, then distributed among his men. When he found the GPS, however, he held it in his hand for a moment then raised his eyes. 'You are spies.'

'No.' I tried to keep the fear from my voice. 'It's a GPS, it helps you find your way.' I reached out a hand. 'Here I'll—'

White light flared in my brain, as I was felled by another vicious blow. 'You are spies,' he said again. He put the GPS on the ground, drove the butt of his rifle down on it, and then kicked it away into the undergrowth.

He flicked his hand in a dismissive gesture and we were pushed and prodded down the hillside towards the village. We were spotted at once and there were shouts and cries of alarm. People began to run, only to find more groups of rebels advancing into the village on all sides. The men and boys who had been out working in the fields were dragged in a few minutes later and the whole population was herded together on the trampled earth at the heart of the village.

I searched the villagers' faces, trying to find some faint ray of hope, but sheer blind terror was written on every one. The rebel leader pushed Layla and me into one of the huts. Two rebel soldiers stood guard over us as the rest went about their murderous work.

I touched Layla's hand. 'I'm sorry I got you into this.'

'You didn't. I got myself into it. It's been the same all my life – meeting everything head-on, shit or bust. And now look where it's got me.' She tried to smile, but her voice cracked and I saw a shudder run through her.

'At least you meet your challenges,' I said, speaking as much to break the unnerving silence as to tell her my feelings. 'What do I do? Run away from one war, where at least we knew what we were fighting for, and where do I end up? In the middle of an even worse conflict where everyone is as brutal and bloody as everybody else.'

She shook her head. 'Not everyone. I'm not here because of the government or the rebels or mercenary thugs like Rudi.

They're as bad as each other – they deserve each other. I'm here because of Njama and his people. They deserve better than what life has dealt them so far. A lot better.'

I nodded. 'But we're not in a position to help them now. We can't even help ourselves.'

She shivered. 'If you make it out of here, Jack, go and see my parents for me, will you?' A tear trickled down her cheek as she spoke. 'Tell them what happened and say that though I wished it hadn't ended this way, I still didn't regret having come here.'

'You can tell them yourself, the next time you're home.'

She gave an impatient shake of her head.

'All right,' I said. 'I promise I will.'

She held my gaze a moment longer. 'And rebuild your own bridges with your family, Jack. In the end, they're all we've got.'

We fell silent and sat huddled together, frightened and alone as the rebels finished looting the village. Food and jugs of palm wine were brought out of the huts and passed from hand to hand, and they were soon drunk. They began to interrogate the villagers, but after a few minutes, they gave up even a show of interest in the answers they were given. They had not come for information, nor to uncover government sympathisers or informants.

They began chanting and singing, stamping their feet, moving ever closer, crowding the villagers together. Pangas began to rise and fall, the sun glinting from the blades. Layla stifled a scream and buried her face in my shoulder as a bloodied man collapsed to the ground, the pangas still whistling down onto his body. The blood mingled with the dust and I could see the white of bone as they struck at him. Then the rebel leader pushed back his men and produced a knife. He stooped over the figure and cut at him, then stood upright, tearing the heart from the man's still living body. He brandished it over his head, then bit into it, making his own face a bloody mask.

I was shaking with fright, and bile filled my throat, but still I could not drag my eyes away.

The leader threw the remnants of the heart to his men, then severed his victim's head with three strokes of his panga. He impaled the head on a stick and thrust it towards us, jeering at the terror he saw written on our faces.

The slaughter went on all that afternoon, until the village was full of wounded, mutilated and dead. The smell of blood hung over it, sweet and sickly, tinged with a metallic note. It was burned into my memory, mingled with the stink of sweat, urine and fear.

The young girls and women were separated and dragged away to be gang-raped. The boys were forced to become recruits. Each was first made to identify his parents and then ordered to kill them. If he refused, he was killed himself. But after this had happened three or four times the boys began killing their parents as soon as they were ordered to do so.

When one boy hesitated with a knife at his mother's throat, she herself pressed forward onto the blade, her eyes locked on his, sacrificing herself for him. The remaining adults were also killed, some hacked to death with pangas, others buried alive in a pit they were forced to dig in the dry, dusty earth.

Tears running down our cheeks, we watched the surviving boys and young men, most too stunned even to cry, being marched away. Now only the girls and young women remained in the village. The leader stayed with the two rebels guarding us. The rest of them dragged the girls away, ripping off their clothes and holding them down as each soldier took his turn. It was like a soundtrack from hell, with cries, groans and screams coming from all sides.

The leader watched for a moment, a smile on his face, then turned towards us. He flung open the door of the hut and his gaze switched from me to Layla as he licked his lips, his tongue darting out like a snake tasting the air. He walked over to me, pulled a pistol and held it against my head.

I felt the cold pressure of the muzzle against my temple and heard the click as he slid off the safety catch. He stared directly into my eyes then turned to look at Layla, watching her expression as he pulled the trigger.

I kept my eyes fixed on her face, wanting my last sight on earth to be of her. The click as the hammer of the pistol came down echoed in my ears like a clap of thunder. I fell to my knees. There was no shot. The chamber had been empty.

The rebel commander laughed and stepped away from me. He signalled to the other two to take my arms, then walked over to Layla and stood directly in front of her, then ripped her shirt from her body. He laid a panga flat against her stomach wall, the keen edge of the blade against her breasts. He clasped her nipple and mimed cutting off her breast. His men greeted the display with cruel laughter.

As I strained against the two holding me, I felt sharp steel prick my throat and forced myself to remain still. I saw Layla catch her lip between her teeth, but she showed no other sign of fear and kept her eyes fixed on the horizon.

The leader moved to the side of her and tongued her breast, watching my face all the time. 'This one is mine,' he said.

He moved round behind her, placing one hand on her hip. Still clutching the panga in his other hand, he began to propel her towards one of the other huts, thrusting his hips against her buttocks to push her forward.

As he reached the entrance he paused and called out to the two men guarding me. 'Do what you want with the white devil.'

They gave another burst of harsh laughter. One of them propped the RPG he was carrying against the wall of the hut and held a blade against my neck. The other stood in front of me. His T-shirt was stained with blood, dirt and sweat and when he spoke he showed a mouthful of black and rotting teeth. He stretched out a hand and stroked my cheek, then said something to the other rebel. They both laughed again.

He took a knife from the sheath on his belt and pressed the point against my chin, forcing my head up. I felt a stab of pain and blood trickled down my neck. The knife point worked lower, tracing a line down my throat and chest. He cut off the buttons of my shirt one by one and then slid the knife down the waistband of my trousers.

I winced as I felt the cold metal against the base of my dick. Suddenly he jerked the blade outwards, slicing my belt in half. My trousers fell to the ground. I stood there, unable to stop shaking with fright.

I felt the cold blade against my balls and he spoke directly to me for the first time in halting English. 'Shall I cut these off, white boy?'

He stepped round behind me, his hands pressing down on my shoulders. I resisted for a second and was rewarded with another blow behind my ear. I sank to my knees and was pushed forward until my face was buried in the dirt.

I heard him hawk and spit. I tried to twist away from him, but at once felt the panga against my neck. I held myself still, trying to focus my thoughts far away, but I could not block my ears to the sound of his heavy breathing close behind me.

Suddenly there was a terrible screaming from the hut where the rebel leader had taken Layla, so high pitched it sounded as if no human voice could have made such a sound. Even my captors were momentarily nonplussed. Then they laughed. 'You never made her come like that, did you, white boy?'

I gave up the last shreds of hope. Layla was dead. I would be next. Better to die fighting than on my knees, humiliated and then murdered. I tensed myself, poised to attack. I might at least get one of them before the other cut me to pieces.

Then I heard a footfall and a thin, sibilant sound, 'Sssst! Sssst!'

I looked up. The face of the rebel guarding me had become a red mask of blood. The sound came again, 'Sssst!'

There was a squeal like a slaughtered hog and the bulk of the other man crashed down on my back. Writhing to be free of his dead weight, I forced myself away from him, then swung around, smashing my elbow back into his head and twisting to drive my knee up into his groin. Then I saw his staring eyes and the gaping gash in his neck. Blood still spilled from it, but he was already dead.

I looked up. Layla stood there, still naked to the waist, her skirt ripped and stained. Blood dripped from the blade of the panga she held in her hand. She met my gaze, her eyes blank and hard, but as she looked down again at the bodies, her face crumpled and the panga dropped from her grip.

I dragged myself to my feet and wiped some of the dead man's blood from my face, then hauled up my trousers. My hands were trembling so much that I could barely tie a rough knot in the waistband. I dragged a T-shirt from the body of one of the dead soldiers and handed it to Layla. She stared dully at it and I had to help her to pull it over her head.

'We've got to get out of here,' I said, my voice cracking. 'Now.'

I ran to the doorway and peered out. The sounds of raping continued around the village, but then I saw a figure emerge from the hut to which Layla had been taken. The rebel commander staggered into view, blood drenching his thighs, his hands clutched to his groin. As he raised his head and saw me, he let out another unearthly scream.

He dropped to his knees but still kept screaming and shouting. I ducked back into the hut and looked around. The soldiers' weapons were still propped against the wall. I reached for a rifle, eased off the safety catch and took careful aim. Then I squeezed the trigger.

Instead of punching a hole in his chest as I had intended, the shot hit him low and slightly left, ripping through the side of his abdomen. The force of the impact spun him round and knocked him off his feet. But the next minute he sprang upright again, shooting wildly from the hip as he tried to bring his own rifle to bear.

His body jerked as I fired again and again. I was surprised how much it took to kill one person and how little to kill another. At last he dropped and lay still, as pools of his blood thickened and blackened in the dust. The rounds that had killed him had torn through his stomach wall and out through his back, trailing lines of torn intestines as if tracing the path of bullets for a police photograph.

I dropped the rifle and stared at my hands. To pilots, war could sometimes seem an arcade game. Remote from the action we fired our guns or dropped our bombs on targets that seemed as small and insignificant as ants. A pilot never heard the screams or smelt the blood. Even in a helicopter – even in Kosovo – I had a sanitised view, isolated from the worst of the sights, sounds and smells of combat. Now I was mired in the bloody, terrifying, ground-level reality of the most brutal and vicious warfare that the mind of man could devise.

'Jack!' Layla's fingers were digging into my arm.

I looked up. A group of rebels were sprinting towards us yelling and screaming. I reached for the rifle, then checked and picked up the RPG instead. I fumbled with it, pressed it into my shoulder, sighted and pulled the trigger. Nothing happened. I jerked it down, groped for the safety catch and then pulled it up again.

The lead rebel was no more than twenty yards away. As I sighted along the barrel I saw his face change as he spotted the RPG. Then I pulled the trigger. There was a roar and a blast. The rocket punched a hole through his guts and then detonated against a rock a yard away from him. The shrapnel practically vaporised the rest of him and cut down all the other rebels within range, but the noise of the blast brought the rest of them swarming back into the centre of the village like hornets around a broken nest.

Smoke filled my lungs and I coughed and choked. The far wall of the hut was on fire, ignited by the back blast of the RPG. I grabbed the panga and, half-blinded by smoke, I began chopping at another section of the stick wall. I hacked and booted at it with my feet until I had made a rough opening, then pushed Layla through it. I grabbed the rifle and a belt of ammunition, and crawled after her. Eyes streaming, still coughing and choking, we got to our feet and stumbled through the savannah towards the forest, hearing the shouts of the rebels in our ears. The first shots whined around us.

As we reached the trees I turned to loose off a burst from the rifle. One rebel toppled but the others did not even falter in their pursuit. I turned again and we ran for our lives along the track, deeper and deeper into the forest, with the sounds of pursuit still loud in our ears.

We ran until I thought my lungs would burst, then I checked at a faint break in the wall of vegetation. We dived through it, then twisted around, spreading the foliage back across the gap. We flattened ourselves, worming our way down into the leaf litter of the forest floor and then lay still.

The wild beating of my heart drowned any sound of pursuit at first, but then I heard the slap of bare feet running towards us. The rebels loped into view, indifferent to their own safety, running steadily, well within themselves, confident of overhauling us. Through the screen of foliage I saw the face of the lead man, his head swinging from side to side as he ran, scanning the jungle for marks that might show where we had gone.

I dropped my head and lay still as they moved closer, though my flesh crept with terror. The footsteps slowed. I held myself motionless, though every instinct screamed at me to run before it was too late.

The seconds dragged by. Then I heard the footsteps move on again down the track. I waited until the sounds had faded and my heart had stopped its pounding, and was about to raise my head when I caught a faint noise, as soft as the breeze stirring dead leaves on the forest floor. I froze. The sound grew louder, a soft scuffing in the dust of the forest track.

The noise stopped. I had closed my eyes like a child huddled under the bedclothes in fright. As I opened them again, I saw through my lashes a bare foot no more than a metre away from my face. It was all I could do to stop myself from starting in shock and fear. My flesh crept and the hairs on my neck rose. I felt an overpowering urge to do something, anything, rather than lie there inches from a man who might even now be raising a rifle to his shoulder or a panga above his head, but I knew that any movement, however slight, would give us away.

I forced myself to remain motionless, gritting my teeth and offering silent, incoherent prayers that the rebel would somehow miss us and move on. There was nothing separating us from death but a single scrubby bush and a thin covering of leaf litter. I could feel a faint trembling in my arm, but could do nothing to stop it.

I heard the soft rustle of cloth and saw the foot move as he turned towards the other side of the track, but after a moment he turned back. The foot was now facing directly towards me. An arm came into my view as he reached down and fingered a broken plant stem. It disappeared as he straightened up again.

A voice broke the silence and I almost jumped out of my skin. He had spoken in the local language, but though I did not understand the words, his tone told me the game must be up. He had seen us and was telling us to come out. If I raised my head I would see a gun barrel covering us.

My mind raced through a score of scenarios to kill him and save our lives. None was remotely feasible. We had no choice but to give up. I was tensing my muscles to ease myself up slowly enough to avoid alarming him and provoking a shot, when he was answered by another man just behind him on the track.

There was a brief, staccato conversation, then a dry, crackling sound as they pushed aside a branch of the bush hiding us. The voices came again as they peered into the undergrowth, but their tone was uncertain. There was a long silence, then an abrupt word of command and I heard again the faint scuffing noise in the dust and saw the feet of first the lead man and then the other, moving away along the track.

I remained absolutely motionless, my heart still hammering in my chest until the calls of birds told me we were safe, for the moment at least. I rose slowly to my feet, peered along the empty track, then took Layla's arm and led her off, away from the track, deeper into the jungle. We moved with painful slowness, measuring each footfall, trying to make no noise, nor leave sign that would give us away, and terrified that at any moment we might blunder into another party of rebels.

Chapter 8

We kept walking for another two hours before I felt it was safe enough to pause. We stopped at the bank of a forest stream and Layla sank to the ground at once. Her face was bruised and cut, and her hair was matted with blood. I took off my tattered shirt, rinsed the sweat and dirt from it and then gently cleaned her face. As I reached over to dab at a cut over her eye, I put a hand on her arm to steady myself. She recoiled and pulled away from me at once.

'Are you all right?' I said.

She didn't reply. Her eyes remained fixed on mine, but she seemed to be staring straight through me.

'Did he—' I checked and changed the question. 'How did you get away from him?'

Her voice was harsh and flat. 'I don't want to talk about it and if we get out of this alive, I never want anyone else to know what happened back there in that village.'

I saw her eyes fill with tears and tried to cradle her head against my shoulder, but she pushed me away, fury in her face. She walked away, turning her back to me, but I saw her body racked with sobs.

I waited in silence until she had grown quiet again. 'Do you want to wash yourself?' I said. 'I'll keep watch.'

She shivered, as if waking from a nightmare, then turned her tear-stained face towards me. 'I'd like that, thanks.'

I moved away a few more yards and stood with my back to her as the stripped off and bathed herself in the stream water.

When she had finished, we changed places. I took off my clothes, crouched on the bank alongside the stream and began washing myself. I scooped up handfuls of sand from the bed of the stream and scoured myself with it, rubbing at my back and buttocks until they were red. I felt I could have washed myself for a week and still not got clean.

After I'd pulled my clothes back on, I was already reaching for my GPS when I remembered that it, and everything else, had been taken from me by the rebels at the village.

'What do we do?' Layla said.

'I don't know. I don't know where we are. We can't find Bohara with no map and no GPS.' I thought for a moment. 'Our only hope is to make for Freetown.'

'But we can't cross the country on foot. And how will we navigate? Even if the rebels don't find us, we'll starve.'

'The river was north of us, wasn't it? All we can do is use the sun to navigate — when we can see it for the tree canopy — and make our way north until we find the river . . .' My voice trailed away.

'And then?'

'I don't know. Try and steal a boat, I suppose.'

'What about food and water?'

'Food we can live without for a while, but we have to have water. I've no Puritabs, the rebels took them along with everything else, so we'll just have to risk drinking the water.'

As if to settle the matter, I moved a few paces upstream and then crouched down and drank a deep draught of water. After a momentary hesitation Layla did the same. Then I took a rough bearing from the sunlight filtering through the forest canopy and we moved off.

We walked slowly and deliberately through the forest, trying not to leave sign, watching every footfall. The twists and turns we had to make to negotiate our way through or around the often impenetrable stands of trees and dense undergrowth made our progress even slower, and it was easy to get disorientated. I paused and tried to check the direction of the sun every few minutes, but it was often obscured by the tree cover.

The dense foliage frequently reduced visibility to no more than five yards, but my other senses seemed heightened in compensation. I paused every few steps to listen for the sound of movement or the distress cries of birds, and I sniffed the faint breeze for any human trace.

At length I heard a faint sound, barely above the threshold of hearing. It grew into the steady ripple of moving water. I caught a glint through the undergrowth and, motioning Layla to drop, I sank to my knees, lay flat and inched forward through the bushes. Parting the leaves I looked out on a broad, slow moving river.

We tracked the bank westwards for three hours. Shortly before sunset I saw a dark shape on the far bank. As we drew closer, the shape resolved itself into the mud walls and rough thatch of a ferryman's hut. Beyond it was a small, roughly cultivated and furrowed plantation for growing mealie.

A battered, rusting metal craft was tied up at the water's edge and a thick wire cable ran from bank to bank, sagging into the river in the middle. It was secured to thick, braced posts driven into the soil on either bank. The cable passed through steel eyes at each end of the boat; the ferryman could row or punt across the river, guided by the cable, or even pull the boat across, hauling in the cable, hand over hand.

I crept back into hiding and we lay down to wait for full darkness.

Half an hour after the faint glow of a candle or lantern in the huddled low building had been extinguished, I left Layla in our hiding place and crawled forward through the vegetation, with the whine of mosquitoes in my ears. I got to my feet next to the post securing the cable and gave the rusting wire an experimental pull. The boat remained motionless, but the protesting squeal of rusty metal penetrated the night.

I dropped to the ground. A second later the hut door opened and I saw the outline of a rebel soldier, his T-shirt grey in the darkness, the barrel of his gun black against the sky. He stared suspiciously at the boat and made a desultory search of the clearing around the hut, but he found nothing and a few moments later I again heard the bang of the door.

I waited another ten minutes, then I knotted the carrying loop of my rifle, clenched the strap in my teeth and lowered myself into the water. I took hold of the cable and began to haul myself out along it, climbing hand over hand, my head tilted back to keep the rifle free of the water.

The dark, muddy river swirled around me, the current trying to drag me from the cable as I inched my way outwards. I winced as strands of the rusty, fraying wire bit into my hands but I kept pulling myself on towards the far bank, fighting the powerful surge of the current.

Dark shapes sent my heart racing as they swirled past me on the flood. They were only branches and deadfalls, but to my frightened eyes in the gloom of the night, each one looked like a water snake or an alligator.

My arms were aching with the effort and I paused to rest for a moment, hanging from the cable. At once I began to shiver with cold. I forced myself on again, but had hardly moved when a half-submerged log carried on the current crashed into my shoulder, driving the air from my lungs.

I lost my grip with that hand and I gasped with shock. I felt the rifle-strap drop as I swallowed water. Coughing and choking, still clinging desperately to the cable with one hand, I flailed frantically at the water with the other. By a miracle my fingers closed around the cold metal of the very end of the barrel as the rifle slid down towards the bottom of the river.

I hauled it back towards me and forced the strap back into my mouth. With what seemed the last of my strength, I dragged my hand back onto the cable, then hung there gasping for breath, draped over the cable like a wet rag.

There was another squeal of metal and a few moments later, above the rush of the water, I heard a faint noise from the bank. I froze. The hut door had again opened and the rebel soldier was once more outlined against the starry sky, staring out over the river towards me.

I lowered my head until my nostrils were only millimetres above the surface and waited. The hairs rose on my neck as I tensed myself, expecting at any second to hear the crack of a rifle and feel the impact of a round.

He still stood motionless facing towards me, but then I saw him lay down his rifle. A moment later I heard a splashing as he urinated into the river. He turned and went back inside the hut, banging the door shut behind him.

I was now too cold to wait even a minute before working my way on towards the bank. Each movement of my hands was an agonising effort. I dragged myself onwards, snail-like, not daring to turn my head, scared not of the rebel soldier, but of the distance I might still have to cover to reach the bank.

Just as I felt I could go no farther and my numbed fingers were beginning to lose their grip on the cable, my right hand bumped against the edge of something cold and hard. The shallow, metal, flat-bottomed ferryboat was no more than ten feet long and less than half that in width. I worked my way along the side of it and crawled out onto the bank. I lay gasping on the mud, waiting for my strength to return, but as soon as I was able, I crawled a little way up the bank and hid in the shelter of some bushes. Then I began to strip down the rifle.

I laid the magazine and the breech assembly on my lap and then tore a long piece of cloth from my shirt. I squeezed as much moisture from it as I could and used it to wipe down the rifle. I reassembled it working by touch, slow and clumsy in the darkness. It took me several attempts to put it back together.

I crept back down the bank. I stared towards the hut, straining my ears for any sound, then laid the rifle down at my feet and began to work on the rotting post that held the steel cable. I heaved at it with all my strength, but it barely moved. I thought of unbraiding the cable but it was as thick as my wrist, and without tools it was impossible. I tried to scrape away the dirt from the base of the post using the butt of the rifle but the earth was too hard-packed.

I crouched there, fighting down a wave of panic, then glanced back across the river, straining my eyes into the darkness until I saw the pale disc of Layla's face watching me from the far bank. I hesitated for no more than a moment, but there was no other way. I had to release the boat. It was our only hope. I knew, what I had to do — for her as well as for me.

I crouched down behind the ferry boat no more than five yards from the hut and set the rifle on automatic. I aimed six inches above the ground and then raked the hut from left to right and right to left. I heard a scream from inside the hut as the sound of the shots echoed from the wall of the forest and rolled away across the river. Then there was silence.

I remained motionless, my rifle trained on the door of the hut as I counted to a hundred in my head. I had reached forty when the door flew open. A rebel trailing one leg behind him burst from it, shooting without aiming as he ran, heading directly for the boat where I lay hidden. I fired another burst at point-blank range. The impacts hurled him back against the wall of the hut and he slumped to the ground and lay still.

I put another burst into the hut to be sure, then I stepped out of cover and moved to the doorway. In the faint glow of the embers from their dying fire, I could see another body lying inside the hut. This was no soldier. The ferryman had been unarmed and unprotected, wearing only shorts and a faded T-shirt. The shots I had fired had hit him in the head, chest and thigh as he lay asleep. He must have died without even raising his head. The burning taste of bile was in my throat as a wave of revulsion and shame swept over me.

I ground my teeth and looked away. Then I stepped over the body and grabbed a handful of kindling from the stack of wood against the wall. I threw it onto the embers, and as it flared up I searched the hut by its flickering light, aware that every second was now vital. The noise of the gunfire would have been heard for miles up and down the river, and even now a rebel patrol might be moving to investigate.

I had hoped to find an axe or a shovel. There was neither,

only a panga, a rusty chisel and a heavy hammer. I took them outside and at once began to hammer at the cable, trying to drive the chisel through the strands. A few of them snapped but then as I pounded at the chisel, its blade suddenly broke with a crack.

I ran to the dead soldier outside the hut, intending to use his rifle as a crowbar, but as I picked it up I saw something else hanging from his belt. I hacked at the post with the panga until I had carved out a rough hollow beneath the cable. Then I forced the grenade into it, pulled the pin and sprinted for the cover of the boat. There was a flash and a blast and I heard shrapnel rattle against the metal hull.

I ran back to the post. Most of the cable had been shredded but a few strands still held. I picked up the panga and hacked at it in a frenzy, driven by the fear that at any moment the rebels would arrive, drawn by the sound of shooting. I knew there would be no escape a second time.

There was a crack as the last strand of the cable snapped. At once the ferry boat began to drift away from the bank. I ran down the slippery mud bank and half-jumped, half-dived for the boat, just managing to catch the gunwale as it swirled away on the current.

I dragged myself up and over the side and fell onto the bottom boards. Still attached to the cable on the far bank, the boat swung in a pendulum curve out across the water, past the midpoint of the river and in towards the far bank. Then the cable tautened and the boat held station, some twenty yards from the water's edge.

I called to Layla but she was already racing along the bank towards me. As she began wading out through the shallows towards the boat, I heard a scraping sound and then a twang as the cable pulled free of the guidehole in the stern. The end whipped my cheek, drawing blood as it snaked past me. It was checked for a moment by the guidehole on the bow of the boat, then it pulled clear and fell away with a splash.

I shouted another warning to Layla and she lunged for the boat as it began to slip away, gathering speed on the current. Her fingers clawed at the gunwale, and I grabbed her arm and dragged her bodily into the boat. We lay flat, gasping with exertion, as our craft moved away downstream.

We were soon well downriver of the ferryman's hut, carried headlong by the rip of the current. Within seconds the fear of striking a rock or capsizing in the darkness pushed me upright. There was no rudder, only a long punt pole lying in the scummy water in the bottom of the boat.

The current carried us along without need of my assistance, but I trailed the pole over the stern and used it as a makeshift rudder. I strained my eyes into the darkness, looking for the dirty white water of rapids or an outline blacker than the surrounding darkness that might show a sunken rock.

The sky was beginning to show the faintest trace of grey and I knew that the sudden tropical dawn could not be far away. We had to find a safe hiding place until nightfall. Low islands covered in thick vegetation were now dotting the surface of the river. Buried by the swollen river during the rainy season, they were inhabited only by the clouds of mosquitoes hovering over them.

As the light grew stronger, I chose an island in the centre of the river, no more than twenty metres long and half that across. We beached the boat and pulled it up among the long grasses and low scrub. Then we used pieces of brush to sweep the sand clear of our footprints and the marks the boat had made.

We lay down alongside the boat and made ourselves as

comfortable as we could, trying to ignore the incessant whine of the mosquitoes. 'You get some sleep,' I said. 'I'll take the first watch.'

Layla turned to look at me, her face grey in the pre-dawn light, and touched her fingers to my lips. Then she nestled down in the crook of my arm and her breathing slowed almost at once. When I looked down again, she was fast asleep. I let my eyes linger, taking in every detail of her face. In repose she was even more beautiful, her skin smooth, wiped clear of the lines of stress and tiredness. It would take far, far longer to erase the memories from her mind.

The first light of day filled me with alarm, for it revealed a village on the bank of the river which had been invisible in the darkness. As the sun rose, women walked down to the bank to fill pots at the water's edge, while others began washing clothes, pounding them on flat rocks. It was a peaceful, timeless scene, yet one filled with menace, for if we were discovered there was every chance that we would be turned over to the rebels.

The people all looked pinched and thin and — a certain sign of hard times — there were no dogs to be seen. Layla had told me that in times of famine or war, or when pollution from the mines had poisoned the river, they became more valuable as a source of protein than as guard dogs.

The lack of dogs increased our chances of escaping detection, but I did not relax my vigilance for an instant, even when the villagers disappeared from the bank to escape the heat of the midday sun. As the shadows began to lengthen again a group of a dozen armed men approached the river bank. I tensed and pressed myself down even lower into the undergrowth.

They stood on the bank, staring up- and downstream and talking among themselves. My heart started to race. Cold logic told me that there was no way that they could have tracked the passage of the boat downstream from the ferry; but my fear continued to rise. Whether through coincidence or blind luck, they were now standing only a few metres from the quarry they were seeking.

Four of the men handed their rifles to their companions and walked down to the edge of the water, dragging what looked like a thick, black rope between them. They stood and waited as two others pulled something from their belts. I saw their arms swing back and then forward, releasing black shapes that tumbled end over end and then splashed into the water a few yards upstream from where we lay hidden.

Next moment there was a double blast and twin waterspouts drenched me as the breeze carried the spray downstream. Layla's eyes jerked open. I clamped my hand over her mouth, keeping my weight on her until I was certain that she was fully awake and aware of the danger we were in.

I shifted my gaze back towards the bank. The four rebels were now advancing into the river, chest-deep in the water as they made their way towards the island.

Still I could make no sense of their actions. Then each of them in turn stopped and stood still, facing the current, their arms raised to show a net draped between them. A few silvery traces showed on the surface of the water – fish stunned by the explosions and carried into the waiting net.

The men stood motionless for another minute, then returned to the bank and tipped their catch onto the red, dusty earth. It looked a meagre haul, but I could feel my empty stomach rumbling as I watched the rebels build a fire, cook and eat the fish. As soon as they had finished, they kicked dirt over the remains of the fire and made off away from the river, into the forest.

Layla kept watch while I tried to sleep, but my hunger, thirst and general discomfort meant that I could do little more than doze. As soon as it was dark we hurried down to the water's edge to drink greedily from the river. I filled my stomach with the brown river water and the hunger pangs that plagued me faded to a dull ache.

We hauled the boat out of its hiding place and pushed off again, drifting downstream with the current. We passed between the crumbling piers of a collapsed bridge, the remaining remnant of the last railway in Sierra Leone, closed twenty-five years before.

A mile downstream of the bridge, we encountered a long stretch of rapids. I tried to steer for the bank, but the strength of the current was already too great. We were carried sideways towards the rocks as I dug at the river bed frantically with my punt pole, trying to bring us around.

The noise of the rapids reverberated around us as we entered a steep ravine, its walls smoothed and scoured by the force of rainy season floods. I could barely steer. The rapids creaming around us showed as a dull grey in the darkness, and the rocks protruding from the river bed were just a darker shade of black in the night.

I shipped the punt pole and Layla and I clung to the sides of the boat with both hands as it barrelled through the water, cannoning off the flanks of the rocks in its path. Finally our luck ran out. The boat was driven headlong onto a massive rock in the centre of the channel. I felt a bone-jarring shock and was thrown forwards and sideways out of the boat.

As it was swept away into the darkness, I heard Layla scream, then I was fighting for my life, floundering to keep my head above water. The rapids hurled me onwards. I was bumped and battered so hard from rock to rock that I could hardly draw breath. My fingers clawed for grip on the smooth, slimy rocks, but each time I was dragged away by the force of the current, carried headlong with the flood until I was thrown against the next boulder with a force that drove the air from my lungs.

I could see nothing in the darkness and hear nothing but the thunder of the water echoing from the bare rock walls of the gorge. It was as much as I could manage to gulp in a fresh mouthful of air before the next surge of water swept over my face and whirled me away again downstream. My struggles only made me weaker and weaker, and I was sure that I would soon slip below the surface and drown.

The thunder of the rapids seemed to fade, as if consciousness were ebbing away from me, then the waters again closed over my head and blackness enveloped me.

I regained consciousness, choking and retching. I could feel water still lapping around my legs, but there was gritty sand against my cheek. Then strong hands pressed down again on my chest and a fresh spasm of coughing shook me as more river water poured from my mouth.

I opened my eyes. Layla sat astride me. Tears ran down her cheeks and dripped on to me as she worked, rhythmically pushing on my chest. When she saw me looking at her, she hugged me and kissed my face. 'Thank God, I thought I'd lost you.'

I raised my head a little. The boat was drawn up on the narrow beach a few feet away. Upstream to my right, I could make out the rapids spilling out of the entrance to the canyon. The river flowed fast and silent past the beach where I lay.

'What the hell—?' I broke off in a fresh paroxysm of coughing. I pushed myself up to a sitting position and took a few deep breaths. 'Let's get out of here.'

She gave me a doubtful look. 'Are you sure you're all right?'

'As long as we don't meet any more rapids, yes.'

We clambered back into the boat and she pushed off from the bank with the pole. We slipped downstream, fast at first, but as we drifted farther from the rapids, the river broadened and grew shallow, and began to meander on a leisurely course across the plain that separated us from the coast.

We drifted with the current, peering into the dark water, trying to discern the telltale eddies troubling the surface as the river passed over shallows and swirled around sandbars and sunken rocks. Three times we had to beach the boat and half-drag, half-carry it over the shallows to the next navigable stretch.

The river bank was now barely a foot above the surface of the water. We passed through a humid, water-filled land of marsh and water-meadows, speckled with islands from which palm trees grew. On the banks of the river was the crumbling ruin of an ancient slave compound. Grey and white herons stalked through the shallows, stabbing at the black mud of the marshes with their beaks.

The low hills and hummocks, rising high enough from the marshes to be above the rainy season flood level, were clustered with garden plots and crude huts. 'They're probably deserted now,' Layla said, as she saw my anxious look. 'Uplanders use them as temporary homes in the wet season. They grow rice and fish the marshes, then go back to the uplands to grow their crops during the dry season.'

We drifted on the sluggish current through the swamp, past thickets of bamboo and the first sprawling mangrove forests. The river divided and then split again, forming a series of near-identical, slow, muddy, channels. At each point where the flow of the river divided, we dropped a leaf or a blade of grass into the water and followed whichever channel moved faster . . . or even moved at all.

Somehow we lost the main channel, however. As dawn approached, we found ourselves drifting through a series of progressively narrower and more sluggish waterways, with the mangroves growing so close around us that they scraped along the sides of the boat. I tried to retrace our course, but only succeeded in disappearing into another maze of blind alleys and dead-ends.

One ended in a mudflat and a slight break in the wall of mangroves. As I stared at the mud in the dim pre-dawn light, I saw a series of footprints leading away from the water. Whatever the dangers it might herald, it at least promised a way out of the swamps. We dragged the boat out of the water.

I took a half-pace forward and then froze. A snake was coiled at the side of the path. The leg of the frog it was swallowing still protruded from its mouth. It stared at me with cold, dead eyes, then turned and slid away into the undergrowth.

Heart thumping, I hurried past the place where the snake had disappeared and began to follow the trail away through the swamp. Clouds of flies buzzed around our heads and I heard the hacksaw whine of mosquitoes. Stumbling over submerged roots, we worked our way at snail's pace through the thickets, trying to steer a course between the main channel of the river and the settlements fringing the shore.

The soft, black, stinking mud sucked at our legs as we forced a way through the twisted stems and breathing tubes of the mangroves. Our clothes were soaked through with sweat and moisture and we were covered in black slime from head to foot.

As we plodded on, exhausted and weak from hunger, the path became better defined. Palm logs were laid as bridges over the creeks and small rivers, and among the mangroves were patches of swamp, and paddyfields studded with vivid green rice shoots.

At last the mangroves began to thin and the track started to open out ahead of us. Dawn had now broken and, after the gloom of the swamp, as we cleared the last of the banks of grey, leathery foliage and stepped out into the open, I had to shield my eyes from the light.

The tide was low and the sluggish river channel was flanked by broad expanses of glistening mud. Boats were drawn up on the opposite bank, beyond our reach. The near bank was empty. The steep hillside hid Freetown from us, but half a mile ahead, I could see smoke rising from the shanty town climbing the slopes just above the water's edge.

The rim of the rising sun was now above the horizon. 'We'll never make it,' Layla said. 'The bank will be alive with people collecting water before long.'

'We have to try,' I said. 'If we can get past here we should be safe.'

'Always assuming the rebels haven't attacked the capital while we've been making our way back here,' Layla said.

'Let's assume the worst, but hope for the best,' I said, bending down to scoop up handfuls of the brown, stinking mud. I rubbed it all over my arms and smeared it on my face and neck. Layla stared at me.

'It'll hide the white of my face and arms,' I said.

After a moment's hesitation she followed my example, and then we struck out along the bank. It was slow going, skirting treacherous stretches of mud that sucked at our legs like quicksand, and picking our way over rotting logs and past shacks and shanties that were perched just above the high water mark. Some were even built out over the water on rotting piles driven into the mud of the river bed.

The path was now a mudslide strewn with refuse and excrement, and so narrow that we could barely walk abreast past the huddled dwellings cobbled together from packing crates, scrap timber, tin sheet and even cardboard. There was little cover, but we used what we could.

Suddenly a figure appeared no more than thirty yards in front of us. We froze and dropped to the ground. The man yawned and stretched and then squatted down on his haunches. A woman emerged a few moments later from another shanty a little farther along the bank. Seemingly indifferent to the man defecating nearby, she walked out to the edge of the river, her footprints black against the wet mud. She filled a cooking pot with water and then returned the way she had come. The man stood up, wiped himself with a handful of leaves and disappeared back into the maze of shacks.

We moved on again, our progress slower and slower as more people appeared to wash or fetch water. I heard the sleepy murmur of voices from a couple of the huts and the crying of children, but no more figures emerged that might challenge us. As we passed the mouth of a filthy street lined with mean shacks and huts, a cur dog barked at us and then slunk away between two buildings.

My heart was in my mouth. If the alarm was raised we would instantly be surrounded by hundreds of people. I had seen some of the inhabitants of the shanty town at work on the way in from the airport the day I had arrived in Sierra Leone. They might hand us over to the rebels, or they might simply rob and murder us themselves.

I was torn between the need for silence to avoid rousing the people and a wave of panic that made me want to cut and run headlong for the mouth of the river and the relative safety of the beaches that lay beyond.

As we rounded a bend we came face to face with a woman carrying a bucket of water on her head. She froze for a moment, her jaw dropping with astonishment at seeing us there. Then she dropped the bucket and turned and ran before us.

I looked at Layla. 'If she raises the alarm . . .'

'But what are you going to do? Kill her?'

The fleeing woman turned up an alley and disappeared from our sight, and we hurried on past the last, ragged fringes of the shanty town. Then I heard laughter behind us. I whipped around. A group of children were tracking us, mimicking our movements. One pointed at our mud-smeared faces then dabbed a spot of mud onto his own forehead. His friends collapsed with laughter. I tried a reassuring smile. The laughter redoubled.

'Keep moving,' Layla said. 'We're free entertainment at the moment but if they get bored and start yelling for their parents . . .'

I smiled again and waved at the children, provoking a fresh outburst of mirth, then we turned and moved away across the mud. I again heard the children following.

Layla laid a restraining hand on my arm. 'There's nothing we can do,' she said. 'Let's just keep moving.'

The mud began to give way to yellow sand, speckled with grey grass stalks. I heard the roar of breakers and saw surf haze hanging in the air ahead of us. I paused and looked back. Our tracks showed clearly in the mud, two accusing arrows pointing the way we had gone. It would be another two or three hours before the rising tide would obliterate them.

The children had stopped a hundred yards behind us. They shouted something at us then turned and ran back the way they had come. 'Come on,' I said. 'We have to get out of here.'

We hurried on, but there were no sounds of pursuit from behind us, and after a few hundred yards we slowed our pace to a walk. Even so, as the sun rose higher, the heat and humidity became unbearable. We stopped to wash the heavy covering of mud from our faces in the surf, then we walked on along a beach alive with small crabs. The fronds of the ragged palms fringing the sands rustled overhead like dry brown paper.

Chapter 9

We worked our way along the deserted beach until we were almost directly behind the hotel. Then we crawled forward through the dune grass and peered out at the building and the city beyond.

My head was pounding. I ran my tongue over my dry, cracked lips. We needed water above everything. I felt an overpowering urge to run straight to the hotel, but I fought it down. We had been out of touch with everything for days. Had a rebel offensive been launched against the capital, we could be heading straight into a deathtrap.

We lay in hiding, watching and waiting. The streets were almost deserted — a worrying sign that something was wrong — and yet there was a disarming air of normality about the few people and vehicles we did see moving about. Two men stopped to talk in the street in front of the hotel and I could see a few stallholders and street vendors touting for custom farther down the hill. It was the arrival of a delivery van at the rear of the hotel that led to my next movements. As the kitchen door swung open, I took in the scent of warm bread wafting to us on the breeze. It set the saliva flowing in my mouth and my stomach rumbled in anticipation.

'Come on,' I said, getting to my feet. 'It's okay, I'm sure of it.' We walked down the slope from the dunes, crossed the concrete access road and entered the building.

There were a handful of people in the lobby. None carried weapons and as I felt the tension ebbing from me, I became almost paralysed by weakness and tiredness. The hotel guests had lapsed into a stunned silence as we walked in. I caught a glimpse of our reflections in a mirror and could see why. Two mud-stained, wild-eyed, near skeletons stared back at me. Our clothes were in rags and even I could smell the stink of the mangrove swamps upon us.

The Lebanese owner peered at me from behind the reception desk, trying to identify the mud-covered stranger in front of him. 'We need water,' I said. 'Lots of water. And food, plenty of food. And then a shower and a bed.'

He continued to stare at me, uncertainty written on his face.

I tried again. 'We were staying here a few days ago. I'm Jack Griffiths. I'm with Decisive Measures.'

His face now wreathed in smiles, he advanced from behind the desk, clapping his hands to summon his staff. 'Mr Griffiths, of course, of course. I will have your room prepared for you at once. But perhaps you would prefer to shower before you eat.'

I shook my head. 'Water and bread now.'

He turned and barked an order at a slouching waiter, then ushered us towards the dining room.

Relief again washed over me. I felt my knees buckle and I had to slump in a chair before I fell. The waiter brought a jug of water and I gulped some down, then fell on the basket of naan bread he proffered. Layla laid a warning hand on my arm. 'Take it easy,' she said. 'Eat and drink a little, then wait a while before you swallow some more. Give your body time.' She sipped at her own glass of water as she spoke, then took a small mouthful of bread.

We sat there for half an hour, hardly speaking a word, just eating, drinking water, and smiling at each other. At length, I pushed back my chair and got unsteadily to my feet. 'I've got to have a shower but I think I'm too hyper to sleep.'

She nodded. 'Me too. Let's get away from these people though.'

As we walked through the lobby, I stopped at the desk and picked up the phone, planning to call the Decisive Measures HQ or the High Commission in the hope of getting word on the situation at Bohara. The line was dead. The owner spread his hands. 'Out of order, I'm afraid.' As I shrugged and started to turn away, he added, 'The phones seem to be out all over the capital.'

I turned back to him, trying to read his expression. 'Is everything quiet here?'

He gave a flustered smile. 'It's very quiet. Not many guests.'

'That's not what I meant. I was talking about the rebels.'

'There is still fighting in the mountains, but they will not dare to attack Freetown.' He darted a glance around the lobby, measuring the effect of his words on the few hotel guests, then leaned forward over the counter and lowered his voice. 'There are rumours though. People are leaving the city.'

'What rumours? Which people?'

'There are always rumours, but . . .' He paused. 'The President is unpopular, the army has not been paid. The President's son flew to Conakry yesterday on a visit.' He tapped his nose. 'They say that the aircraft that took him there has returned without him to await its next passenger.'

'What do you think?' I said to Layla as we walked towards the stairs.

'I don't know,' she said. 'It could be significant, it could just be rumour. The whole place seethes with rumours most of the time.'

'We'll get a better idea in the morning,' I said. 'If the phones are still knackered I'll go to the High Commission and make contact with Decisive Measures from there.'

'And I'll go to Medicaid International,' she said. 'I should have reported in already, they'll be worried about me.'

'To hell with it,' I said. 'Let's catch up on the world tomorrow. We've earned a bit of rest after what we've been through.'

We staggered up the stairs, leaning on each other for support. When we reached the first floor, we stood in silence on the landing, looking at each other. I ached to take her to my room, crush her to me and bury myself in her body, then sleep with our arms wrapped around each other all night, cut off, if only for one night, from whatever awaited us in the hard light of day. But still I hesitated, unsure of her response. 'Would— Do you wa—' I began at last.

She stood on tiptoe, took my face in her cool hands and kissed me, but when she felt me responding, she stepped back. 'I'm sorry,' she said. 'I can't, not yet. It's too soon.'

'I know,' I said. 'I'm in no hurry. I'll wait as long as it takes.'

'But I don't want to be on my own. Can we just . . . ?'

For answer, I put my arm around her waist, supporting her as we shambled away down the corridor to my room. The rifle I had left behind a week before was still propped in the corner of the room, down the side of the wardrobe. Less surprisingly, the bed was still unmade from the last time I had slept in it, but I couldn't have cared less. I sat down on the edge of the bed. 'You shower first.'

She emerged twenty minutes later, her hair damp and her body wrapped in a threadbare towel, barely long enough to cover her. I saw the marks of lacerations and dark, purpling bruises on her thighs and felt anger burning in me again. As she looked towards me I averted my gaze, as if I'd been caught spying on her.

I stood under the trickling shower for a few minutes, washing off some of the filth from my hair and body, but when I dried myself, the towel still came away black with mud. I took another long shower, soaping my hair and body over and over again, until the last of the dirt had been washed away. I checked myself in the bathroom mirror and was shocked at my condition. There were black, sunken hollows under my eyes, I had lost several pounds in weight and my skin was a mass of abrasions, bruises and insect bites.

I threw my old clothes into the bin, pulled on some clean ones, and walked through to the bedroom. She was lying on the bed covered by the sheet. She held out her arms to me. 'Come and hold me while we talk.'

I lay down next to her, feeling the unaccustomed softness of the bed beneath me, and very aware of the warmth of her body against mine.

She lay watching me in silence for some time. 'I—' Layla began. 'There's something I have to ask you. The last time we were in this hotel, you spent most of the evening avoiding telling me why you were in Sierra Leone. After all we've been through, do you feel ready to tell me yet why an otherwise apparently sane and decent human being would want to become a mercenary here?'

I hesitated, buying myself a few more seconds. 'All right.' I paused, choosing my words. 'I suppose I fell out with the RAF and—' I hesitated again. I didn't want to lie to her but I was afraid of what she might think if I told her the truth. 'There was an operation in Kosovo,' I said at last. 'It went badly wrong.'

'Was that your fault?'

'It was my decision.'

'But that doesn't really answer my question. Tell me about it.' Sensing my hesitation, she hurried on. 'Only if you want to, of course, it's none of my business, but I would like to know because . . .' Her voice trailed away.

I held her gaze. 'No, I want to tell you. It was when the Serbs were really tearing the country apart. We were flying non-stop missions looking for opportunity targets — tanks, artillery, anything that presented itself to us. We'd been flying virtually non-stop since dawn and it was close to sunset. Then base picked up Intelligence — either from satellites or overflights, or from people on the ground — on some suspected hostiles. My wing-man and I were sent to investigate.'

I paused, half-closing my eyes. I could see the scene as clearly as if it were spread out in front of me as I sat there. 'There was a small hamlet surrounded by dense woodland. The houses were burning; the columns of smoke rising into the sky led us straight to the place. There was no sign of any people. We made a few passes over the area and I glimpsed something hidden in the woods.' I broke off to look at her. 'You almost get an instinct for these things after a while — unusual shapes or outlines that are just a little too straight or regular, concealed within the natural pattern of light and shade among the trees.

'There were a number of vehicles hidden in the forest, and there was something projecting from one of them; it could have been a tank barrel or maybe just a tree trunk. I made another pass, then another, trying to decide. I was also hoping to draw some fire that would have confirmed them as hostile.

'My wingman was already more certain than me. He said they were definitely hostile, but I still wasn't sure. I went round again, put the heli into the hover near the wood and then I saw some movement. It looked like people sprinting for the vehicles.

'We were cleared by base to attack and my wingman was pressing me too, but it was still my decision to make. I hesitated a little longer, then I made up my mind. We attacked.

'We flew in at low level and I fired my rocket pods at the vehicles. I was circling for another attack when I saw a figure running out of the trees. It was a woman wearing a long black skirt. She was on fire. She raised her arms above her head as if she were pleading with me. Then she fell to the ground.' Tears were now streaming down my face. 'She was one of the few who'd managed to escape from the Serbs. A group of them were hiding in the woods with their farm trucks and tractors and their horse-drawn carts. If the Serbs had found them, the men would have been killed and the women raped. But they'd survived. The Serbs had gone. Then I killed them.'

Layla didn't reply, but she reached up and stroked my face as I got myself under some sort of control. 'I'm sorry,' I said again. 'I've never told anyone about that before.'

We lay in silence for some time. 'I used to dream that one day I would be really famous,' Layla said. 'An astronaut or a film star or a Nobel Prize winner. I imagined leaving behind a monument to my life so that years after my death, people would still remember my name and what I'd done.' She smiled. 'I'm getting a bit older and wiser than that now, I've realised that I'm never going to blaze a trail across the heavens. Even if I did, what difference would it make to me once I'm dead and buried? Nelson's Column is still standing, but aren't his bones as cold as the stone it's made from? Is Andy Warhol any less dead because his paintings are still hanging on gallery walls?

'The older I get, the more I realise that life is about really small things. God knows, I'm no Mother Teresa, but I feel that if we can do a little bit more good than harm while we're passing through, that's probably about as good as it gets for most people.'

'In that case, my personal ledger is way out of balance,' I said. 'Helping a couple of old ladies across the road doesn't really begin to compensate for the people I killed in Kosovo.'

She gripped my arm, her fingers digging into my flesh, trying to impress the importance of what she was saying on me. 'Then that's all the more reason to start balancing the books now. You can't change the past, but you can change the future. You don't want to be looking back over your life in old age and still be seeing that burning woman in Kosovo before anything else.'

She fell silent, studying my face, and when she spoke again, her voice was little more than a whisper. 'I killed a child once. It was when I was training as a doctor. I was a houseman, a junior doctor, at—' She paused. 'Well, it doesn't matter where, does it? I was dog-tired at the end of a very long shift, but of course that's no excuse. Somehow – I don't know how, I knew what the right dose should be – I gave the baby three times the normal dose of a drug. Her heart stopped. I killed her.'

'But you've saved hundreds of others since.'

'I killed that one. When I close my eyes I can still see her little crumpled figure in the cot and the bewildered faces of her parents turning to look at me and asking, 'Why? What happened?' And do you know what? I didn't even have the guts to admit what I had done.

'The hospital administrators hustled me away at once and one of their bereavement counsellors came to talk to the parents.

They never found out. They could have sued me, sued the hospital. But it wouldn't have made any difference. It wouldn't have brought their child back.' She fell silent again, staring past me. 'So, we've both had to learn to live with the consequences of our mistakes,' she said. 'I can understand why you left the air force, but that still doesn't explain why you came to Sierra Leone.'

'I didn't want to be put in the position of having to make that kind of terrible decision again.' I paused. 'Who am I kidding? What I really mean is that I didn't ever want to be in a position where I could get it so terribly, horribly wrong again. But flying helicopters is what I do. There's no work on civilian helis; there are thirty or forty trained pilots for every job that's going. I thought this would be a safe option; not many people want these kind of postings, but it suited me.'

She gave me a gentle smile. 'If the reasons you joined the air force were good ones, what happened in Kosovo shouldn't negate them. It was a tragic accident, but you can't just run away from it.' She paused. 'I ducked my responsibilities to the family of that dead girl and I'll never forgive myself for that, but I didn't give up medicine because of it.

'I know that nothing I can ever do will bring the child back to life, or end the heartbreak her parents must feel every single day. All I can do is try to help other sick children to get better and make sure I never make such a terrible mistake again.' She held my gaze as she spoke. 'You've got to do the same kind of thing, Jack. We all have a few skeletons in our closets. You can't keep using what happened in Kosovo or the fact that your parents divorced when you were young as a reason not to commit yourself, any more than I can blame my mixed parentage for my failings. It's down to us, Jack, no one else.

'You can't just sit on the sidelines, least of all in Sierra Leone.

If you're here at all, you're either part of the problem or part of the solution. There isn't any neutral territory.' She fell silent. 'I'm sorry,' she said. 'I'm a fine one to lecture you, aren't I? I spend my life butting my head against every obstacle that presents itself. Half the time, maybe more, it's completely counter-productive. I'd achieve a lot more if I didn't contest every single issue as if my life depended on it.'

'We make a good team then,' I said. 'We cancel out some of each other's weaknesses.'

She gave me a long, thoughtful look. 'That's one way of looking at it. But what if we cancel out each other's strengths instead?'

'If we did, we wouldn't be having this conversation now. We'd be lying dead back there in that jungle somewhere.'

The light was fading now. She kissed me again, then sat up. 'I'm going back to my room,' she said. 'I need to sleep now.'

'Sleep here,' I said.

She shook her head. 'I need to be alone for a while to think things through.' She held on to my hand a moment longer, then stood up.

I watched her all the way to the door and as it closed behind her, I whispered, 'I love you,' to the empty corridor.

Despite my exhaustion, it was a long time before I fell asleep. When I did, I was soon in the grip of the familiar nightmare: the thunder of guns, the burning figure, and the crushing feelings of helplessness and guilt as I saw the woman slump and lie still, her clothing still ablaze. Then I was awake, with the sound of explosions and gunfire in my ears. This was no dream.

'Christ no. Not again. Not again.' I rolled off the bed onto the floor and lay still for a moment, then crawled to the window and peered out. Dawn had not yet broken, but I could see the flash of explosions and the lurid glare of flames. I picked up the phone. It was still as dead as a hammer, either faulty or . . . I let that thought go at once.

I crawled back across the room, dragged on some clothes and picked up the rifle and the spare clips of ammunition. Then I let myself out into the darkened corridor. As I felt my way along the wall towards Layla's room, I heard a door open and saw her silhouetted in the flash of light from another explosion in the heart of the city. I called her name and we clung to each other.

'I was just coming to find you,' she said, her voice shaking with fear. 'What do we do?'

'Get in the safest place we can find in the hotel, and then try to find out what the hell is going on.'

'Are we safe in the hotel?'

'I guess so, as safe as anywhere. If we go charging out into the night, we're just putting ourselves in greater danger. We'll stay here until we know what's happening.' I cursed as another explosion lit up the night. 'Why is this shit following us around?'

'In Sierra Leone it follows everyone around.'

We groped our way to the stairs and went down to the lobby. There was no one to be seen. The hotel staff and, more worryingly, the security guards paid to protect the building had obviously reached their own conclusions about the shooting. All had fled.

The owner's office was unlocked. I tried to dial the British High Commission, but the phonelines were still dead. There was a transistor radio on the desk, but when I turned it on, there was only the unbroken hiss of static from the local channels. It was another ominous sign. If a coup was under way, the telephone exchange and the radio station would be among the first targets.

I tuned the radio to the BBC World Service instead. We had to endure forty minutes of magazine programmes before the next news bulletin. We were the lead item: 'Reports are coming in of an attempted coup in Sierra Leone. Sections of the armed forces led by junior officers and NCOs have mutinied and made simultaneous attacks on the airport, the radio station and Government House in the capital, Freetown.

'Another group detonated a car bomb outside the gates of the Pademba Road jail, releasing hundreds of prisoners who have joined the rebel forces. There are unconfirmed reports of killing and looting in the capital. The Liberian-backed rebels recently began a renewed offensive in the Eastern provinces of the country.

'Sierra Leone's President is reported to be alive, but has fled to Conakry in Guinea. Sierra Leone has experienced years of turmoil since . . .'

Layla shook her head. 'He's done that so often, they must keep a suite permanently on standby for him.'

There was a whistle of static as I returned to the local channel. A scratched recording of martial music was playing, but a few minutes later it was replaced by the first broadcast by a rebel spokesman. Speaking in thick, lugubrious tones, he announced that the government and 'key installations' were already in rebel hands, and declared a new republic of Sierra Leone. The identity of its leader was not revealed. He proclaimed an immediate curfew, breaches of which would be punished by death and warned 'foreign troops not to get involved with the internal affairs of the new republic of Sierra Leone'.

I forced a smile. 'I guess that means me and the rest of the boys.'

'What do we do now?'

'We wait. We'll have to reach a safe haven like the High Commission eventually. But we need to know a bit more about what's going on first. Meanwhile we stay put. We'd be safest from the firing somewhere near the heart of the building, but I guess we'll be better off up where we can see what's happening. If the rebels decide to storm the hotel, we need enough warning to be able to make a break for it. I don't fancy our chances' — I held her gaze — 'especially yours — if they find us here when they're looting the place.'

We went back to the lobby. The handful of other residents had now congregated there. They had dressed in haste and jammed their possessions into their bags, but now stood irresolute, debating what to do like package tourists waiting for a coach that hadn't turned up. Some were for making a dash for the airport at once, others preferred to wait for daylight. Two others, businessmen — or so they said — advocated sitting tight and awaiting the arrival of a rescue force of US Marines. 'We're American citizens,' they kept repeating like a mantra. 'The US government will make sure we're safe.'

The hotel owner fussed around the edge of the group, a sheen of sweat on his forehead. He kept imploring them not to panic, to stay and see what daylight brought. It was hard to tell if his concern for them was personal or financial. When he caught sight of me, he greeted me like a long-lost relative. 'This man works for Decisive Measures,' he announced. 'Tell them that soldiers will soon come to protect them. Please.'

'I don't know if they will,' I said, provoking fresh consternation. 'I'm a pilot, not a soldier, but if it's any help, until the situation on the streets becomes clearer, I'd say you're as safe here as anywhere.'

We left them still arguing about what to do, and went down to the kitchens. We collected some food and water, and I liberated some rolls of parcel tape from the luggage room, then we went up the service stairs to the first floor. The door to the corner suite was locked, but I kicked it open. The suite had windows to both the south and east, looking out along the beach road, where some of the expatriate houses were clustered, and down the hill into the city centre.

I took the fire extinguishers from the corridor and placed them inside the room, then closed the door. We covered the windows with strips of parcel tape and then drew the curtains, leaving only a chink through which we could see out. Layla helped me manhandle the bed onto its end, and with the tables and the other furniture we constructed a primitive blast screen. Then we sat back to watch and wait, huddled close together, her head resting on my arm.

Explosions continued to light up the dying night and there were regular, sustained bursts of small-arms fire. It convinced me that the shooting was coming from very poorly trained soldiers; professional fighting men used short aimed bursts, rather than emptying their magazines into a target.

Just before dawn, two vehicles crammed with people stormed out of the hotel car park and away down the hill. The group advocating an immediate break for the airport had obviously won the day.

'Do you think they'll make it?' Layla said.

I shrugged. 'I don't know. Even if they do, the airport might already be in rebel hands.'

We tracked the taillights of the cars until they disappeared from sight at the bottom of the hill. Shortly afterwards there was a prolonged burst of gunfire from the direction they had taken and the crump of grenades or rockets. Our eyes met, but neither of us spoke, though I felt Layla's shoulder shaking as she cried soundlessly.

The first light of dawn confirmed the impression we had formed in the last hours of darkness: the shooting and explosions were moving steadily closer to us. The rising sun revealed a pall of grey smoke hanging over the city, and we could see flames licking around some of the taller buildings in the centre.

Peering out through binoculars from our hiding place, I saw the first rebel soldiers advancing along the road. Most of them wore sunglasses, T-shirts and stolen clothes piled, despite the heat, layer upon layer over their threadbare fatigues. Like the rebels we'd encountered earlier fragments of mirror and bits of multi-coloured plastic were woven into their hair. They also had juju emblems, feathers and fragments of cloth or paper, attached to their clothes.

As they moved through the streets, they searched each building by shooting wildly into it. Then the looting began. The streets lower down the hill were soon part-blocked with rough barricades and strewn with debris, smashed glass and burning wreckage. Fires broke out in several buildings and bonfires were also lit in the road to signal trouble or summon help. I saw waves of people pouring through the streets, heading towards the beacons of oily black smoke rising from pyres of burning tyres.

'Where the hell are the government troops?' I asked.

'Don't hold your breath. They defected to the rebels en masse in the last uprising. They're on whichever side they think will win.'

From the windows facing the beach road, I could see the homes of expatriates also being stripped. The Lebanese traders, like the Asians in Uganda or the Chinese in Indonesia, were the richest and most vulnerable targets. Those who had not already taken the precaution of buying the protection of the rebel leaders – and perhaps even some who had – were robbed of everything.

The rebels commandeered any vehicle they could find to carry off their plunder. Some were stolen only to be crashed within yards and abandoned by their inexperienced drivers, but I saw a steady procession of jeeps, lorries, cars, and even an ambulance and a fire truck, driving off laden with booty. As well as food, clothes, furniture and bedding, they looted things for which they could have no conceivable use. Fridges and washing machines, computers and televisions were piled on trucks and taken away to sit blank as dead men's eyes in some shack or jungle clearing far from any source of electrical power.

Most people had already fled or gone into hiding. Those who remained behind, whether from foolish optimism or paralysis by fear, were dragged out of their homes. We watched, powerless to intervene, as some were forced to kneel in the road and then shot or beheaded. The terrible screams we could hear echoing through the deserted streets told of the fate many others were suffering.

I tried to drink some water, but my hands were shaking so much that I spilled more than I drank. In the end Layla took the bottle from me and held it for me.

'I'm sorry,' I said. 'I guess I'm not as brave as I used to think I was.'

She silenced me by placing a finger against my lips, and then held me in her arms as the thunder of shots and explosions continued to rumble around the city.

Two groups of rebels even fought a gun battle with each other over possession of a liquor store. An argument over the spoils erupted into a fight and they turned their guns on their comrades with the same murderous indifference they had showed when killing others. Already high on drugs, the victors began drinking every bottle of wine and spirits they could find.

Another large group attacked the Bank of Sierra Leone. Boxes of explosives and RPG rounds were carried into the bank – enough to blow up half the town. The detonation killed several rebels waiting outside the bank. It also lifted the roof off the building and sent burned and singed bank notes flying high into the air. As they fluttered down, carried west on the breeze, they were pursued by a rabble of rebels. They jumped to try to pull the notes from the air as they drifted down, stooped to pick up undamaged ones from the dust and tried to stamp out the flames on the remnants of burning notes.

Late in the morning, the sustained firing began to die down, replaced by brief isolated bursts, suggesting that either the two sides were regrouping or that the major resistance had been overcome. It took the rebels until noon to complete the clearance of the streets at the bottom of the hill. Then they began to advance towards the hotel.

The few remaining residents panicked at the sight. I heard an engine start and a moment later a battered Toyota came storming out of the car park. There was a blizzard of gunfire and a crash, as it slewed off the road and hit a wall.

I did not stay to see what would happen to the surviving occupants. 'Come on,' I said. 'This is our chance. If we stay, we're finished. Let's get out of here.'

'To where?'

I shrugged. 'The High Commission or the airport, if they're still in friendly hands. We need to get some information on what's going on and where the rebels are in control.'

She gave me a doubtful look. 'I think our best destination is the Medicaid International compound. I'll be needed there anyway. There'll be a lot of wounded. And whatever else the rebels are destroying, I'm sure they won't attack there.'

'I wish I shared your confidence,' I said. 'The High Commission has well-armed guards to protect it. The rebels are likely to leave it alone because they won't want to provoke a direct intervention by British troops. It's a much safer bet.'

Layla shook her head. 'For you maybe, but if there's a way to reach Medicaid International, I have to go there. I'm a medic, Jack, I'm needed there.'

We ran down to the lobby. It was now empty. Every other resident had fled, and only the owner remained, sobbing and wringing his hands. He ran across to us and seized my arm. 'What will I do?' he said. 'Please bring help, bring soldiers before it is too late.'

I gently disengaged his hand. 'You should get out now,' I said. 'If you stay, you'll be in great danger.'

'If I leave my hotel, it will be destroyed.'

'Perhaps, but if you stay, they will loot it anyway. Don't let them kill you too. You must leave now.'

He turned away and disappeared into his office. A moment later, I heard the sound of the key being turned.

Layla looked at me. 'Come on,' she said. 'It's his choice.'

We went downstairs to the deserted kitchens, took some more water and a little food, and then slipped out of the back door of the hotel and ran off down the access road. As it began to curve round towards the front of the hotel, we clambered up the sand bank separating it from the beach. I dropped flat just below the summit, wormed my way forward and peered out across the white sands. To our left, I could see smoke rising from some of the expatriate houses, but the approach road and the beach itself seemed to be empty.

Bursts of gunfire still sounded behind us as we crept along, almost bent double, using the low wall of the approach road as cover. We had almost reached the beach when there was a sudden movement in front of us. I swung my rifle up, then exhaled as a vulture flapped lazily into the air. Others followed as we moved closer, their beaks and heads stained dark red.

I knew what we would find before we rounded the end of the wall. Clouds of flies rose from six battered corpses, their blood staining the white sands around them. Each had been mutilated. Hands, ears, noses, and a woman's breasts had been hacked off with bush knives. The eyes and tongues of two others had been ripped out, and a man's genitals had been cut off and then stuffed into his mouth.

Shards of mirror glass had been forced into the empty eye sockets of one of the victims. It gave his corpse an even more horrible, macabre air, as the reflected sky shone like glittering blue eyes in his tortured, screaming death mask.

The vultures we had disturbed congregated in the trees at the edge of the beach. In the lulls of firing behind us, I could hear the dry, leathery rustling, of their wings as they changed position on the branches or another flew in to land. They could wait all day to resume their feast, secure in the knowledge that they and all their kin throughout the city would grow fat on the day's gruesome harvest.

As I stared again at the bodies littering the beach, I felt Layla's hand on my arm. 'Come on, Jack. We can do nothing for them. We must get away.'

I shivered, then turned and ran after her. My legs felt like lead and I was crushed by a numbing weariness. We had found safety after a terrible ordeal only to be cast back once more to the edge of the abyss.

We sprinted along the sands, using the dunes flanking the beach to screen us from any pursuers. We ran for half a mile, then threw ourselves down, gasping for breath.

'We can't stop yet,' I said, as soon as I could speak. I grabbed a handful of dead palm fronds. 'Come on. Down to the sea.'

Layla looked at me as if I was crazy, but followed me without protest. When we reached the water's edge, I turned and ran through the shallows for another few hundred yards. Then, lungs bursting, I stopped again.

I turned to make sure the beach was still empty behind us, then gave Layla the rifle and sent her on ahead into the dunes. I followed, walking backwards, erasing all trace of our tracks with the palm fronds.

Layla had already found a hiding place in a hollow among the dunes, from where we could keep watch. I swept away the last marks we had made and then lay down beside her. I was so close I could feel her heart pounding against my side as she reached forward to part the dune grass and stare back down the beach, but when she turned to speak to me, her voice was level. 'What now?'

'We wait for nightfall and then move out.'

Chapter 10

We lay there throughout the heat of the day, eking out our precious water supply and using the palm fronds to give us a little shelter from the sun. The hideous, faraway sounds of shots, screams and explosions, continued intermittently, but the only visible movement was the flapping and squabbling of the vultures over their feast.

Then in late afternoon, a utility truck crammed with soldiers cruised slowly out of the end of the approach road and drove down the beach. I sank back deeper into hiding, my heart thumping as they slowed and stopped at the line of tracks leading down to the sea. The engine died and four rebels jumped down and began pacing the beach, staring down towards the sea and back towards the dunes. I inched the rifle forward and eased off the safety catch, but to fire at a truckful of well-armed rebels would have been a suicidal last resort.

I felt Layla tense beside me as one of the rebels appeared to stare directly at us. 'Keep still,' I said. 'I'm sure they can't see us. Don't move and give us away.' I squeezed her hand and felt a slow answering pressure.

It seemed an eternity before the engine restarted and they began to drive on slowly down the beach. I saw their heads swivel from side to side as they scanned the surfline and the edge of the dunes. I froze, hardly daring to breathe as they drew level with us. From high in the dunes I could still see faint marks where I had brushed away our tracks. I could only pray they were invisible from beach level.

The truck slowed and then moved on, out of our sight, but we remained motionless, listening to the engine note. It faded then swelled again, as they turned and began to make their way back.

I jumped at the sudden sound of a shot, though it could have been the truck backfiring, which came back into our line of sight, moving even more slowly, and stopped again at the line of tracks. We heard the murmur of voices rising as an argument began, then there was a crash of gears and it drove off again, speeding away up the beach towards the city.

We saw no one and nothing else all day, but even when nightfall came we remained where we were, for in the darkness we still heard the occasional burst of firing and the sounds of shouts and brute laughter, carried to us on the breeze.

We drank the last of our water just after sundown. Mosquitoes buzzed and whined around us, adding to the discomfort of our thirst, but still we lay there, waiting until midnight in the hope that by then, sated with killing and looting, most of the rebels would have fallen into a drink- and drug-induced stupor.

I kept looking at my watch as the hands inched towards midnight, and peering through the fringes of the dune grass. Still

I hesitated, reluctant to leave even this flimsy refuge for the dangers that might lie in wait on the city streets.

'Come on,' Layla said at last. 'We can't stay here for ever.'

We moved off through the dunes, advancing with painful slowness, working our way along the fringes of the beach. We could last without food if we had to, but we needed drinking water badly. The nearest point where we could find some was the hotel. My plan was to get some from there if it seemed safe to do so, and then strike across the city to the Medicaid International compound.

If, counter to my expectations, we found that it was untouched, I would leave Layla there and make my way on alone to the High Commission, to obtain both some Intelligence on the situation in the country and the means of communicating with Decisive Measures HQ. I cursed myself for not taking the hotel owner's transistor radio with me when we left, for I was sure it would by now have been looted.

We inched our way along the edge of the approach road from the beach and lay in the shadows behind the hotel for some minutes. The already battered walls were marked with holes from fresh gunfire and several windows gaped emptily. Lit by the starlight, the shattered glass glittered like diamonds in the dust around the base of the walls.

There were no lights in the hotel and no sign of movement. After watching for ten minutes, I took a last careful look around and then reached across and squeezed Layla's hand. 'Okay,' I said. 'Let's go for it.'

We broke cover and sprinted for the back of the hotel, flattening ourselves against the wall at the corner of the building. We edged our way along, ducking under the windows, until we reached the rear door. It hung slightly ajar, banging softly in the breeze.

I slid the safety catch off my rifle and eased the door farther open with my toe, then paused and listened. There was no sound but the faint drip of water from somewhere inside. We moved into the dark building. The entire basement of the hotel was deserted, but the walls and ceilings had been riddled with gunfire, the doors forced open and everything looted. The kitchens were stripped and even the sink and cooker had been ripped from the wall and carried off. All that was left were broken pipes and smashed tiles.

We slaked our thirst and refilled our empty water-bottles from a dripping pipe and then crept up the stairs to the ground floor. It was deserted, but everything of value had again been torn out in an orgy of destruction. As we moved through the lobby, our boots crunching on broken glass, I heard a faint noise from the owner's office.

I motioned Layla to silence and crept round the broken brick plinth on which the reception counter had been standing that morning. I listened at the door, eased it open a chink and then burst into the room.

A bruised, bloodied figure sat in the far corner half-burrowed into a pile of broken furniture and fallen plaster. He was rocking slowly to and fro, keening to himself. The voice died away as he looked up. The hotel owner stared blankly at me for a moment then scrambled to his feet. 'My English friends, thank God, you have come back.'

His speech was slurred, and as his mouth gaped open, I saw by the moonlight the stumps of broken teeth.

'Are there more soldiers with you?' His smile faded as I shook my head.

'Are the rebels still here?' I said.

He shuddered and shook his head. 'All gone. Everything gone.'

'Other people?'

Again he shook his head. 'I don't know. I don't know.'

'Do you have food?'

He didn't reply and I shook his arm. 'Do you have food?'

'Nothing. Nothing.'

I turned away and left him there. We hurried through the rest of the ground floor searching for food, but the rebels had stripped the place bare. We paused just inside the broken doors of the hotel, peering out into the darkness. I hesitated a long time before moving out. Even the hotel's echoing, empty concrete rooms offered some illusion of safety, and I had to force myself to move. At last I stepped out again into the heat of the night.

The telephone poles lining the street still sprouted a stubble of short strands of wire; the rest of the cables had been pulled down. Doors, locks, doorknobs, hinges and window frames had also been looted from the buildings we passed.

The streets were almost deserted and the handful of people we did see were as nervous and frightened as we were, scuttling away into hiding as soon as they saw us approaching. Through the gaping windows of one looted three-storey building I could see the flicker of a dozen fires lit by squatters, who had moved into the ruined offices as if they were caves in a rockface, but elsewhere we saw no one and heard nothing but the howling of a dog in the distance.

'Where is everyone? Where are the rebels?' I said.

'Asleep probably, dead drunk on palm wine or high on drugs. Their bloodlust might be sated for now, but don't be fooled. They haven't gone away.'

We kept to the deserted sidestreets as much as possible and moved a few yards at a time, pausing to scan the way ahead from each doorway or alley. We stopped before every intersection and I stole forward, moving soundlessly through the shadows, to make sure our way was clear.

Twice I saw barriers to our right, blocking the main road, but if they were manned, the figures guarding them were asleep or motionless and invisible in the darkness, and there was no challenge as we crept across the open space and disappeared into the next alleyway.

The closer we got to the Medicaid International compound, the less sanguine I was about finding it untouched. There was devastation on all sides and mingling with the stink of smoke was the sickly stench of blood. Several times we had to skirt or step over corpses sprawled in the gutter, but we saw no other living thing save the rats sharing the fruits of the rebels' victory.

The double doors of the World Food Programme's warehouse stood wide open and the building had been completely emptied of rice. Layla's workplace lay a few yards farther down the street. Here again the gates of the compound were unmanned and gaping open. We crept across the yard, stumbling over rubble and debris, and entered the darkened building.

We searched it from one end to the other. There were no signs of struggle, no bloodstains, and few bullet holes, as if even the blood lust of the rebels had been muted here, but there was no trace of the doctors and nurses who had worked here either and, not unexpectedly, the store rooms and cabinets had been stripped of every last drug and dressing.

Layla's shoulders sagged. 'What's happened to them?' she said, her voice so low I barely heard her.

I went to her and cradled her to my chest. 'They'll be all right,' I said. 'Even if they didn't get away in time, the rebels aren't stupid. They know the value of them both as medics and as hostages. They'll be kept alive and well treated.'

She pulled away from me to search my face. 'Do you really believe that?' she said. 'Or are you just trying to comfort me?'

'I really believe it. They're alive, I'm sure of it.'

She exhaled heavily, still staring around her. 'So what now?'

'The High Commission. Let's hope that hasn't been looted too.'

There seemed to be no roundabout route we could take there. The only way to avoid the main streets was to work our way up the hill through the shanty towns — an even more frightening alternative.

We moved slowly across the city, pausing in the shadow of each building to scan the streets ahead. We had been walking for about twenty minutes when we reached the junction of a broad street and a narrow alley running up the hill in roughly the direction we wanted to follow. I hesitated, weighing up the benefits of using the alley.

It was bound to be less frequented than the streets, but had few openings in which we could take cover. The cracked walls of the concrete buildings fronting one side of the alley were two storeys high and the doorways were blocked with steel shutters or iron gates. On the other side, a high wall of mud bricks interspersed with a few old stone buildings was pierced only by stout wooden doors.

The sound of an engine in the main street decided me. I ducked into the alley, pulling Layla behind me. We inched our way along, paused at the corner listening and looking, then sprinted across a broad street and dived into another alleyway. As we did so, I heard a shout and the sound of running feet.

We sprinted up the alley. I could hear Layla's footfalls echoing from the walls as she ran after me. Then there was another shout followed by the crack of a rifle. I heard the howl and whine of the bullet as it smashed against the wall and ricocheted away.

The words of a combat survival briefing I had been given as a rookie pilot came into my mind: 'Bullets ride walls. If you're trapped in a street and you have no cover, you're safer in the middle than pressed flat against the walls.'

The theory was fine, the practice less attractive. More shots rang out and more rounds whistled past us. I dived into a doorway, heaving at the door and battering it futilely with my shoulder. A bullet struck the wall inches from my head and stone fragments needled my skin.

I ran on again, ducking and weaving in the hope of making myself a harder target, as I scanned the walls for any opening that might give us refuge from our pursuers. I came to another wooden doorway almost flush with the wall. It was locked, but again I put my shoulder to it, trying to ignore the running feet and the hail of bullets whining around us. The wood creaked, groaned and at last gave way and we tumbled inside. The door opened into a single deserted room. There were two tiny windows in the rear wall, barely large enough to squeeze through, even if we had had time.

Which we did not. The running footsteps stopped. There was a moment's silence, then a grenade exploded outside the sagging door. The blast threw us against the wall. I heard a thunderous concussion and a flash of heat seared me. There was the sour taste of chemicals in my mouth.

We dragged ourselves up. The stout door now hung from one hinge, part-blocking the doorway. It had absorbed much of the shrapnel that would otherwise have shredded us. We were both scratched and cut but otherwise unhurt.

Through the ringing in my ears, I heard the sound of running feet again. I looked around. There was no way out but the way we had come. The back windows had been blown out in the blast, but if we tried to crawl through them and became stuck . . .

I looked up. Thick beams supported the shallow, pitched roof above us, so blackened and ancient they might have been the timbers of some wrecked slaver or sailing barque. They sagged in the middle and sprouted fungus where they joined the walls. I could only pray that they would bear our additional weight.

There was no time to wait. The running feet were closer now, almost at the doorway. I threw myself upwards and my fingers grabbed and caught on a beam. I hauled myself onto it, squeezing between the beam and the roof, the muscles of my arms screaming with the effort, then reached down and pulled up Layla. Her feet dangled in the beam of moonlight from the doorway for a moment, then with a further heave I hauled her up and alongside me.

I put my mouth close to her ear. 'Lie on your side along the beam and don't move, no matter how frightening it gets.' I could barely hear my own voice for the ringing in my ears, and was unsure if I had whispered or shouted, but she gave a small nod and did as I said.

We lay lengthways, head to head, our hands clasped. A moment later, the remnants of the door were kicked aside and there was the thunder of automatic weapons. The walls below us seemed to explode as rounds ripped into them, sending fragments of stone and mud whining around us.

The shooting stopped. The walls were riddled with bullet holes, and dust motes danced in the pencil beams of moonlight from each one. There was a pause, then two figures darkened the doorway. They again raked the room with gunfire, bullets smashing into the walls and ricocheting away with a sound like screaming.

Another lull, then they began firing upwards. Rounds blasted through the roof on either side of us, perforating the slates and punching holes through which I could see the glimmer of stars in the black sky. More rounds smacked into the beam beneath me. I felt it twitching with the impacts and shards and splinters of wood filled the air.

The shooting seemed to go on for ever. I shook with fright, wanting to scream out my terror, beg, plead, anything to make it stop. There was a sudden pause. In the silence I heard the faint metallic scraping of magazines being changed. I heard voices too, though my shell-shocked ears could make no sense of the sounds. Then the dark shadows disappeared from the doorway. I fought the urge to raise my head and peer down.

The next moment there was the thunder of another grenade below us. I heard a rumble as part of the rear wall collapsed and a crash as one of the other roof beams toppled and fell. The beam we were lying on twisted and I clasped it in a bear hug with one arm, clinging grimly to Layla's hand with the other as I felt her start to slide away from me. The beam stopped for a moment, hanging at a steep angle, then it shifted again and I lost my grip.

We fell together, crashing down among a torrent of falling masonry and timber and disintegrating mud bricks. I hit the ground with a thump that drove the breath from my lungs and lay there helpless as fragments of stone and tile crashed down around and on top of me. I closed my eyes and waited for the end.

I heard rough laughter, though it sounded as faint as the buzzing of an insect beneath the roaring in my ears. A few moments later there was the faraway sound of footsteps retreating up the alley.

I waited, counting to five hundred as the ringing in my ears slowly subsided, exploring the sensations in my bruised and battered body. Then I tried to raise my head. It would not move. I panicked, imagining that I had shattered my neck or spine, but realised that I could move my legs. I tried again and managed to raise my head a fraction, and I heard the rattle of stones falling away and found I could raise myself a little more.

I forced my right arm up through the dead weight of rubble

on top of it, then clawed at the mound covering me. It took several minutes of gruelling work to prise myself free. My eyes and mouth were gritty with dust and I suffered cuts and almost certainly livid bruises, but I was alive.

I looked around, my panic returning as I realised that Layla still lay somewhere under the rubble. Then I spotted a foot protruding from the mound and hardly dared to breathe as I felt for a pulse at the ankle. Almost sobbing with relief, I began tearing at the rubble that covered her. As I cleared more and more of it, I found that she had fallen under the beam which now lay across her chest.

I dragged and scraped at the stones and dirt covering her head and found myself looking into Layla's eyes. They were red-rimmed and lined with dirt, and her face was covered in blood from a score of cuts. She was shaking with fright. I wanted nothing more than to take her in my arms and drive away the fear.

'Are you badly hurt?' I said.

She was slow to reply and I suffered an agony of suspense before she found the strength. 'N – no, I don't think so. Just very fr—' Her voice faltered and died.

'Can you move your legs? Your body? Your chest?'

Each time there was hesitation, then the faintest of nods. I felt for the underside of the beam and moved my hand along it. I could feel the softness of her stomach and breasts and the thumping of her heart against her ribs. There was a fraction of an inch between her body and the beam, no more.

I heard a faint noise in the darkness and glanced around. It was the first time I realised what had happened. The building had almost completely collapsed. We were out in the open air, lit by the stars and the setting moon. The oak beam on which we had been lying had slid down and outwards, projecting through what had been the back wall of the house into the open space beyond.

I put a finger to my lips, and waited in silence. After a few moments, a rat showed itself, a few feet away. It froze, half-rising onto its hind legs as it stared at me, then it turned and scuttled away.

I turned back to Layla. 'I can't lift the beam off you, it's too heavy. I'm going to try to pull you out from under it.'

The lower end of the beam was wedged fast against the ground, buried in a mound of stones. Moving with exaggerated care, I began clearing the dust and smaller rubble away from the upper end. It was precariously poised, resting on a mound of loose material. I packed it as well as I could, forcing rocks and broken timbers under it. When I was satisfied that it wouldn't shift, I started to clear the rubble away from one side of Layla's body. I managed to make a small space, but there was a large rock I dare not move without the risk of dislodging the beam.

'You'll have to move to the rock,' I said, 'then twist sideways and worm your way out towards the foot of the beam. I'll help you.'

Her frightened face looked up at me. I leaned over and kissed her forehead. 'It's all right, you can do it.'

I pulled gently on her upper arm as she wriggled and strained to free herself. Each movement set off tiny avalanches of dust and stone fragments, causing me to look anxiously at the beam above her.

She worked her legs and hips free, but her upper body was still directly under the beam. 'I can't get any further,' she said, panic rising in her voice.

I reached underneath her, but the stones seemed jammed solid. It was problematical in that any piece I removed might make the rest collapse.

I took hold of her ankles. 'I'm going to try to pull you out. Turn your head sideways. If you can't bear it, tell me to stop.' I could see her face in the faint moonlight. Beneath the streaks of dirt, it looked deathly white. I took hold and began to pull, steadily increasing the pressure on her legs. She moved a little towards me, stuck, then moved again. Her shoulders were now directly under the beam and she became wedged again, and though I increased the pressure still more, I could not move her. I saw her bite her lip as she tried to stop herself crying out with pain.

I let go of her legs. 'It's no good. You're well and truly stuck. I'm going to have to try and lever the beam up a fraction.'

'No!'

'What else can I do?'

She was silent, but at last I heard her murmur, 'All right.'

I clambered back over the rubble towards what had been the front of the house. One side of the doorway still stood; the rest had collapsed. I leaned out and peered up and down the alley. It seemed hours since we had sprinted up it as the bullets howled around us. There was now no one in sight and not a sound to be heard.

I took hold of the thick post that had formed one upright of the doorframe and began to heave on it, working it to and fro. Dust and mortar dropped away from it and each time I was able to rock it a little further. Finally the fixings gave way with a groan that seemed to thunder through the alley. I froze and remained motionless for five minutes, watching and listening. No one came. I pulled the timber free, and carried it back to the rubble heap where Layla was buried.

I forced it in under the beam as close to Layla's head as I dared, then braced it with a pile of rocks. 'When you feel it lift,' I said, 'scramble for your life. If it slips . . .' I left the rest unsaid. 'Ready?'

I took the strain and then heaved down on one end of the timber, it creaked ominously and for a moment nothing happened. I redoubled my effort and saw a piece of stone roll down the mound as the beam lifted a fraction. 'Now,' I said.

Her legs writhed as she tried to force her way out. 'I can't.'

I poured all my reserves of strength, all my desperate hope, into one final heave. The blood was pounding at my temples and the veins stood out on my arms. I felt myself shaking as I tried to sustain the effort. There was a creak and a rustle of dust and stone and the beam rose another inch. 'Now, now!'

Her legs kicked again and her head disappeared from my sight under the beam as she wormed her way downwards. The timber creaked once more then split with a crack like a pistol shot. The beam crashed down, the mound of stone and rubble collapsing beneath it. I dropped the useless end of the timber and dragged my eyes towards the other side of the beam.

The top of Layla's head was a bare inch from where the beam had smashed down. She rolled over and dragged herself to her feet.

'Thank God,' I said. I crushed her to me and kissed her face, clinging to her, as our tears made tracks in the dust on our cheeks.

She returned my kiss then eased my arms from around her and began gingerly feeling her ribs.

'Anything broken?'

'I don't think so.'

I tore my eyes away from her. The sky was still dark, but the eastern horizon was tinged with the faintest trace of red. 'We have to move,' I said.

'Where to?'

I hesitated for no more than a second. 'The High Commission, as fast as we can. It'll be daybreak soon and if we're caught on the streets . . .'

'What if the rebels are there ahead of us?'

'Then we'll think of something else. Come on,' I said, not leaving either of us time to dwell on our uncertain future any more.

Chapter 11

Hugging the wall, we moved away through the deserted street. Layla limped as she walked. She caught my worried look. 'I'm all right,' she said. 'Bruised, but okay.'

We paused before each cross-street then hurried on, moving up the hillside using whatever cover we could find. Often there was none. We kept to the margins of the city — deserted streets and narrow alleyways — whenever possible, but several times we were forced to cross bigger roads that lay across our route. Each time we waited — sometimes for minutes on end — until the road was clear, then hurried across and ducked back into the shelter of the nearest alley.

As we neared the intersection with the main road to the east, we lay flat and crawled our way forward, then paused by the edge of the road, hidden by the rubble from a collapsed shopfront. In the far distance I could hear the crack and whine of small arms and the thunder of heavy weapons from the direction of the airport.

Layla's expression was bleak. I squeezed her arm. 'It gives us some hope. It shows the rebels are still being resisted.'

As I spoke, I glimpsed two shapes outlined against the sky over the airport and heard the distant howl of jet engines. A moment later there was the faint crash of rockets, and black plumes of smoke rose into the air. It lifted my spirits at once. 'We might be in with a shout,' I said. 'The rebels don't have any ground-attack planes. The Nigerians might be on the way in.'

We lay in cover a few more minutes, watching and listening. Peering through the tangle of broken timbers on top of the mound of rubble, I could see a steady stream of people moving along the road. They were unarmed civilians, refugees from the fighting, not soldiers or rebels, and most looked shocked and disorientated, walking slowly, heads lolling.

There seemed no sense or purpose in their movement. If they were fleeing from the fighting, they were fleeing in both directions, for as many were heading towards the hills as were trudging onwards towards the centre of the city.

Old men, women and children carrying bags, cases, pots and pans on their heads plodded past us. Many of the women clutched babies to their breasts. There were no teenage boys or girls or young men or women to be seen, however. I could guess what their fate had been.

As the last of the long lines of refugees disappeared from sight, we were once more preparing to cross the road when I heard a faint engine note. We both froze for a moment and then dived back into cover as a truck labouring up the hill came into view, its engine groaning under its load.

The back of the truck and the cab were piled high with loot — sacks of rice, pots and pans, furniture and mirrors, all lashed down with rope. A score of rebels were sprawled among their booty.

I crouched down even deeper into cover as they drew closer to us. Above the noise of the engine I could hear their laughter as they gesticulated at something behind them, hidden from us by the bulk of the truck.

It drew level with us, moving barely above walking pace up the steep gradient, and I saw a rope stretching from the back bumper of the truck. Its other end was tied in a hangman's noose around the neck of a man. His hands were tied behind his back and he shambled after the truck, jogging to keep pace. I could see his chest heaving with exertion. Rivulets of sweat ran down his naked torso and his bare feet left bloodied prints in the dust as he ran.

The truck slowed and as the driver tried to change down to first, there was a crunch from the gearbox and a grinding of gears. The rope slackened and the man shambled closer to the back of the truck. Then it jerked taut again as the driver found his gear and the truck lurched forward. The prisoner on the end of the rope lost his balance and tumbled forward. Unable to break his fall with his hands, he hit the road with a sickening thud. It provoked only laughter and jeers from the rebels on the truck. The man struggled desperately, trying to haul himself back to his feet as the noose tightened around his neck, but the relentless onward progress of the truck dragged him forward and the rope tightened still further.

I caught a glimpse of his face, mouth wide open, tongue protruding, then the truck crested a small rise and accelerated away. The man was dragged after it, his body bumping and jolting over the ruts and loose rock of the road surface. Soon he disappeared from sight, leaving a red, glistening snail's trail of blood marking the surface of the road.

I tasted bile in my throat and spat.

Layla touched my arm. 'We can't help. We must move on.'

I nodded. 'You go first,' I said. 'I'll cover you as you cross, but don't stop for anything. Keep low and go like hell until you hit that alley on the far side.'

I took another look up and down the road. It was deserted. Layla took a deep breath, gave me a brave, frightened look, then sprinted off across the road. I kept my gaze travelling left and right, but there was no sign of movement in any direction.

As soon as she was in cover I ran after her. Safe on the other side we set off again climbing through the city. With the sky lightening by the minute, there was no longer time to find the safest route. We just had to press on, hoping there would be no rebel patrols or roadblocks.

We worked our way higher and higher up the hillside. At last, when I looked up, I could see a glow illuminating the darkness ahead of us at the top of the hill. It had to be the lights from the High Commission.

As I stumbled forward, quickening my pace as our goal lay almost within reach, I saw movement ahead. I froze for a second and then dragged Layla into the cover of a doorway. A figure had appeared from the side of the street. He stood looking up the hill for some time, but as he turned towards us I saw the dark shape of the barrel of a gun etched against the sky.

Layla put her mouth close to my ear. 'What shall we do?' she whispered.

'We can't go past him.'

She peered at the sky. 'It's almost dawn. We can't wait. We'll have to go back and find another way.'

I cautiously leaned my head out of the doorway. The man was in profile to me, looking away from us. I worked my way out and along the wall, back down the hill. Layla followed and we inched our way out of sight and earshot. I grudged every yard of hard-won ground we had to give up.

Eventually we found a break in the wall, opening the way to a burned out and collapsing building. It took several minutes to negotiate the ruins, picking our way through the rubble, testing each footfall on the shifting, uneven surface. Finally we reached a sagging fence barring the way to the neighbouring street. I hauled myself up and over it and Layla followed a moment later and we moved off up the hill.

Starting at every faint sound in the lightening darkness, we climbed towards Spur Road. I almost wept with relief when at last I heard the dull thud of a diesel generator and saw again the harsh white light over the gates of the High Commission.

It was too soon to relax our guard, however, as we still had a hundred yards of open ground to cross before we reached the gates. I took a careful look around us and then we sprinted over the open ground and across the road, the sound of our footfalls seeming to thunder in the darkness as we ran.

The High Commission was a concrete blockhouse of a building, protected by steel-barred gates and an eight-foot wall topped with razor wire. The bullet-proof windows of the guard house just inside the gates bore the marks of recent impacts.

The gates were locked and the door of the guard house was closed, but shielding my eyes against the glare of light, I saw a dark figure outlined behind the glass of the guard house and I could hear the faint strains of music from inside. I called in a low voice, torn between the need to attract the guard's attention and the danger of alerting the rebel in the street behind us. There was no response. I took another look around and then shook the gates. The metallic rattle seemed deafening to me but still the man did not look up, his head nodding in time to the music.

As I searched around my feet for stones that I could throw at the window, I heard the faint noise of an engine lower down the hillside behind us. I scrabbled frantically in the dirt and at last my fingers closed round a clod of earth. I picked it up and hurled it through the gate at the window. There was a dull thud and the guard started and jumped up.

I again rattled the gate and he came to the window and peered out through the glass. He stared at us, shaking his head with disapproval, but then moved across the guard house and opened the door. He held his rifle loose in his right hand. 'What do you want?'

My heart sank. What we needed right now was a trained British soldier, not some menial local recruit.

'We're British citizens. We need to speak to the High Commissioner.'

He shook his head. 'My orders are to admit no one.'

I heard the noise of the engine growing louder behind us. The guard's expression had not changed. 'Then get your boss here now,' I said.

'He's asleep.'

'This is life or death. Fucking wake him up.'

'If I do that, I'll be in trouble,' he said.

The noise of the engine grew still louder. There was no time for further discussion. We had not come so far, endured so much, to be captured or killed now through the truculence and stupidity of a jobsworth of a guard. I swung up the rifle to cover him. 'If you don't, you'll be fucking dead. Now drop your rifle and keep your hands away from your sides as you walk towards the gate.'

He put the rifle down, but as he did so he made a quarter turn away from me.

'One more step towards the guard house and I'll shoot you dead,' I said.

He hesitated, then I saw his shoulders drop. He began to move slowly towards the gate, a sheen of sweat on his brow. The glow of headlights lit up the sky behind us and the engine note grew to a roar.

'Faster,' I said. 'Now open the gate.'

He opened his mouth to argue, but then closed it with a snap as I pushed the rifle forward and the barrel dug him in his ribs. He stepped to the side of the gate and pushed a button. There was the whine of an electric motor and a rumble as the massive steel gates began to slide slowly apart.

As soon as the gap was wide enough, we edged our way through. 'Now shut it.'

Never taking his eyes from the gun barrel, he pressed the button again. As the gate stopped midway and began to close again, the vehicle I had heard cleared the top of the hill behind us.

It skidded to a halt. There were shouts and then a ragged volley of shots as we dived for the cover of the guard house. Rounds pinged off the steel gates and one smacked into the bullet-proof glass of the window. After another volley of shots I heard the pick-up drive on. The rebels in the back kept jeering and firing into the air.

Another noise behind me made me whip around. The guard was back on his feet and grabbing for the weapon he had dropped.

I swung up the barrel of my rifle to cover him again. 'Now get your superior,' I said.

We followed him into the guard house. He picked up the phone and dialled a number, his eyes still fixed on the muzzle of my rifle. I heard a distorted voice giving a sleepy reply, and the guard gabbled out an explanation. 'I'm being held at the gate by armed gunmen,' he said.

'British armed gunmen,' I shouted.

A moment later a siren began to sound. The seconds ticked by with no sign of movement from the building. Then suddenly the door of the High Commission swung open, spilling a pool of light into the darkness. As it did so, I saw a flurry of movement to either side of the building, and armed soldiers sprinted out and dived for cover.

After escaping the rebels, I had no wish to be shot by British soldiers so I kept myself clearly visible through the armoured windows of the guard house as I held the rifle away from my body and dropped it to the ground. Then I raised my hands over my head and Layla did the same. The guard hurried to pick the rifle up and covered me with it as we emerged slowly from the guard house.

A voice barked at us from the darkness. 'Step forward, five paces. Now down! Down!'

I spread-eagled myself in the dirt and heard Layla drop alongside me. There was the sound of running feet, and my arms were grabbed and jerked up behind my back. I winced as the flexi-cuffs bit into my wrists. Then I was hauled to my feet.

'Who are you?'

'Jack Griffiths. Helicopter pilot with Decisive Measures.'

'Who's she?'

Layla replied for herself. 'Layla Edwards, a paramedic with Medicaid International.'

'We were shot down up-country a few days ago,' I said. 'We E & E'd back to Freetown just in time to be caught up in the coup.'

'It's not been your lucky week, has it? Where's your ID?' Already the voice was friendlier.

I jerked my head towards my pocket. One of the soldiers took our documents and passed them to his boss. He checked them as they patted us down for concealed weapons.

'Okay,' he said. 'Bring them inside.' We were hustled in through the main door of the building. 'And you can lose the cuffs,' he said. As they were removed, I rubbed the feeling back into my wrists, then glanced up.

He smiled. 'Was it really necessary to put the shits up our guard like that?'

'He wouldn't let us in,' I said. 'I didn't have time to argue.'

We were shown into one of the rooms in the High Commission. A moment later an attaché strode in. I took his outstretched hand. 'Glad you made it,' he said. 'We were worried about you.'

Two staff members looked up and eyed us with curiosity for a moment, then went back to their task of methodically shredding documents.

The attaché followed my gaze. 'The Foreign Office version of Groundhog Day,' he said. 'They must have carried out the same task at least half a dozen times before. We pack up ready to withdraw at each coup and counter-coup, then return to pick up the pieces afterwards – business as usual, whatever the complexion of the government. Gold, diamonds, iron, bauxite and rutile will be mined and sold whoever's in power. The only change is usually the name on the Swiss bank account into which the ruler's percentage is to be paid.'

I nodded, privately surprised at his candour. The instability of the country was obviously even getting to the diplomats; I had never heard one speak with such frankness before.

'How did you make it back?' he said.

'Overland to the river, then we stole a boat and drifted downstream to the coast. The city seemed quiet and we were starving and dead beat, so we ate some food acquired in the hotel and then flaked out there. I was planning to report in the morning.' I paused. 'Yesterday morning, that is. Not a smart idea, was it?'

'Anything you can tell us about rebel movements up-country?'

I shrugged. 'Not a lot, and anything we can tell you would be well out of date. I expect you already know most of it anyway. The Bohara compound was still holding, last we heard.'

He nodded. 'It's still holding.'

I talked for a few more minutes, outlining our experiences and the little we knew about the rebel positions. When I fell silent, he looked at the two soldiers alongside him, then nodded.

'Thank you. I don't think there's anything further we need to know from you.' He wrinkled his nose. 'Now, from the state of you both, I'd say the things you need most right now would be a shower, something to eat and a stiff drink. Get yourselves cleaned up and then I'll have someone show you to the dining room. You'll find someone else there who will be even more pleased to see you.' He had turned and walked out before I could ask him who he was talking about.

I spent a long time in the shower, soaping the filth and sweat from my body. I was covered in cuts, bruises and even more mosquito bites, some already turning septic in the heat, but it could have been a lot, lot worse. When I was ready I dressed in clean clothes – not my own, but approximately the right size – and followed a soldier to the dining room on the first floor.

As I entered, Grizz leapt up from a table and clasped me in a bear hug, nearly crushing my ribs. 'I didn't expect to see you again,' he said. 'You're either a military genius or the luckiest bastard alive. Let's hope it's luck; we need all of that we can get.'

'You must be a bit of a lucky sod yourself,' I said. 'How the hell did you get out of that clearing in one piece?'

He shrugged. 'Those rebels are brave as hell, but they're not soldiers. They were blazing away in all directions with everything they'd got, emptying magazines like it was Christmas. I just kept firing and moving, picking them off one at a time. They tried to rush me a couple of times and I think they'd have kept it up until they either got me or the last one was killed, but their leader called them off in the end. I watched them pull out and then took off across country.

'I probably had the same idea as you – head for Freetown, not Bohara – but I took the overland route. Luckily, when I hit the road I was able to – he paused and smiled – 'to borrow a pick-up from a group of rebels I came across. They didn't look like they had any further use for it by then. I was parked up here waiting for orders from HQ when the coup started.'

He broke off as Layla came in and he hugged her. 'Great to see you,' he said. 'Now, you two eat, and I'll talk. Here's the situation.' He gave a grim smile. 'As you've probably already noticed, the city's disintegrated – no police, no army, no one in control. The Nigerians are holding the airport and have flown in some of their crack troops – that's what they call them anyway. They've apparently started a push out towards the city, but how far they'll get will depend on the opposition they meet. I'm not too optimistic about their enthusiasm for a fight if the rebels make a stand.'

'Do you think they will?'

'Hard to know. Their usual practice is to loot everything they can carry and then take off for the hills with it. The Nigerians won't pursue them there. The rebels might let them have Freetown for now; what they really want are the diamond mines.

'Anyway, we've been given three objectives: to help secure the existing government in power if possible, to evacuate the European expatriate workers if necessary – but only if necessary – and to hold the diamond mines at all costs.' He gave a sour smile. 'Not necessarily in that order. Our first job is to get ourselves and as much ammunition as we can carry up to Bohara as quickly as possible.

'The garrison's still holding off the attacks at the moment, but once the rebels have finished looting the capital, the odds are they'll join forces to begin an all-out assault on the mines. We need to be there to help fight them off, or get our guys out of there before they're wiped out.'

'And securing the existing government in power?' I said.

He shrugged. 'We've other priorities. The Nigerians'll have to take care of the Freetown end of things, but it boils down to this: in the long term, whoever holds the diamond mines holds the country.'

I glanced towards Layla. 'What about the Medicaid International people?' I'd lowered my voice as I spoke, but she heard the question and leaned closer to us to hear the reply.

Grizz shrugged. 'No sign of them and no ransom demands yet.'

Layla said nothing, but I saw her expression as she turned away.

'Try not to worry,' I said to her. 'Like I told you, they won't be harmed. They're too valuable to the rebels.'

'Anyway,' Grizz said, 'the boys at Bohara are in shit street. They're low on supplies and ammunition and already being hard pressed by the rebels. A convoy from what's left of the Sierra Leonean army tried to resupply them by road yesterday, but it was ambushed – or at least, that's what they said – so we finished up arming the rebels instead.

'Now we've got you back though, we're in with a shout, apart from one big problem. The shit has hit the fan at the UN and after the ruckus last time Her Majesty's Government are running even more scared about being seen to support our activities here.'

I paused from shovelling food down my throat. 'Which means?'

'It means that despite our friendly welcome here, the supply of helis or heavy weapons is not going to be permitted. They won't even look the other way this time while we bring them in from elsewhere.'

'There are still ways, though.'

He shook his head. 'Not this time. There are spooks and journalists crawling all over the airport. You couldn't get a pea-shooter in without an end-user certificate.'

'So what can we do?' I said. 'The only heli we had is in pieces in the jungle.'

He shook his head. 'There is one more.'

I stared at him for a moment, then I shook my head. 'Oh no,' I said. 'You're not thinking of that wreck at Camp Seventeen, are you?'

He nodded. 'Exactly.'

'We'd never get it off the ground.'

'We'll have a bloody good try. What else can we do? The rebels are pounding Bohara with heavy machine guns. We need to give our guys some fire support.'

My heart sank at the prospect, not so much through fear for my own safety — though I was certainly concerned for that — as that I would be going back into a place I didn't want to go. I had no wish ever again to be seeking opportunity targets among the chaos and confusion of civil war, with rebels, government soldiers and a displaced, panic-stricken population all criss-crossing an area where dense forest offered refuge to those fleeing and ample scope for fatal confusion to a helicopter pilot.

I looked around. Layla was sitting at the other end of the table, sipping a cup of coffee as if it were the most beautiful thing she had ever tasted. I turned my back to her and lowered my voice. 'What about Layla?' I said.

'She comes with us, of course. There are wounded at Bohara.'

'No!' I almost shouted it.

'You were happy enough to have her along before,' Grizz said.

'That was different.'

'I don't see how.'

'I think I'm entitled to a voice in this,' Layla said. She had walked down the table and now stood directly behind me. 'I'm going back to Bohara with you. There are wounded there and patients who need treating at Boroyende.'

'It's all-out war there now, Layla,' I said. 'It's a free fire zone.'

She inclined her head. 'All the more reason that you need me, then.'

'It's too risky, too dangerous.'

She smiled. 'More dangerous than what we've been through already?'

'But we had to do that; you don't have to do this.'

'I'm a medic, Jack, of course I have to.'

'But you can't—' I began.

Her eyes flashed. 'Don't presume to tell me what I can and can't do. I'm doing my work, just as you're doing yours. I'm going to Bohara with you. End of story.'

I was ready to go on with the argument, but her expression showed me I'd be wasting my time.

'Right,' she said. 'That's settled. The only problem I can see is that you're short of a co-pilot.'

'That's no problem,' Grizz said.

I gave a grudging nod. 'The only problem we'll have is if I'm hit. If that happens, we're probably all dead.'

'But why not have Grizz in the cockpit? He at least knows a bit about helicopters.'

'Not enough to fly one,' I said. 'And anyway, someone's got to man the door-gun. If that's the only choice I have, I'd sooner have you up front and Grizz on the gun than the other way round. He can't fly a heli any more than you can, but he can at least shoot straight.' I tried a change of tack. 'Anyway,' I said, turning back to Grizz, 'how do we even get to Camp Seventeen without a vehicle?'

'We've got the one I borrowed.'

'And what do we do for weapons? There's been a coup and a rebel offensive, in case you hadn't noticed. We can't just head out onto the roads as if we're going for a Sunday drive.'

He winked and tapped his nose. 'The High Commissioner is not unsympathetic. Officially he can't do anything, of course, but unofficially . . . he's been looking the other way while I've called in a couple of favours from the garrison here.'

'But what about spare parts for the heli? The High Commissioner hasn't got any of those lying around here as well, has he?'

He shrugged again. 'What we have, we'll use. What we don't, we'll improvise.'

'So when do we leave?'

'As soon as we're ready,' he said. 'I'll just get the latest sit-rep here and call HQ for an update, then we're on our way.'

He returned to the room a few minutes later. 'The Nigerians' push out along the airport road ended after a couple of miles,' he said. 'They pulled back at the first sign of resistance. No surprises there. HQ reckons they'll just hold the airport and await developments.'

He led the way to the compound at the back of the High Commission. A battered utility truck was parked there. Two general purpose machine guns had been lashed onto it, on either side of the roll-bar. 'GPMGs,' I said. 'Those favours you called in were pretty big ones, weren't they?'

He grinned. 'Okay, Layla will drive. You and I'll take charge of the guns. Have you fired one before?'

I shook my head.

'With luck, the threat should be enough anyway. But if we

meet any roadblocks and the usual cigarettes and bribes don't do the trick, we're going to have to shoot our way through. If you have to fire, use very short bursts. It'll save ammunition and it'll stop you from shooting up the tree-tops instead of the rebels.'

I helped him load fuel, water and rations, and we shoved a few cartons of cigarettes under the dashboard. Then we climbed on the back as Layla gunned the engine. We drove round to the front of the building and at our signal the guard opened the electronic gates. It was the same man I had threatened, and he gave me a baleful stare as we passed.

Chapter 12

We bucketed out of the gate in a cloud of dust and I hung on to the roll-bar for support as we bounced away down the road. Pillars of smoke were still rising from different parts of the city, but it was early in the morning and most of the rebel soldiers were off the street, no doubt sleeping off the previous night's looting and drinking.

We tore through the outskirts of the city, with Layla swerving expertly around piles of rubble, abandoned vehicles and the remains of barricades. As we turned onto the road towards the mountains, however, we hit a road block. A rough barrier of logs and old tyres had been thrown across the road, which was guarded by eight soldiers. Seven had Kalashnikovs, the eighth an RPG.

Grizz swung the barrel of his GPMG to cover them. I followed suit, keeping a particularly wary eye on the man with the RPG. 'Government soldiers or rebels?' I said out of the corner of my mouth.

'Who knows?' Grizz said. 'They look more like government men, but it doesn't necessarily make any difference anyway.'

With the forefinger of his right hand curled round the trigger of his weapon, he raised the other hand, palm outwards in a gesture of friendship.

The soldiers eyed us, impassive. Layla pulled out one of the cartons of cigarettes and held it out of the window. After a moment one of the soldiers advanced and took it from her. They shared the cigarettes out, but still made no move to raise the barrier.

'We have no quarrel with you,' Grizz said. 'Our orders are not to fight with you.'

Their leader weighed up his words. 'Where are you going to?' he said.

'Just to the hills to try to buy food.'

'Not to Bohara?'

Grizz shook his head. 'See for yourself, we have nothing here, just water and a little fuel.'

The soldiers debated among themselves, staring at the GPMGs as they spoke. Finally the leader shrugged. 'Twenty dollars and you can pass,' he said.

'We have only leones,' Grizz lied.

The leader motioned one of his soldiers forward and Grizz reached into his pocket and handed him a bundle of crumpled notes. There was another long pause as the leader counted them, licking his thumb as he flicked over the notes. He stared at Grizz again, then jerked his head to his men, who began dismantling the barricade.

As we drove through the gap, the RPG tracked us. Grizz swung around, raising an arm in farewell, but also bringing the

GPMG to bear on the soldiers as we sped away up the track. When we were safely out of sight he eased the safety catch back on to the weapon and winked at me.

'Would you have fired first?' I said.

'Hell, yes. Would you?'

'I don't know. I think so.'

We ground on up the hill, leaving a plume of red dust hanging in the air behind us.

'What if the base has been overrun?' I said.

'Then we'll have to come up with another plan.'

We turned off the main road and followed the winding track through the forest. We were on maximum alert as we approached the base, but though the decrepit gates sagged from their hinges, the familiar listless soldiers still sprawled in the dust by the fire-blackened buildings inside the fence. They jumped to their feet and shouldered their weapons when they heard our approach, but at the sight of Grizz and the production of yet another carton of cigarettes they dragged the gates open.

We drove into the compound and across to the rusting helicopter, half-hidden beneath a dust-laden camouflage net. Layla and I stripped the net from it as Grizz disappeared into the Nissen hut and began dragging out spare parts, tools and a pile of what looked like scrap metal.

I looked the heli over and shook my head. 'We'll never fix this.'

Grizz grinned. 'Never isn't a word in my vocabulary.' He brandished a roll of metallic tape. 'There's nothing that can't be fixed with speed tape – mends everything from bullet holes to a broken heart.'

I began checking over the heli externally, greasing the rotor hubs, topping up the oil and the transmission and hydraulic fluid levels, while Grizz worked on the engine. Then I began bolting lengths of aluminium section across the worst of the holes in the cab walls.

It was three or four hours before Grizz was satisfied with the condition of the engines. We paused for a brew and a bite to eat then I ran through the cockpit checks while Grizz removed the GPMGs from their makeshift mountings on the pick-up and began fixing them to the door frame of the heli. The mountings for the door gun had been blown away by the stray round that had demolished the door of the cab, but Grizz improvised a bracket from scrap metal and bound the gun to it with swathes of speed tape.

Next he beckoned to me and I climbed down from the cab and followed him into the Nissen hut. Together we dragged a rocket pod from the hut and levered it into position on the underside of the nose of the cockpit. I tried to blank off the memory of what had happened the last time I had fired a rocket pod in action, but the thought kept returning to me.

When it was securely attached, Grizz connected a firing cable, running it across the skin of the cockpit and then through the door frame, fixing it at intervals with more speed tape. He connected it to the firing trigger on the stem of the collective, holding it in place with another swathe of tape.

Layla shook her head in disbelief. 'You'd not win any design awards for that job,' she said. 'I've seen cowboy builders with more pride in their work.'

I grinned. 'We're going for functional, not fashionable. It's the season's new look.'

I helped Grizz to load the rocket pods and we took on maximum fuel and maximum ammunition for the mini-guns. When we had finished, Grizz stood back to admire his handi-work. The whole helicopter looked as if it had been assembled from scrap metal and Meccano, and bound together with speed tape. 'Fantastic,' I said. 'If Trabant built a helicopter, this is what it would look like.'

'Let's just hope it doesn't fly like a Trabant,' he said.

I did the pre-flight checks, then sat motionless in the cockpit for a moment, trying to calm the tumult of my thoughts and focus only on the task in hand. Then I pressed the starter. The turbine stuttered and whined like an old banger on a frosty morning. Then the engine coughed and died as a cloud of black smoke belched out and drifted away across the base.

I exchanged a glance with Grizz, then tried again. Once more it faltered, spluttered and then caught. I tried the other engine and the whine of the turbines swelled to a roar as it also caught and fired. Grizz gave the thumbs-up sign and ran for the cab. I let the engines idle for a good five minutes as I checked the gauges, watching for any warning signs. The oil and hydraulic pressures were both low, but not dangerously so, and for a heli that had not flown in months it seemed in surprisingly good mechanical nick, though the bodywork was another story.

Before we took off, I glanced across at Layla. Her expression was relaxed, but the whiteness of her knuckles and the way she caught her lip between her teeth showed how nervous she was. I tested her harness and checked that the armoured panel under her seat was fully extended.

I reached across again to squeeze her arm with my gloved hand, then I pushed the lever into flight idle. The rotors began to move, carving ponderous sweeps through the air at first, then accelerating to a blur. Red dust rose around us as the rotors thundered, and the airframe of the heli juddered, poised between earth and air. I raised the collective and eased the cyclic forward as we rose from the ground, and I paddled the rudder pedals, banking us to the east.

The Huey's response to the controls was sluggish, but given

the amount of speed tape and scrap metal attached to the fuselage, it was hardly surprising. Even through my helmet I was deafened by the noise as the slipstream howled through the bullet holes and rips in the body, setting metal vibrating against metal in a cacophony of noise.

There was only sporadic ground fire as we flew over the outskirts of the capital. Looking down, I could see the scale of the devastation that had been inflicted. Whole blocks had been laid waste and smoke was still rising from scores of fires. Ragged lines of vehicles were moving in both directions, empty trucks and pick-ups heading into the city, and heavy-laden ones making for the mountains to the east.

The airport road was scarred with the marks of recent fighting, the road surface blackened, burned and part-blocked by the wrecks of vehicles. Bodies still lay sprawled in the dirt around them and the vultures barely moved from their feast as the helicopter thundered overhead.

The two Hawk jets I had seen flying sorties the previous night were drawn up on the hard-standing at the far side of the airfield, near a couple of Nigerian military transport planes which were unloading supplies. Groups of soldiers were dug in around the perimeter and a large force of men was milling about near the arrivals hall.

I kept the heli at height until the last possible moment, then made a steep descent over the heart of the airfield. There was no fire from beyond the perimeter, however, and we touched down safely.

We climbed down from the Huey and followed Grizz over to the main airport building, pushing our way through the crowds of soldiers lounging around it. A group of Nigerian officers had commandeered the airport administration offices for their own use.

Grizz introduced himself to the senior officer, a bulky figure in combat fatigues and the inevitable mirrored sunglasses.

'What's the situation here, Major?' Grizz said.

He looked Grizz up and down without speaking for a moment, his expression suggesting that something particularly repellent had just been placed under his nostrils. 'We have secured the airfield,' he said, his voice cold. 'And when we are ready, we shall advance on Freetown and drive the rebels back into the hills.'

'A further push now and they'll break and run,' Grizz said.

The Nigerian turned a cold stare on him. 'We will decide the military priorities here,' he said, 'not mercenaries.'

I saw Grizz's lips tighten, and he looked as if about to argue, but then inclined his head. 'And the President?'

The Nigerian spread his hands. 'That is for the politicians to decide. No doubt he will return when the situation merits it.' He gave the faintest of smiles.

There seemed no more to be said so we turned and walked away.

'Looks like the Nigerians have their own agenda,' Grizz said.

I nodded. 'And their own presidential candidate-in-waiting.'

We walked over to the small barbed-wire compound that Decisive Measures maintained at the airport. Some of the Sierra Leonean soldiers detailed to guard it were still there, but they seemed cowed by the presence of the Nigerians.

There was no sign that there had been any fighting in the immediate area, but there had been a serious attempt to force the locks on the heavy steel doors of the store bunkers. In one case it had been successful. The doors hung off their hinges and the interior of the bunker had been stripped bare.

'The rebels?' I said.

Grizz shook his head. 'They never breached the airport perimeter. More likely our saviours here.'

He walked over and spoke to the Nigerians. All shook their heads or shrugged their shoulders.

'No one knows anything about it,' Grizz said. 'Now, there's a surprise.'

He led the Sierra Leonean soldiers off to one side and began talking to them. I couldn't hear what they said, but their body language showed their uneasiness. They kept their faces averted from Grizz's probing stare and raised their eyes only to dart nervous glances at the Nigerians.

Grizz raised his voice, and pointed a finger towards the city. 'You want to keep working for us? Or do you want to take your chances out there?'

A couple of the men hesitated, then muttered something in reply. He walked back to us. 'Come on.'

We made our way back to the administration building. The Nigerian officer made no attempt to conceal his impatience as Grizz stated his grievance. 'One of our store bunkers has been looted of grenades, rifles and ammunition.'

'White adventurers who come here should realise that there is sometimes a price to be paid. But of what concern is this to me?'

'Your men are the culprits.'

The Nigerian drew himself up as if about to strike Grizz. 'You dare to accuse my men of this? Where is your proof?'

'The word of the soldiers we pay to guard it.' He paused. 'If we don't get them back, those weapons will be sold to the rebels who have been robbing, raping and killing in Freetown, while your men sit here doing nothing. Are you here to protect the people or are you waiting for the rebels to leave so that you and your men can take their turn at whatever is left?'

The Nigerian strode from behind his desk and stood toe to

toe with Grizz. 'We are Africans.' He jabbed his stubby thumb into his chest. 'I am African.' He fixed us in turn with his bloodshot eyes. 'These are my people, they have my protection. We Africans know who the real oppressors are. Get out before I have you arrested.'

'Go ahead. See how much shit hits the fan after that. With the amount we pay in bribes to Nigerian generals, I don't think we'll have any difficulty in finding one willing to bust you back down to private.' He paused. 'We want those weapons back, Major, and if any of those other bunkers are tampered with again, we'll be asking our generals for a favour.'

'Do Decisive Measures really have some Nigerian generals on the payroll?' I said, as we walked back across the airfield.

Grizz laughed. 'I don't know, but you'd have to be a very brave major to call the bluff, wouldn't you?' He opened one of the other bunkers and we loaded more ammunition and RPG rounds for the garrison at Bohara. Then I fired up the engines and took off, once more staying above the safe haven of the airport perimeter as I maintained a tight spiral climb to height.

I levelled at 2,000 feet and set the nose of the Huey directly towards Bohara. The landscape of savannah and forest that had looked so tranquil on my first flight over it had now been transformed into a scene of devastation. The once-neat villages had become blackened ruins, their patchwork of fields scarred and stripped bare of the crops they had carried.

Everywhere there were fleeing figures, scattering in panic at the sight of the helicopter. Whether they were rebels, government troops or simply refugees it was impossible to know, until they paused in their headlong flight to loose scattered rounds at us as we overflew them. We had neither the time nor the ammunition to retaliate; our targets were elsewhere.

In the distance ahead I saw columns of smoke climbing into

the clear sky and red and orange flames still licking around torched houses and villages. One blaze had spread to the forest and swathes of trees were on fire, sending a pall of smoke into the sky.

I had been flying at 2,000 feet and 120 knots, but closer to Bohara I took the heli down to treetop level and accelerated to 150. It was the ultimate white-knuckle ride, hugging the trees, tilting the rotors to ride up and over the onrushing branches of some giant protruding above the level of the forest canopy. Out of the corner of my eye I saw Layla flinching at the sight of each fresh obstacle in our path.

The blur of foliage came back into focus as we slowed and started to drop into the Bohara valley. I kept the Huey moving, taking it left and right, rising and falling – small differences, but enough, I hoped, to unsettle the aim of any rebel gunner. Even so, after the rush of speed the slow-moving heli felt impossibly vulnerable, the sitting target for any gun. Shots rattled around us, but it now felt almost routine, no more than an annoying insect buzz around my ears.

Grizz and I began a three-way conversation with the radio operator at the mine compound, and Grizz was also talking to Rudi on the net.

'We need to get the expats out of here,' the operator said. 'The mines have been shut down for the last week anyway and we're taking a shit-storm of incoming fire. We can't guarantee their safety any longer.'

'Have them ready to ship out,' I said.

Grizz chipped in. 'The guys are taking heavy fire from the ridge to the north-west. Let's see if we can quieten those bastards down first before we start worrying about the expats.'

I raised the collective and put the heli into a steep climb. We passed over the compound and swung away over the wilderness of bare rock and gravel towards the ridge Grizz had indicated.

It was a jumble of boulders, screes, broken rock and stunted trees. An army could have been hiding there invisible. I circled over the area flying lower and lower. Nothing happened. I spoke to Grizz on the intercom. 'Fire a few rounds from the door gun.'

A moment later, I heard the rattle of the GPMG and saw puffs of white dust as rounds ricocheted from the rocks below us. That provoked an immediate response and orange tracer rounds seared upwards at us.

'Cease fire,' I said. I kicked the rudder pedal to swing us away from immediate danger and radioed the position back to the compound. I kept circling and within ninety seconds, their mortar rounds began crashing down.

I radioed a correction and the next rounds were right on the money. When the mortars ceased firing I again circled over the site, dropping lower and lower as Grizz raked the ground with the door gun. This time there was no answering fire.

I thumbed the transmit button. 'Bohara, that problem seems to be sorted. Any more trade for us?'

'Yeah. Hostiles are reported advancing twelve miles.'

I raised the visor of my helmet for a moment to wipe the sweat from my eyes, then set the heli on to that bearing and dropped to low level. I heard the clank of ammunition links as Grizz reloaded.

We swooped over a ridgeline and down towards the target valley. As if my Kosovo nightmare had again become reality, I saw a burning hamlet ahead of me, the ruined buildings standing stark among the flames and smoke. Beyond it was dense woodland and forest.

As I banked around and skimmed along the edge of the treeline, the downwash lashing at the branches revealed shapes moving in the shadows of the trees. There were no muzzle flashes, no tick of rounds against the Huey's skin. I could see figures running between the tree trunks but I had no way of telling if they were refugees from the burning village or rebel soldiers.

Not again, please God, not again, I thought. I made another, slower pass. Still there was no fire from the woods.

I flicked the intercom switch. 'What do you get, Grizz?'

'Figures. Hostiles.'

'They could be villagers.'

'Negative. I can see men with weapons.'

'They might be sticks or spears,' I said. 'Hold your fire, I'll make another pass.' I did, and then another, putting the heli into a hover directly in front of the half-hidden figures, inviting them to shoot.

Above the thunder of the engines, I heard the clank of the ammunition links for the door gun.

'Hold your fire.'

'What?' Grizz said.

'Hold your fire.'

'Jesus, Jack. What are you trying to do?'

I ignored him, my thoughts echoing in my brain: Why don't they shoot? Why don't they shoot?

I glanced at Layla. Her face showed her fear, but her voice was firm and level. 'This isn't Kosovo, Jack,' she said. 'Trust your judgement. Do what you have to do.'

I strained to look beyond the camouflage of the foliage, using my peripheral vision to pierce the shadows. I saw a few angular shapes and what might have been the glint of metal. Then the sunlight glancing from the metal fuselage of the heli was picked up and reflected by a score of tiny mirrors, gleaming like Christmas lights in the darkness of the forest.

That decided me. I had seen enough rebels with mirror fragments woven into their hair or dangling from their clothing, part of the juju they believed would keep them alive.

I swung the heli up and away from the forest then banked in a sweeping turn and dropped to minimum low level. 'Are you ready in the back?' I said.

The answer from Grizz was immediate. 'Yeah, I'm set. Just give me the word.'

'On my shot.' My finger began to close on the trigger. A micro-second before I fired, a figure came sprinting from the treeline. A woman ran blindly out of the wood, blundering directly into the cross-hairs of my sights. Without knowing it, she had been a fraction of a second from death.

The vision of the burning woman from Kosovo flooded my mind. 'Abort! Abort! Abort!' I pulled my hand from the trigger as if it had been burned, stamped on the left rudder and jerked the cyclic back, banking us up and left, away from the wood.

'Jack? What's going on? Jack?'

I couldn't answer him for a moment. My hands were trembling so much I could barely grip the controls and my body shook with shivers. I offered a silent prayer of thanks that I'd been saved from repeating the terrible crime I'd committed in Kosovo.

I glanced back over my shoulder and saw the woman still running. Then she stopped, jerking from side to side as if some giant invisible hand was shaking her. She toppled forward and lay still. I swung the Huey round, unable to believe the evidence of my eyes. I had not fired, yet the woman lay dead.

Then there was a red flash from the edge of the wood and I heard Grizz's warning shout. 'Missile launch! Evade! Evade! Evade!'

I had no more than a heartbeat to respond. Reacting by an

instinct honed by years of repetitions in training, I was already throwing the Huey into a savage right-hand break as the RPG round blasted up at me trailing a plume of dirty grey smoke. I watched it with a curious detachment as it flashed towards us. I even thought I could see the dull sheen of its gunmetal exterior and the blurring motion of its fins.

It knifed past us, so close it appeared to pass through the whirling disc of the rotors. Then it was gone, diminishing to a black speck in the sky, before it exploded in a ball of orange flame.

I levelled the heli and glanced down. At once I glimpsed the stooping figure of a rebel soldier, a squat black tube extending from his shoulder. He had fired from almost directly underneath us. It was a near-suicidal shot; the back-blast from the RPG rebounding from the ground could easily have killed him and the smoke trail marked him out as a target to anyone, but he had almost succeeded in shooting us down.

I could see him fumbling with another round in his haste to load for a second shot. I swung the heli back to face the forest and set it dropping towards ground level.

'Arming weapons,' I said. 'Fire when ready.'

'Weapons armed,' Grizz said.

The rebel soldier had succeeded in reloading and was raising the launcher back to his shoulder. He froze as he looked up and saw the Huey blasting in towards him. I nudged the nose of the heli right a shade, and as the cross-hairs intersected, I squeezed the firing trigger. There was a whoosh as the rocket blasted from the pod. The soldier disappeared in a burst of crimson flame, and clods of earth were blasted into the air, scattering dust and fragments like black rain.

I was already searching for my next target. I jinked slightly left, watched as the cross-hairs intersected on the gap in the trees

I had sighted, then pressed the firing trigger again and then again. White smoke trails marked the course of the rockets, ending in angry red flashes of flame as they detonated around the target.

I heard the clatter of the GPMG as Grizz began raking the treeline. He gave a warning shout. 'Muzzle flashes four o'clock.'

I swung the heli right to bring my weapons to bear and squeezed the trigger of the rocket pod again. Driven by a cold, murderous rage, I circled and attacked over and over again, rocketing and strafing, indifferent to any danger, as I laid the ghosts of my past. I was wreaking vengeance as much for what I had done in Kosovo as for the terror the rebels had inflicted here.

Some rebels broke cover and ran for their lives. I hunted them down without mercy, cutting them to pieces with short bursts from the nose gun. Then I banked and returned to the attack against those still hiding among the trees. Fires burned in a dozen different parts of the wood, and as the heli passed over, I would make out twisted and contorted bodies sprawled below.

I kept on firing long after every trace of resistance, every sign of movement from the rebels had ceased. I launched all the rockets from the pod and would have emptied the nose gun too had Grizz not called me to my senses.

'That's enough, Jack. That's enough.'

I came to, as if waking from my dream.

'Wha—? Okay.' I pulled back the cyclic and eased the collective down to drop our speed, then turned away from the burning forest back towards Bohara.

I flew the Huey automatically, barely aware of the controls in my hands. Suddenly there was a flash and a blast strong enough to throw the Huey sideways. Shrapnel ripped into the side of the cab.

'What the fu—' I froze. In the corner of my eye I glimpsed a black shape just above the forest canopy, as sinister and ugly as a tarantula, but far more deadly. The twin black holes of its air intakes reared above the cockpit like bulbous, sightless eyes.

It was a Hind helicopter-gunship. The markings on its flanks had been painted out, but there was little doubt about where it had come from. The rebels had no access to aircraft, and certainly nothing of the calibre of the Hind. The Liberians had obviously decided to gamble on an intervention to tip the fight for the diamond mines in favour of their protégés.

There was another flash and a streak of smoke and flame. 'Flares! Flares! Flares!' I yelled.

Layla's hand hovered over the buttons, then pressed one.

'Not chaff, flares! The next button!'

She pressed the correct button and the fierce light of miniature stars burned at the periphery of my vision as a burst of flares ignited in our slipstream.

Reacting without thinking, I jerked the cyclic and kicked down on the right rudder, putting us into a dive towards the forest canopy even as I spun the heli around to mask the heat of the engines from the missile streaking towards us.

The Huey screamed downwards. I held the dive until my vision was filled with the sight of onrushing trees, then I yanked back on the cyclic, almost breaking the Huey's back as I pulled the steepest climbing turn I could manage. I could feel the blood draining from my brain as the G-force bit, but I held the turn until the colour began to wash from my vision. It was the grey-out – the prelude to unconsciousness.

I eased back on the controls and as my full vision returned, I whipped my head round searching for the Hind. 'Where is it? Where is it?' I shouted.

'In your five,' Grizz said, hanging out of the door of the cab to keep the enemy in sight. 'Go left. Go left.'

I stamped down on the rudder again, forcing the Huey into

another juddering turn. The Hind flashed across my sights. I'd have given a year's wages for just one of the rockets I'd blasted into the forest only a few minutes before, but the pod was empty.

As the cross-hairs intersected on the Hind I squeezed the trigger of the nose guns and rounds spat out, punching a rising line though the Hind's fuselage. Then the firing stopped abruptly. I squeezed the trigger again, holding the turn to keep the enemy heli in my sights, but the guns were useless — empty or jammed.

I could barely control a mounting wave of panic. I had no rockets and now no guns — no armaments of any sort to take into a duel with one of the most deadly gunships ever built. I needed a few moments' respite to think, but there was none to be had. The Hind was already turning to bring its own weapons to bear once more.

Still jamming the collective up to the stops, I held the climb for another five seconds then sent it spiralling down, jinking left and right. I turned the heli through 360 degrees and began another climb. We twisted and turned, soared and plummeted, each of us trying to second-guess the other pilot.

This was no long-range battle like fast jets in combat. This was more like a bar-room knife-fight: two rivals circling within arm's length of each other, each one looking for the opening for a fatal thrust . . . except that even if the opening came I had no weapon that I could use.

I tried to manoeuvre to bring Grizz's guns to bear, but though he loosed off a couple of bursts, sighting through the doorway of the cab barely gave him enough time to bring the gun to bear, as the Hind came into view, before its momentum had carried it past and out of his line of sight again.

'Jack, what's happening?' Layla said. 'Why aren't we firing back?'

I didn't have time to answer. The Hind flashed towards me again. I faked a left turn, then kicked hard right and dived, passing under the Hind, its blindspot. We were so close that its downwash shook the Huey like a terrier on a rat and my own rotors scythed the air within feet of its metal belly.

In that instant, I saw one glimmer of hope. I dived again, accelerating towards maximum speed and set the nose due west as if bugging out from the fight and running for home. The Hind immediately turned in pursuit and the gap that had begun to open narrowed again. He was now in perfect position to plant a heat-seeking missile straight into the exhaust of the Huey's straining engines, but still I held the course, imaging myself in the pilot seat of the Hind, my fingers closing on the trigger. I would wait that half second more to be certain of a kill, and then . . .

I dumped the collective and booted the right rudder, sending the Huey into the most savage break yet. There was a strangled cry from Layla alongside me as the force of the turn threw her against the side of the cockpit and I heard a thud and a curse behind me as Grizz lost his footing and fell against the wall of the cab.

The Huey's momentum carried it through the turn and as the nose dipped and we started to drop, a flash of fire trailing a column of smoke blasted past the cockpit mere feet from my face.

It detonated with a blinding flash behind us, but I had no time to spare it a thought. I was already yanking the collective back to the stops. We were now nose to nose, a mile apart and closing fast. If neither of us evaded, we would impact in a handful of seconds.

The Hind opened up again with a burst from its nose gun and then jinked left. I matched the move exactly. We were still nose to nose. He went right and left again, then climbed, and each time I matched him, focusing only on the helmeted figure I could just glimpse through the tinted Perspex bubble of the Hind's canopy. We were now no more than 200 yards apart. I sensed as much as saw him start to climb and once more matched his move.

'Jack! No! What are you doing?' Layla screamed. 'You'll kill us all.'

A fraction of a second later I saw the Hind's nose dip. I twitched the cyclic upwards as the Hind's ugly black shape filled my vision. The disturbed air threw the Huey around, but I held the controls with rigid arms as I saw the nose of the Hind slide towards us. I could see the pilot's face behind his visor and his mouth opening to give an order as he craned his neck to keep us in sight. Then I saw his expression freeze as I jerked the cyclic forward and the Huey began to drop towards the blur of razor-edged motion – the rotors of the Hind.

There was no margin for error. A couple of feet too low or too high, a fraction of a second early or late, and we would all die together. I started to panic. I had left it too late, I had missed.

My hands twitched instinctively on the controls even though I knew the Hind would be long gone before any correction I made now could take effect. Then there was the crack and whine of metal on metal from behind and below me. The back of our skids had caught the very tips of the Hind's main rotors. It was not enough. The Hind was damaged but still flying.

I was powerless to do anything but wait. If I had misjudged our angle of dive, I would have set us on an irreversible path to destruction. Our own tail rotor would be destroyed, cut to pieces by the massive blades of the Hind's main rotors.

There was a deafening crash and my helmet smacked against the edge of the canopy as the Huey was thrown bodily sideways as if hit by a truck. The floor of the cockpit beneath my feet was torn and buckled by the impact.

I heard Grizz curse and yell as he was thrown around. 'What the fuck's going on?'

Shaking my head to clear it, I kicked the rudder pedals and worked the controls in a frantic attempt to regain control. The force of the impact had spun us round so that the Hind again filled my vision. Its main rotors were still turning at blinding speed, but the tail had disappeared, smashed away like rotten wood. With no tail rotor to control the torque, the giant body of the Hind was already beginning to spin out of control. Whipping around its own axis, it drilled downwards towards the ground and then disappeared in a massive orange and yellow flash. Smoke belched up towards us and once more the Huey was tossed around like a leaf in the wind as the blast wave of the explosion tore past us.

I fought to stabilise the Huey again, as my gaze raced across the gauges and warning panels, looking for danger signs. We had minor damage, but that was all. I eased back on the controls and pushed up my visor to wipe the sweat from my eyes. 'Jesus,' I said. 'That's the first and last dog-fight I ever want to go into with no ammunition. If they've got another Hind, we're finished.'

I heard Grizz's rumbling laugh over the intercom. 'I think you just wrecked at least fifty per cent of the Liberian air force. I don't think there's much danger of them risking the other half as well.'

Layla, too, tried to join in the laughter, but her face was chalk white and there was a catch in her voice as she spoke. 'What now?' she said.

'Back to Bohara.'

Chapter 13

I set the heli climbing to clear the ridge, sighting on a notch in the skyline where a landslip had cut away a section like a small quarry. Beneath it the slopes were barren and strewn with scree. 'A great place to hide,' I said as we flashed over it. 'You could lie up there for weeks and never be found.'

As we cleared the ridge, I raised the collective and pushed the cyclic forward, picking up speed as we flashed down towards Bohara. I felt the turbulence increase as we moved away from the rocky upper slopes back over the dense forest.

The rotors beat the air just above the tree tops and I kept the Huey jinking so hard I could feel the pressure of my guts forced against my rib cage. Tree trunks flashed past in a continuous blur. Then we were out over the moonscape of the mines. The ground fire from the rebels began at once and rounds clipped the rotor blades, tracing a brief fiery trail of sparks in the sky.

I pressed down lower and kept the heli weaving from side to side as I radioed the compound, 'Grizzly One, coming in.'

Almost at once the garrison put out a barrage of fire at the rebels. Despite the fighting, I could make out people gathered in knots around the perimeter wire, and a jostling mass pressing against the gates of the inner compound. The scene within it looked almost as chaotic.

As I dropped fast and low towards the helipad, the downwash tore bushes from the dry sandy earth and sucked metal sheets from the roofs, sending them spiralling away like missiles through the air. I flared the heli for the landing and the strength of the downwash physically blasted the crowd back.

Chickens were blown head over heels and a woman's clothes were torn off by the force of it. Another held a baby in her arms; it was snatched from her grasp by the windstorm from the Huey and fell in the dust. The mother stooped over it, her hair whipped around her face. I gave a gasp of relief as I saw the baby's mouth open in a howl of rage. It was alive.

The crowd still mobbed the fence. The pressure from the rebels had driven villagers and mineworkers alike towards Bohara. They were pinned between the advancing rebels and the mercenary garrison protected within the ring of steel and razor wire. I could see them shouting, pleading and waving fistfuls of leone notes. It felt like the fall of Saigon.

We flared and landed. As the engines wound down, I looked at Layla. 'End of the line,' I said. 'Your patients are waiting. You haven't got long, though.'

As I spoke, I cast an uneasy glance out of the cockpit. The arrival of the helicopter seemed to have driven the already desperate people into a fresh frenzy. They were throwing themselves at the fence, clawing at the wire, indifferent to the cuts on their hands as they tried to haul themselves up and over.

One boy succeeded. He sprawled in the dust and then pulled himself to his feet only to be clubbed to the ground again by a mercenary. I recognised Rudi's powerful figure standing over the prone figure of the boy. As he raised his face from the dust, Layla stared through the cockpit, then began tearing at her harness.

'What is it?' I said. 'Layla, wait.'

She was already jumping down from the cockpit and sprinting towards the fence, ignoring the crackle of small-arms fire. I hurried after her. She was crouching over the boy. I helped her carry him towards the bunker at the centre of the compound.

We laid him down at the side of the doorway and, screened by the wall of sandbags, Layla first tested his skull for fractures and then began to bandage his torn and bleeding hands. There was also an older, ugly knife wound across his cheek. Flies were clustered around it. Only when he opened his eyes and spoke did I realise that the boy was Kaba.

Layla was trying to calm him, but he kept gabbling out the same refrain, 'You must come to Boroyende. You must come to Boroyende. Njama is wounded.'

'What happened?' I said.

He turned his bleak gaze on me. 'The rebels came. They knew you had been to the village; they'd seen your truck. They said we were spying for you.' He stared me out. 'They found the knife you gave him. They said it was payment for spying. They tried to kill everyone. A few of us managed to get away; the rest of them are still hiding now.'

A sick feeling grew in my stomach. 'But Njama?' I said. 'He is alive?'

He nodded. 'He was in the fields, otherwise they would have killed him too. But he is sick, wounded. He needs medicine.' He turned back to Layla. 'He needs you. I ran here. It has taken two days. You must come.'

Layla took my arm and led me off to one side. 'We have to go there,' she said. 'What's happened is our fault, our responsibility.'

'I can't,' I said. 'I have to take the expat workers out of here.'

'And then?'

'Whatever my orders are next.'

'And the black mineworkers?'

'You know the answer to that, I'm afraid. They're on their own.'

'In other words, you're going to leave them to die.'

I couldn't hold her gaze.

'And Boroyende?'

Again, I couldn't meet her eye as I answered. 'The same.'

'So, you look after the expats and the diamonds and leave the people themselves to die.'

'It's not that black and white.'

'You're wrong, Jack. Black and white is exactly what it is.'

She stared at me for a moment. There was a look in her eyes I could not read.

'What is it?' I said.

She looked away. 'Nothing,' she said. 'I made a mistake, that's all.'

She turned her back on me before I could reply.

Grizz had been conferring with Rudi and now came racing back to the Huey. 'Let's get things moving, fast.'

A group of white expatriates, each clutching a single case, stood waiting for the signal to load. Fear and anger vied for control of their faces as they stared at the mob inside and outside the compound, held back only by the threat of the mercenaries' guns.

I walked over to Layla who was huddled in a corner talking to the boy. I touched her shoulder but almost flinched at the look she gave me. 'We have to get ready,' I said.

She shook her head. 'You mean you do. I'm staying here.'
'You can't do that. It's crazy.'

She gave me a level stare. 'You're coming back for the mercenaries, aren't you? Or are they to be left to die too?'

'Of course I'm coming back.'

She shrugged. 'Then I'll return with them.'

'Layla, you can't . . .' I said. My voice trailed away.

'It's time to choose sides, Jack,' she said. 'Whose side are you on?'

Grizz came charging over. 'Jack, for God's sake get out there before that heli's overrun.'

I hesitated, still holding Layla's gaze, then I turned and ran for the Huey. As soon as they saw me climb into the cockpit the crowd renewed their efforts to breach the wire. People threw themselves bodily at the gates or thrust money and possessions at the impassive mercenaries.

The expatriates hurried from the bunker and ran for the heli as I fired up the engines. A group of black workers began trying to force the gates of the compound. The massive figures of Hendrik and Reuben were at the heart of a group of mercenaries firing over their heads and into the dust at their feet, trying to hold them back. Still they inched forward.

I saw Rudi raise his hand and as he let it fall again, Hendrik, Reuben and the others fired a volley of shots. Several of the workers sprawled in the dirt, the rest turned and ran. Heartsick, I tore my eyes away. Everywhere I looked, every place I went, dead bodies were strewn, innocent lives sacrificed.

Even after the deaths of the workers, other people continued to press against the wire; the mercenaries' bullets were less terrifying than their prospective fate if they were left to the mercies of the rebels.

At another command from Rudi, Reuben had turned and jogged to the helicopter. He swung himself up into the cab.

'Grizz? What's going on?' I said into the intercom. 'The Huey's already seriously overloaded with the expats and their kit. You're the door gunner. We don't need that murderous bastard riding shotgun as well.'

'I'm also the boss,' Grizz said. 'We've two GPMGs. I can't fire both of them and we need every gun-hand we can load onto this crate. There'll be the biggest shit storm of firing you've ever seen when we get airborne.'

'And if we're too overloaded, we won't get airborne at all.'

'Just try it, will you?'

I had the rotors blurring overhead now, waiting for the signal to go. They threw up a pall of red dust through which figures moved like wraiths in the mist.

'Okay, that's it,' Grizz said. 'Everyone loaded. Let's go.'

I hesitated, sick at heart, staring back towards the entrance to the bunker where Layla's slim figure was still hunched in the shadows next to the boy.

'What are you waiting for? Let's get the hell out of here,' Grizz said. 'Go! Go! Go!'

The turbine whined its way up the octaves and the drooping rotor blades straightened and blurred as they picked up speed. I raised the collective to bring the Huey to a hover, but it barely lifted on its springs. I pushed the collective right up to the stops but though the heli felt lighter on its skids, it remained rooted to the ground, shuddering with the vibrations of the engines as they strained at maximum power.

Cold, dry air at sea level gives the easiest take off, hot, humid air at altitude the hardest. In such fierce heat and humidity there was much less than normal lift. Ten men and their equipment was the prescribed maximum load for this air density, altitude and temperature. There were at least fourteen piled on board.

'I'll have to try a running take-off,' I said.

I used the cyclic to set the heli lumbering slowly towards the compound. It ground its way slowly forward, the skid plates scraping and rattling at the earth. The noise and vibrations made it feel as if the Huey was disintegrating around me, but I kept it moving forward. If I could squeeze enough speed and forward momentum out of it to lift the rotors into clean, undisturbed air, free of the turbulence of the ground effect, in theory we would achieve translational lift – the rotors would bite and send us soaring upwards.

That was the aim. At the moment, we were still bumping along the ground, carving furrows in the red dirt of the compound with the skids. Just short of the perimeter fence I paddled the right rudder – turning with the torque increased the available power to the main rotors – and came around. We moved back across the compound, having gained a fraction more speed from the manoeuvre.

I made another right-hand turn at the far side of the compound and felt our speed increase a little more. 'One more turn,' I said as we approached the fence. As I swung the heli around again I could see the faces pressed against the chainlink, mouths opened soundlessly as they shouted desperate appeals that were drowned in the thunder of the rotors. The downwash whipped at them and dust clouds billowed around them, but still they clung to the fence.

One pair of eyes seemed to lock onto mine with an expression not of anger nor of hate or despair, but of infinite sadness. Then we swung around and I lost sight of her. I evened the rudders and we accelerated again across the compound. The heli rocked as the skids rumbled over the rutted ground.

I tried the collective: nothing. We were moving too fast to make another ground turn and the fence was now looming ahead. I hauled on the collective again. For a moment the heli remained earthbound, but then I felt a sudden jerk as the rotors bit into clean air, free of the turbulence of the downwash.

As the perimeter wire seemed to rush towards us, we crept a few feet above the earth. I swung the heli around just in time to miss the fence and nosed it back across the compound, barely airborne and still trapped by the fence surrounding us.

We crawled back across the compound, not gaining another inch of altitude. We were still nowhere near high enough to clear the fence. I brought the Huey to an engine-grinding hover a few feet above the floor of the compound. The vibrations increased and after a moment the by now familiar screech of the low RPM warning began to sound.

The battle between power and weight was being lost, and inch by inch the Huey was slowly sinking back towards the ground. I pulled on the collective until it almost came off in my hand, but still the heli settled lower and lower. I had to find a way to reduce the power demand for a moment or I'd lose control of the ship altogether.

I eased the collective down a fraction, letting the Huey drift downwards even closer to the ground. My reward was to hear the turbines pick up and I saw the rev counter rise a little. The warning siren died away and as soon as the heli stabilised, I eased the collective up again and the Huey rose back into the air.

Once more, however, even though I pulled in maximum power, as soon as the Huey began to rise out of the ground effect, it started to settle back down again. I repeated the manoeuvre and, perhaps also helped by the loss of fuel weight as I kept the engines bellowing, this time I managed to squeeze a few more revs and rose a fraction higher in consequence.

After half a dozen repetitions, rising and sinking back down, only to rise again, I at last got the Huey level with the top of the compound fence. I kept parallel to it, building the revs as much as I could. Then I took a deep breath and banked hard right, praying that the power boost I could nick from allowing the Huey to swing with the torque would be enough to lift us clear of the fence.

The coils of razor wire along the top disappeared beneath us. I was just beginning to exhale when there was a savage jerk. The nose dipped and I saw the ground rushing up at us. I fought the controls to stabilise the heli, holding it in a hover as the engines screamed under the load.

Grizz's voice came over the intercom. 'We're caught. One of the wheels has snagged the fucking razor wire.'

I glanced behind into the cab. He was hanging out of the door with Reuben lying across his legs. 'I'll have to free it. Get me roped up.'

He wriggled back in and Reuben tied a rope around his chest, padding it with his shirt. Grizz picked up a pair of metal shears from the toolkit and Reuben lowered him out of the door. He hung suspended for a moment out of reach of the wire and the skids. Then Reuben began to swing him like a pendulum.

Slowly at first, Grizz swung away in a wider and wider arc. I heard him grunt as he grabbed and missed the shaft of the skids, then he grabbed again and held.

In the gusting wind I was flying blind, holding the heli in a hover against the anchor of the fence, but unable to see my exact position. His voice came again over the intercom. 'Back five.'

I eased the heli back. I saw a strand of wire curl up into my vision as he cut through it and heard his laboured breathing and grunts of effort.

'Come on, you bastard,' he said.

A gust hit the heli, pushing it a few feet. 'Hold it,' I said into the intercom, working the controls to bring us back. Just then I heard the snap of the razor wire parting, followed immediately by a scream. The heli lurched and one end of the severed wire lashed the side of the cockpit like a whip. It left a bloody trail across the Perspex.

Reuben's voice cut in on the intercom. 'We've got to land again. Grizz is down there.'

I swung the heli around, craning my neck to look down. A figure lay sprawled in the dirt, one leg twisted underneath him. The flying razor wire had sliced through the rope and sent Grizz plunging to the earth, but the fall was not what had killed him. The wire had also cut clean through his neck, severing his head like an executioner's axe. It lay a few feet from his body, eyes open, mouth wide in a final scream.

I froze, still staring downwards at the once powerful figure lying broken on the ground. I had relied utterly on his character and strength, his wisdom and humour. I'd sleep-walked my way through the combat missions, leaving virtually all decisions to Grizz. Now he was gone. There was no one else to whom I could turn now, no one to rely on except myself.

The downwash whipped up a red mist from the blood still spouting from the severed neck. I shuddered and looked away.

Reuben's voice came again. 'We have to land.'

'We can't,' I said. 'We're overloaded already and the fence is down. If we land there those guys will rush us. Besides, there's nothing we can do for Grizz. He's dead. We'll have to leave him here.'

'You don't leave a comrade behind, even if he is dead.' The voice was angry, threatening.

I paused for a second, astonished at the loyalty Grizz inspired in almost everyone. When Reuben had screwed up, Grizz had broken his nose with a punch, yet Reuben was now demanding we retrieve Grizz's body, whatever the risk to ourselves.

'This time you'll have to,' I said. 'I thought the world of Grizz too, but if we try and land to pick up his body, we'll never get airborne.' I raised the collective again and pushed the cyclic forward, ending the argument.

The ship groaned and shook as it climbed slowly away from the compound. Grizz's last, inadvertent contribution to the cause had been to lessen the load we were carrying sufficiently to lift us clear. The ground blurred and the prone, broken figure disappeared from my sight.

I flew in a daze, only dimly aware of the landscape passing below me and the feel of the controls in my hands. I felt again the lurch as the Huey tore from the fence and Grizz's already lifeless body tumbled to the ground. I could still see Kaba's eyes boring into me, Layla's hard stare and Rudi's arm falling, condemning yet more innocents to death, and I heard again in my head Layla's words, 'There comes a time when you have to choose sides, Jack. Whose side are you on?'

The clamour of the fuel warning intruded on my thoughts. With such a load aboard, I was not surprised that we were low on fuel. I peered ahead into the haze, searching for the first sight of the airport. We still had some distance to go.

I jabbed the radio button. 'Mayday! Mayday! Tower, this is Grizzly One. Fuel critical, request clearance to land. Over.'

'Clear to land,' came the imperturbable voice of the tower. 'Emergency services standing by.'

The fuel needle was still dropping. At last, in the distance ahead, I saw the surf haze hanging over the coast. Then the grey rutted concrete of the airport runway came into view. As we made our approach, a few bursts of ground fire greeted us, but it was sporadic and barely threatening. The rebels were either saving their ammunition, or regrouping before a fresh assault.

With such a load, there was no question of hovering; I had to come in and land like a fixed-wing aircraft. As I slowed, preparing to land, the low RPM warning again began to sound in counterpoint to the fuel alarm. I gunned the straining engines, squeezing a few more revs from them, but they almost seemed to groan with the effort of holding the craft in the air.

I eased down the collective, increasing the rate of descent but giving the turbines a precious couple of seconds to wind up. The sirens died and the engine speed picked up. Then I increased the power again, slowing the rush towards the ground. The sirens shrieked, but I ignored them, and flared and landed with a thud that set the heli juddering on its springs.

I killed the engines and slumped in my seat, feeling the sweat soaking through my flying suit. I shut my eyes then jerked them open again as I saw the image of a severed head lying in the African dust.

The expats tumbled from the heli, laughing and joking as they hurried across the concrete towards the terminal. I went the other way, to the edge of the airfield where I bought some food and a drink from a stall on the other side of the fence. The stall owner had cut a small square hole like a serving hatch in the wire. He handed me through a can of drink and a fiercely spiced sandwich in chapati bread.

I sat down in the shade of a fuel bunker and began to think. Layla's words still echoed in my head and, worst of all, I knew she was right. I buried my face in my hands.

Then I heard the scrunch of feet on the dusty concrete and a shadow fell across me. I looked up. Reuben was staring down at me with an expression of contempt. 'You gutless bastard,' he said. 'There's good soldiers fighting for their lives at Bohara, while you're sitting here in the dirt. If you don't get off your arse and fly that helicopter straight back to Bohara, I'll shoot you myself.'

'I'm going back,' I said, 'but not because you've got a gun pointing at my head.' I pointed to the fuel bowser trundling across the hard-standing towards the Huey. 'If it's all the same to you, I plan to put some fuel in it first. Then I've got some unfinished business at Bohara.'

He walked over to the Huey and stood watching the fuel being loaded. I heard another set of footsteps and looked up again. 'Don't get up,' said a clipped, English voice. 'Taking a few minutes' well-earned rest, eh Jack?'

The voice and the words grated with me at once.

'Henry Pleydell,' he said. 'We met at Bohara when you first came out here.'

I nodded. 'I remember you, Colonel. I just wasn't expecting to see you among the welcoming party here.'

'You've done a great job for us, Jack,' he said. 'Grizz has told us.'

'Grizz is dead.'

He hesitated, pursing his lips, and a bead of sweat trickled down his forehead and splashed on to the front of his neatly pressed shirt. 'I'm very sorry to hear that,' he said. He paused and nodded to himself, then went on, his manner once more brisk and businesslike. 'We have reports that Liberian troops are massing on the frontier. Some may even have crossed it. The mining company is no longer prepared to meet the cost of countering a full-blown invasion, should it eventuate. The Nigerians appear to be willing to commit enough troops to get the job done in the long-term, but we don't have the resources. So we're pulling out, Jack, and leaving them to fight it out.'

'Until the next time,' I said.

'Oh, I'm sure we'll be back when the situation permits. But in the meantime we need you to fly just a couple more missions, to bring out the rest of the garrison and a package.'

'What sort of package?'

He rolled his eyes. 'It *is* a diamond mine, old boy.' He paused. 'Get airborne as soon as you can. There'll be a healthy bonus in it for you when they're safely delivered.'

'The diamonds or the men?'

A fleeting look of irritation passed across his face. 'Both, of course. You don't think we'd leave them to die, do you?'

'I need a door gunner and a co—' I said.

'Door gunner is no problem. Take Reuben. But a co— Well, I'm afraid you'll have to keep flying solo. We've moved heaven and earth to try to find one in these last few days. We even offered double rates, but there were still no takers. Just shows, even the Afrikaaners have a sensible streak.'

His smile twisted as he realised his mistake. 'I – I just meant that people who don't know the reality of the situation tend to believe all sorts of wild rumours.'

'Quite,' I said. 'So what ordnance have you got here? Are there rockets for the pod?'

He shook his head. 'Just rounds for the guns, I'm afraid.' He glanced at his watch. 'Now I must go and sort out another mess. The charter airline say they won't ferry the expats out until they've been paid in advance. Well, I've told them they'll be paid as soon as we land in Nigeria and not a second before. So it's a bit of an impasse at the moment.'

'I'm sure the expats will be very understanding of your accounting problems,' I said.

He hesitated and gave me a curious look. 'Well, good luck then. I'll be here when you return.'

As he walked away, Reuben jumped down from the doorway of the heli, where he'd been sitting swinging his feet. I could hear him whistling to himself under his breath as he began to load boxes of explosives into the cab.

'Demolition charges?' I said.

Reuben didn't even turn his head. 'You fly the helicopter,' he said. 'We'll take care of the rest.'

Chapter 14

It was dusk before we took off and I made the customary transition to night vision goggles for the flight. For once there was little gunfire to greet us as I flew in towards Bohara. It was as if, secure in their impending victory, the rebels had pulled back to rest and recuperate before the final assault.

Rudi supervised the unloading of the demolition charges. They were at once packed into bergens and Raz, Reuben and Hendrik, their faces obscured with cam cream, slipped out of the gate and disappeared into the darkness, moving down the hillside towards the mine workings.

Rudi spat into the dust. 'Waste of good plant,' he said. 'The kaffirs couldn't use it anyway.'

I turned and walked away from him into the bunker. I searched it from one end to the other, then walked right around the compound. There was no sign of Layla.

I began stopping everyone I passed. 'Where's Layla?' I said. 'Where's Layla?' All shook their heads or shrugged. I reached the main gate. 'Where's Layla?' I said to the guard.

'She went out an hour before dusk' he said. 'She insisted she had some medicines for a patient in the workers' compound and wouldn't take no for an answer.'

'And you just let her go?' I said.

'You think I haven't got enough to worry about without nurse-maiding some crazy medic?'

'Was there a boy with her, an African kid with a big scar on his cheek?'

'Yeah.'

I knew at once where she had gone and I cursed myself for my stupidity. I should have forced her into the helicopter, flexi-cuffed her if I had to. Now she was gone.

I returned to the bunker sick at heart. Rudi was sitting at a table, cleaning his fingernails with the point of a knife.

'Layla's missing,' I said.

He shrugged. 'So?'

'I have to find her.'

He laughed. 'When you've done the job you're paid for then you can go walkabout in the bush, cry-baby. Right now, we've enough to do without worrying about some coloured bitch who's gone native.' His look challenged me to either fight or shut up.

I looked away, waiting until I had controlled my anger. 'How soon do we leave?'

'The first group will go as soon as the demolition teams are back in.'

'And the rest?'

'We'll hold the bunker until you come back for us.'

I raised an eyebrow. 'For us? I never had you as the selfless, heroic type.'

He didn't reply.

We sat in silence for an hour until the demolition teams returned. Rudi selected eight men and sent them out to the heli. With all their kit and weapons, it was once more going to be dangerously overloaded. 'There's one more passenger,' Rudi said. As I began to protest, I saw two men running from the bunker, carrying a burden between them. I knew at once what it was.

Grizz's corpse had been flexi-cuffed at the wrists and ankles to make it easier for them to carry. They ran stooping with it to the heli and tossed it inside without ceremony. Hendrik returned a final time with the severed head wrapped in a piece of sacking. He threw it onto the floor of the cab and I saw one of the mercenaries push it under the seat with the toe of his boot.

Only Rudi, Raz and Reuben now remained to hold the compound. 'Make sure you're back to lift us out before dawn,' Rudi said. 'When the charges on the mine equipment go up, the rebels will be round here like flies on shit.'

I held out my hand. 'The diamonds.'

'Oh no. The diamonds stay here.'

'What do you mean?'

'I mean, if we let you fly out of here with the diamonds, what guarantee do we have that you'll ever come back for us? If we keep the diamonds here, we know you'll be back.'

'I don't give a shit about the diamonds,' I said. 'All I want to do is get everybody out alive.'

'I'm touched by your concern, but perhaps Decisive Measures might have other priorities.' He paused. 'This way we have an insurance policy.'

I turned away and pulled on my helmet. I fired up the helicopter and took off into the night. Somewhere in the blackness below me was Layla, if she was still alive.

As soon as we landed back at the airport, Colonel Pleydell and the Decisive Outcomes quartermaster strode out to meet us. The colonel was immediately surrounded by the mercenaries, airing the traditional soldiers' grievances about pay. While they argued, I shouted for a body bag. The quartermaster sauntered to a bunker and began rummaging among the stores.

He came back with a black rubber body bag. It had not been cleaned since the last time it was used. I spread it out on the ground. 'Help me carry him out of the cab,' I said.

We lifted Grizz's body and laid it down on the rubber. 'We need to cut the flexi-cuffs off him,' I said.

'It doesn't matter to him.'

'It does to me. Just do it.'

He stared at me for a moment, then shrugged and cut off the flexi-cuffs with a knife.

I climbed back into the cab and pulled out the head from under the seat. I unwrapped it from the sacking, but could not bring myself to look at the face as I tried to arrange it in the body-bag to give it some semblance of dignity. As I closed the bag, the sound of the heavy zip seemed to echo in the night.

'Make sure anyone who handles that shows some respect,' I said.

The quartermaster nodded, but didn't speak. We lifted the bag onto the back of his jeep and he drove off across the airfield towards the waiting charter jet.

The colonel was still surrounded by the increasingly angry mercenaries. He eventually brushed them aside and pushed his way through to me. 'You have the diamonds?'

'They're coming on the next trip.'

His thin, bloodless lips tightened. 'Those were not the orders you were given.'

'I know that. Rudi and his mates back there weren't too eager about the original arrangement. They reckoned that without the diamonds, there'd be less incentive to go back for them.'

'That's ridiculous,' he said.

I shrugged. 'Maybe, but Rudi wasn't budging from it.'

He made a visible effort to control his anger. 'How soon can you be airborne again?'

'As soon as I'm refuelled.'

He glanced at his watch. 'Then you'll make it back there before dawn?'

'I certainly hope so. I'd hate the rebels to see how few men there are left there.'

He turned away and started barking orders at the ground crew. They responded with sullen indifference and it was a good forty minutes before the fuel bowser had been brought out to fill up the tanks.

There was an understandable lack of enthusiasm among the mercenaries for one of them to act as a door gunner for the final mission to Bohara. They had seen more than enough action for the moment. The colonel tried bluster, cajolery and bribery in turn.

The plan that had been forming in my mind crystallised as I listened to the arguments. 'Don't sweat it, Colonel,' I said. 'I've managed without a co-pilot for the last few missions I'm sure I can fly this one without a door gunner. There was no groundfire on the last run and besides, once I get to Bohara I'll have four men to look after me on the return trip.'

He gave me a puzzled look. 'You can't fly a heli with a crew of one.'

'Oh, you can,' I said.

'But what if you get hit?'

I shrugged. 'Since the door gunner can't fly a heli, he'd just go down with me anyway. This way you only risk one life.'

He shook his head again. 'Too risky. We need those diamonds.'

'And those men,' I reminded him. 'Fair enough then. Find me a volunteer and we're off.'

He rounded on the mercenaries. 'Either one of you flies this mission or none of you will ever work for Decisive Measures again.'

An Afrikaaner mercenary practically laughed in his face. 'Pay us the wages we're owed and we'll consider it.'

'You will be paid. Do you think I'm going to wander around here with a sack full of dollars?'

Finally one of the other mercenaries stepped forward. 'I'll do it,' he said. 'For five thousand dollars.'

'You must be joking,' the colonel said.

'You're the joker, man. Those diamonds are worth millions and you're arguing about a few thousand.'

I interrupted. 'Look, I don't have time to listen to any more of this crap. If I don't get airborne now, it's going to be dawn before I get to Bohara, never mind get back. I told you, I'll fly it alone.'

I settled the argument by turning away and pulling on my helmet as I hurried towards the cab. As I wound up the engines I could see the colonel's mouth moving as he shouted something to me, but I didn't want to hear what he had to say. I raised the collective and the rotors thundered. His hat was whipped from his head by the downwash and sent bowling away across the concrete.

I checked in with the tower, then I was airborne in a cloud of dust, banking south-east, back towards Bohara. Assuming I made it there, what happened after would depend entirely on Rudi, but I was pretty confident that I had his measure.

I switched on the night vision goggles when still at 2,000 feet, allowing time for my eyes to become accustomed to the green-tinged, negative vision of the world below me before I began the descent. I felt the Huey lurch and then settle into its familiar gut-wrenching rhythm as it soared and swooped over the dark land ahead.

As I flew on, I found the lack of the normal cross chat between pilot and door gunner strange and unsettling. Although there was the usual roar of the engines and the thunder of the rotors overhead, I felt – or imagined – a growing, brooding silence.

I maintained radio silence until I was only a few miles from Bohara, then jabbed the radio button. 'Bohara, this is Grizzly One. Time for the last bus home. Give me a little light there, will you?'

Rudi's guttural Afrikaaner tones came up at once through the static. 'You took your time. Stand by, we'll light you in. There'll be a little diversion too.'

I saw the specks of green light flare in the distance as they began the prearranged signal: two long flashes, one short, three long. It was changed every day; helis had been lured into ambushes before by rebels mimicking the signal from a base. A US heli-crew I had flown with on exchanges had all been killed in Somalia while trying to rescue a downed pilot. They had been following the signal from the tracking beacon stitched into his clothes and had pinpointed it as coming from a clearing in a patch of scrubby forest. When they landed they had been cut to pieces by cross-fire. The Somali warlords knew about tracking beacons. They had captured the pilot, killed him, stripped him of his uniform and ripped it apart until they had found the beacon. Then it was carried into the forest and pinned to a tree trunk to lure the rescue helicopter into the trap.

As I slowed, preparing to land, the darkness beyond the base was lit by a series of blinding flashes as the demolition charges on the mine equipment erupted in succession.

I jabbed the radio. 'Great diversion, Rudi, why don't you just shine a searchlight on me? Wouldn't it have been smarter to wait until we were taking off before you sent that lot up?'

'Just fly the helicopter,' he said. 'And leave the tactics to us.'

A moment later the first groundfire cracked around me. I jinked and dodged mechanically, keeping the Huey moving around. The compound loomed ahead of me and I flared and landed in a flurry of dust as close to the bunker as I could manage.

The shanty town outside the wire already stood empty and abandoned. The black mineworkers knew they had been left to their fate, and none wished to be there when the rebels took control. In the bush they had some hope of survival; if they stayed at Bohara they would all die in reprisal for their collaboration with the whites.

Heavy weapon rounds were already crashing down around the compound and the incoming fire redoubled as the remnants of the garrison – Raz, Reuben and Hendrik – sprinted for the cab, the rebels perhaps sensing their last chance to destroy the hated mercenaries.

Rudi was the last to leave the bunker. He sprinted low to the ground, clutching his rifle in his right hand and a chained steel case the size of a small cash box in his left. He dived through the door of the cab, yelling 'Go! Go! Go!'

I rammed up the collective, the engine screamed and the Huey was airborne again. Torrents of tracer fire ripped through the night around us and the guys in the back blazed away in reply. I fired a few rounds from the nose guns as well, aiming at the muzzle flashes, more to keep the rebel heads down than with any realistic hope of hitting a target.

We were a bare 300 feet above the compound when the bunker detonated. A pillar of flame climbed halfway towards the Huey and we were tossed around like a leaf in the turbulence. I fought the controls to maintain flight trim. When I finally had it stable again, I jabbed the intercom. 'Thanks again for the warning, Rudi.'

'Did you think we were going to leave anything for the rebels? And we've another little surprise for them as well. We've laid claymore mines right around the perimeter. When they detonate, they blast out thousands of wire fragments. All the rebels within range will be shredded.'

'Not forgetting any returning mineworkers unfortunate enough to trigger the mines the rebels miss.'

He didn't reply.

The lack of return fire from the base must have told the rebels the last of the garrison had gone, and the groundfire ceased all at once, as if it had been switched off. I imagined them running through the darkness, tearing down the gates to loot whatever was left.

'Next stop R 'n' R,' Rudi said. 'Man, I'm going to drink the world and screw every whore in town.'

'Come up front a minute,' I said. 'I want to talk to you.'

'What about?'

'I'll tell you when you're up front.'

He pushed his way through the gap between the seats and slumped into the co-pilot's seat.

'Put the helmet on,' I said.

He gave me a suspicious look, but picked it up from the floor of the cockpit and pulled in onto his head.

'It keeps it private,' I said. 'Just between us. I've got a proposal for you.'

'And what do you propose?'

'A deal,' I said. 'I need your help to reach Layla.'

'You don't even know where she is.'

'I do know that. She's at Boroyende. I want you to help me find her and bring her and everyone else there to safety.'

He laughed. 'What have you got that could interest me?'

'Nothing much. Only ten million pounds' worth of diamonds. Colonel Pleydell is waiting to collect them at Freetown airport. But we're here, while he's hundreds of miles away.' I paused, trying to measure the effect of my words. 'So stuff him,' I said. 'I don't give a shit about the diamonds. You guys can split them between you. I'll ditch the heli and say we got shot down, the rebels got the diamonds and as far as I know they got you too. You'll be posted missing in action. Just one of those diamonds'll buy you a new identity and a one-way ticket to a new life anywhere in the world.'

He laughed again. 'Aren't you overlooking one thing? I have the diamonds, not you.'

'Sure you do, but at the moment we're at two thousand feet and heading for Freetown. When we land there, Decisive Measures and their friends will share the spoils and you will be left with a few thousand dollars in back pay and bonuses . . . if and when Pleydell gets around to paying you.'

I shot a quick glance at him and could see the predatory glint of his eyes in the darkness. I smiled to myself; I had him. 'All you've got to do is persuade the other guys to come with us,' I said. 'They'll get their share of the diamonds too, there's enough to make everybody rich for life.'

'You're still overlooking something,' Rudi said. 'What's to stop us taking off with the diamonds anyway, and leaving Layla and her kaffir friends to rot?'

'Nothing, except as I said, we're at two thousand feet in a helicopter which only I can fly. If I set you down here, it'll take you three weeks to walk out . . . if you make it at all. But do as I ask and I'll drop you anywhere you want to go. We've got the range to go to Guinea, Liberia, the Ivory Coast, even the Gambia or Senegal, if you want. We've plenty of fuel, I made sure of that.'

He sat in silence for some time, thinking it over. 'And if she's dead?'

'The same deal applies. We search for her and if she can't be found, I take you where you want to go anyway.'

'Okay. You've got yourself a deal. But we'll keep it between ourselves for now. As far as the other guys go, this is part of the mission. Okay?'

I thought about it for a moment. 'Okay, it's your choice,' I said. 'As long as you're sure you can persuade them.'

'I don't have to,' he said. 'They're soldiers, they take orders, and I outrank all of them.'

I shot another sideways glance at him. 'All that stuff you were giving me about not leaving your comrades; you were planning to take off with some diamonds all along, weren't you?'

Once more I heard his laugh. 'You're not as dumb as you look, you know that?'

I glanced at my watch and gave an anxious look towards the eastern horizon. The stars were already beginning to flicker and fade as the first hints of dawn appeared in the sky.

I switched my gaze back to the steep rocky ridge ahead of us, scouring it for the notch in the skyline that I was seeking – the landslip I had spotted some days before. Then I saw it, a little right of the nose and a few miles ahead. I set the heli into a climb to clear the ridge just west of it and raked the hillside around it with my gaze, searching for any sign of fires or any other indications that rebels or villagers might be in the area, but the screes and the steep mountainside were a uniform black.

We cleared the ridgeline and I pressed the heli down for a moment, dropping from sight behind the ridge. Then I banked it around through 360 degrees, and climbed back over the crest. The instant that the ridgeline cleared beneath me, I flared the heli and dropped it into the notch in the hillside.

I eased the heli back a touch and set it down. The noise from the engines and rotors was overpowering as it reverberated from the rocky walls of the mountain but, screened on either side and hidden from below by the lip of the landslip, the heli was invisible except from the air.

I ran my eyes over the gauges then shut down. Rudi was already climbing through to the cab. 'One more patrol, guys,' he said. There was a chorus of groans and argument. I heard Raz's nasal tones as he argued with him, then Rudi's guttural voice rose, cutting through the dissent. 'I don't like it any more than you do, but those are the orders. We just get in and out; we get the job done, then we go home. And there's a bonus in it,' he said. 'Ten thousand dollars a head if we bring the coloured nurse out alive, five thousand if we don't. She has some powerful friends.'

As they began to clamber down from the cab, I jumped down myself and walked round the side of the Huey. Reuben and Hendrik helped me to drag out a camouflage net from the cab and drape it over the heli. We then spent several minutes studding it with branches of the dry, twisted scrub we tore from the rock face. I took particular care to obscure the Perspex canopy, covering it with branches and showering it with handfuls of dust to prevent it shining like a searchlight when the sun's rays struck it.

When I'd finished, I stepped back and looked it over. It was far from perfect camouflage at close range, but from a distance — or from the air — I reckoned it would be well enough hidden unless someone directly overflew it.

I glanced around. Rudi was standing off to one side, the case of diamonds still clutched in his left hand. 'Let's get moving,' he said. 'We need to be off this mountainside before the sun gets much higher in the sky.'

I walked over to him and lowered my voice. 'Just one more thing first,' I said. 'We leave those diamonds here.'

'Are you crazy? What if there's a contact and we have to cut and run?'

'If you're hit while carrying them, we'll lose them anyway,' I said. 'It's much better this way. If the diamonds stay here, we've both got an incentive to get back here,' I paused. 'Alive.'

He studied me for a moment, then gave a brief humourless laugh. 'You're off your head. The diamonds stay with me. End of story. If you want them, you'll have to kill me to get them.'

To settle the argument, he stuffed the case into the bottom pocket of his combat trousers, fastened the chain around his ankle and snapped the lock shut. He held the key in his closed fist for a moment, then turned and hurled it outwards, over the lip of the landslip. It glittered as it caught the light, then dropped from sight, tumbling down somewhere into the screes below us.

I stared at him for a moment, then shrugged and turned away. We formed up into a column and moved out at once, bathed in the strengthening grey light of dawn. Rudi and Raz led the way with Hendrik and Reuben bringing up the rear. I had the novice's position in the centre of the column, the safest place if we were ambushed and the one from where I could also put the others in the least danger through my inexperience.

Rudi paused for several minutes at the lip of the landslip, scanning the scree-strewn hillside below us, then he led us out of the shade into the fierce heat of the rising sun. We moved left along the slope for half a mile until we reached a dry stream bed. Then, half-hidden by the cover of the jumble of rocks in the stream bed, we began to descend towards the distant line of the forest at the foot of the slopes.

Stones and dusty earth slipped away from beneath my feet as I scrambled down, and sweat drenched me as I hauled myself over the large boulders dumped in the stream bed by the wet season floods. I left wet handprints on the warm rock, but they evaporated almost at once in the burning heat of the sun.

I paused at the head of a twenty-foot chute, a dry waterfall ending in a hollow that would have a been a deep pool only a few weeks before. As Rudi and Raz moved clear of the bottom I let myself go and slithered down behind them, sending small avalanches of dust and pebbles ahead of me.

The gradient eased as we descended. We passed the first stunted bushes and trees on the scree slopes, and we moved more slowly and cautiously as we neared the treeline. Still the landscape was empty of people, and the only noise was the sound of bird calls carried to us on the breeze from the forest.

We crossed the last stretch of open ground and paused on the edge of the forest to give our eyes time to adjust to the dim light under the tree canopy. Then we began to advance through the trees. Birds and the occasional monkey moved through the roof of the forest high above us and butterflies fluttered through the pools of light where a fallen tree had pierced the canopy and allowed the sun to break through. For the first few minutes it was cool and pleasant after the fierce heat of the open sun, but then the drenching humidity and the sticky heat made the sweat pour from me.

Insects whined around my ears, feeding hungrily on any exposed flesh. We moved even more slowly through the forest, advancing in total silence and communicating only by hand signals or clicks of the tongue. We paused every few yards to watch and listen, and check the GPS. We drank the last of our water and stopped to refill our canteens from a stream, adding Puritabs to sterilise the water.

Boroyende lay no more than fifteen miles ahead of us, yet it would take us at least the rest of the day to reach it. The road from Bohara cut through the forest a couple of miles south of our position, but it was certain that the rebels would be watching it and manning road blocks. Our best hope was that, with the mines at Bohara abandoned, the last thing the rebels would be expecting to see would be a patrol of mercenaries pushing through the forest east of there.

I had given no thought to what would happen if we reached Boroyende only to find it deserted, with no trace of Layla, Kaba or Njama, or the few other villagers that still remained alive, but as we moved closer, the prospect of it began to prey more and more on my mind.

I could scarcely believe my recklessness in placing my trust in Rudi, but I could see no way that I could have made it through the forest and back without the help of his mercenaries. Whatever else I might be, I was no soldier and for all their brutality, these men were trained and experienced jungle fighters.

The fact that Rudi had lied to the others also concerned me. I did not care whether the thieves fell out over their spoils afterwards – the mercenaries were as bad as each other – but if Rudi was planning some double-cross he would certainly not want any witnesses to it.

My gaze rested on his powerful shoulders as he moved ahead of me through the forest, hemmed in on all sides by the green walls of vegetation. The tension was a constant draining factor; any bush or branch could have been concealing an enemy lying in wait a couple of metres from where we stood. Rudi insisted on acting as lead scout himself, not trusting any of the others to do the job.

Although a big man, he made virtually no sound as he walked, easing his way through the undergrowth, moving aside and then replacing branches of leaves. He was following the faintest of animal tracks, almost invisible to my inexperienced eye except where a hoofprint showed in a patch of damp earth.

As the slope grew more gradual, the ground underfoot became wetter and wetter. We crossed sluggish, trickling streams and waded through the first shallow ponds. Then, spreading over the forest floor ahead of us, I saw the beginnings of a swamp. There was no way round it, for it spread for miles across the valley floor. We just had to go through it.

We waded into the murky, stinking water and moved on, our pace even more slow and deliberate. We made no sound as we inched our way forward, barely sending a ripple across the scummy surface of the swamp.

Chapter 15

We were still two miles short of Boroyende as night began to fall. We huddled together, thigh deep in swamp water, as we discussed in whispers our next move.

'It's only two miles,' I said. 'Can't we just keep going?'

Rudi turned a scornful look on me. 'Have you ever tried to move through a jungle at night? It's as black as your hat. All you would do is alert every rebel for miles around by the noise you made blundering through the undergrowth and scaring the wildlife.' He shook his head and looked away as if the mere sight of me was more than he could bear. 'We find some dry ground and we bivouac there till morning.'

I knew he was right, but the thought of spending another night so near and yet so far away from Layla – if she was still alive – tore at my heart.

We moved on for another half-hour but then stopped for the

night at a low hillock rising above the surface of the swamp. We remained motionless, watching and listening for several minutes, before Rudi gave the signal to begin unpacking our kit. He and the others had hammocks, brew kits and survival rations in their bergens. I had almost nothing.

As dark fell we ate some rehydrated rations and drank a mug of tea, then Rudi ordered Raz and Reuben to keep guard as he and Hendrik settled themselves into their hammocks slung between the trees. I curled up on the ground, separated from the wet earth only by a half-inch layer of plastic sheet.

The swamp was alive with the noise of frogs and insects, and mosquitoes were so thick they fogged the air around me. Unprotected on the ground I was also kept awake by my fear of snakes. I barely slept and it was a relief to see the emerging light filtering through the forest canopy as dawn broke.

We ate a frugal breakfast, brewed up some tea with more swamp water sterilised with Puritabs, and then moved out again on the trek over the last two miles to the village. After a mile we met the rising ground and emerged at last from the dank waters of the swamp into the leaf-litter of the forest floor.

The trees began to thin almost at once. There were patches of blue sky overhead and sun-dappled clearings in which butterflies danced in the columns of light, but I had no eyes for the beauty of the scene. I felt the tension rising in my throat until I could barely breathe.

As we reached the cultivated land around the village, we advanced even more slowly, fearing at any moment that we might blunder into an encounter with a rebel patrol. We crossed overgrown garden plots slashed and burned from the forest by the villagers, and finally reached the track I had taken with Layla two weeks before; it seemed like two years.

With Rudi again acting as lead scout we inched our way

forward through the forest at the edge of the track and stopped at the treeline, looking out on to the village. It appeared utterly deserted, so still and silent it could have been abandoned decades before. There was not even a scrawny chicken rooting in the dust.

The mercenaries fanned out and worked their way through the village, covering each other, guns at the ready, as they cleared each hut. I followed them, the sense of foreboding growing inside me with each step. I peered into the village carpenter's hut. The neat rows of carefully polished tools had disappeared. The family's earthenware pots and bowls had been smashed to pieces on the floor and the beautifully crafted rocking chair also lay in bits.

I stepped back outside and moved on to Njama's hut. The yellowing Perspex over the window opening was cracked and starred with bullet holes and there were the stains of dried blood in the dust just inside the doorway. Once more the interior of the hut had been wrecked and the lovingly recycled storage jars, bowls and plates, made from shell canisters and pieces of truck body panel, had disappeared.

I looked up at the ceiling. The light bulb still hung there, but the glass had been shattered, leaving only a dangling bent and broken filament. It was a similar tale of destruction in every hut in the village; there was no sign of the occupants, no human trace to be seen.

As I came out of the last hut, I saw Rudi and the other mercenaries standing just beyond the edge of the village, staring down into something at their feet. Such a feeling of dread overwhelmed me that I could barely move my legs to walk over to where they were standing.

It was obvious a crude pit had been dug in the ground where a mound now rose from it, covered in something black that seemed to glisten, move and shimmer as I looked at it. As I reached the edge of the pit, Rudi stretched out the barrel of his rifle and prodded at the mound. The black shimmering curtain rose into the air, a cloud of flies lifting to reveal the pile of corpses beneath.

I found myself staring into the face of one of Njama's dead sons. Before I knew what I was doing, I had climbed down into the pit and begun to tear at the bodies, pushing them and dragging them aside, barely aware of the terrible stench of decaying flesh. As I heaved and pulled at the bodies, bloodied, mangled fragments of flesh came away in my hands.

Three of Njama's four sons were dead. I dragged their bodies aside in turn and searched through the rest, finding old men and women, children and even babies buried there. I was on my hands and knees, crawling through the last of the putrefying corpses at the bottom of the pit. Forty bodies must have been thrown there, but among them I could find no sign of Layla, Njama or Kaba.

As I began to crawl out of the pit, one of the babies I had thrust aside, stirred and made a small sound. It began a feeble, fitful crying. I lifted the child and held it against my chest, but its cries grew ever weaker and more hoarse. 'Water,' I said, holding it out towards Rudi. 'Give it some water.'

Rudi and Hendrik stared back at me without moving, but Raz opened his canteen and wetted the baby's lips with a few drops of water. It tried to swallow, but then gave a shudder and lay still.

'Not now,' I said. 'Don't give up now.'

The baby lay limp and motionless in my arms, its head slumped forward on its chest. I felt for a pulse in its neck. There was not the faintest tremor and the flesh already felt cold. I brushed away the flies crawling over its eyes and laid it down on the ground, covering it with a palm frond.

As I straightened up, tears scalded my eyes. I turned and walked away from the others and stood alone, staring into the forest, as they moved away from the pit. The clouds of flies at once settled again on the heaps of bodies.

Rudi walked over to me. 'That's it then,' he said.

I shook my head. 'There's no sign of Layla or Njama or Kaba here.'

'That doesn't mean they're alive. The rebels could have killed them somewhere else, or taken them away with them.' He paused, studying my face. 'They'd certainly have wanted to have their fun with Layla before they killed her.' He was almost laughing at me.

My fists clenched, but this wasn't the moment to fight him. I kept my voice low and even as I spoke again. 'They could still be alive. We have to search for them.'

He laughed. 'How? Where? Even if they are alive, they could be anywhere.'

'They won't have strayed far from the village. We could light a signal fire, or fire a shot.'

'Don't be stupid. The only people that would bring running would be the rebels. Now I've kept my part of the bargain, it's time for you to keep yours.'

I thought of Layla lost somewhere in the forest and jungle around us. I threw back my head and cried out her name. I heard the scrape of steel on steel.

Rudi's rifle was pointing towards me and the safety catch was off. 'You do that again,' he said, 'and I'll leave you on the pile with the other bodies. Now, we've wasted enough time.' He wrinkled his nose as he stepped closer to me. 'Get down to the river and wash that shit off yourself or the rebels will be able to track us from the stench of dead meat and the trail of flies following us.'

I walked down to the river bank. Njama's makeshift generator had also been destroyed. The metal shaft still projected into the river, but the paddle wheels had been torn away. I sluiced the stench of death from me with river water and turned to walk back towards the village.

As I did so, I glimpsed a face peering at me from the undergrowth. I froze. Then the leaves parted and Kaba walked into the open. His hair was matted and filthy and his ribs showed through his skin, as if he hadn't eaten since I'd last seen him, but his scarred face broke into a lopsided grin at the sight of me. 'You have come for us,' he said.

'Layla?' I hardly dared ask the question.

'She is safe.'

Relief washed over me. 'How many others?'

'Twelve.' The population of the village had been at least eighty.

'Where are they?' I said.

'In hiding a little way from here. I will take you to them.' He turned to go.

'Wait,' I said. 'We must bring the soldiers with us.'

I led him back into the village. His expression darkened when he saw Rudi. 'Why is he here?'

'He's here to help you – to help us all.'

'They're still alive,' I said to Rudi. 'They're nearby. We must go and get them.'

His expression was unreadable. He studied me for a long time in silence. Then he shrugged his shoulders. 'Then let's get on with it.'

The boy led the way. 'How did you know we were here?' I said.

'I've been keeping watch for days. I heard your voice shouting for Layla.'

He led the way into the forest, along a narrow path leading down to the river. Without hesitation, he stepped into the current and began to wade upstream through the chest-deep water. We followed, holding our rifles above our heads. The river narrowed as it curved away out of sight. Both banks were smothered in vegetation, and branches and lianas hung down over the water, forming a tunnel through which we moved. It was as dark as dusk under the dense vegetation, but ahead I could see the glow of daylight.

We were approaching the apex of a sweeping bend in the river. On the outside of it, the foliage and lianas still overhung the water, and trailed across the surface. On the inside of the bend, silt and sand had formed a small beach a few metres deep, ending in a sheer rock face. The beach was only a dozen metres wide and at either end it was screened by a curtain of tree branches and lianas, and driftwood carried down by the winter floods.

I glanced up and downstream. The curve of the river hid the main beach from sight; the only way to come upon it was to wade the river as we had done or to fight our way through the jungle down to the bank opposite.

Kaba called softly from the shallows then moved up onto the beach. I saw the foliage stir at the far end and an old woman stepped into the open. She gave an uncertain look from the boy to the semi-circle of mercenaries flanking him, then she saw my face. She smiled, turned and said something to the people still hidden behind her.

Then Layla stepped into view. A moment later she was in my arms. I pulled her close and kissed her. She stiffened for a second, then leaned into me, holding my face in her hands, staring into my eyes. 'I'd given you up,' she said. 'I'm sorry that I doubted you.'

'You were right to doubt me,' I said.

She glanced over my shoulder at Rudi and the others. 'But why are they here?' she said. 'Don't try and tell me that they've suddenly discovered a conscience; I don't believe that for a moment.'

'It's strictly business for them. I bribed Rudi: diamonds for lives.' When I released her and looked up I saw that the other survivors from the village had also emerged from hiding.

There were two small children, a girl and a couple of teenage boys, and a number of older women. The only adult men were Njama and his last surviving son, who hardly seemed to register our presence. He sank down at once on the ground, holding the stump of his arm across his chest as he rocked slowly backwards and forwards, crooning to himself in a voice that seemed barely human.

Njama was the last to emerge, leaning heavily on the shoulders of two of the women. There were dressings over wounds in his stomach, chest and arm, and his face bore the ravages of pain and grief, but he managed a flicker of a smile as he saw me.

I turned back to Layla. 'Is he fit to travel?'

'Not really, but if he stays here he'll die.'

Rudi took my arm and pulled me to one side. 'If we try and take the old man, we put all our lives at risk.'

'Just the same, he comes with us. I'm not leaving him to die.'

He stared at me in silence, then turned away. 'Come on.'

I stood on one side of Njama and Kaba took the other as we helped him down to the edge of the river. Then I lifted him onto my shoulders. He was so frail that he weighed almost nothing at all.

I waded out into the river and followed Rudi and the others back downstream. When we reached the village, I climbed out of the river and lowered Njama to the ground. Kaba and I helped him as he hobbled up the track and into the clearing at the heart of the village.

Rudi led the way straight through and disappeared into the forest on the far side of the clearing. As we made to follow him, Njama stopped us. He turned around and took a last look at what had once been his village. His eyes filled with tears as he turned his back and walked with us into the forest.

The four mercenaries spaced themselves through our ragged column with Rudi once more at the head and Hendrik again bringing up the rear. We were very vulnerable to attack, however, strung out over thirty or forty metres in forest where the visibility was no more than five or six.

We made painfully slow progress at first, working our way through the dense vegetation, but after a while we found an animal track made by foraging pigs or brush deer. It was an easier and quicker passage, but there was a price to be paid. I could see the glistening heads of leeches waving as they sought a free ride and a meal. At first I tried to avoid them, but it slowed my progress so much that in the end I just walked straight ahead. I would have to deal with them later.

Njama never once made complaint about his injuries or the pace Rudi was setting, but his face was drawn and the sheen of sweat on his forehead owed as much to his pain as to the heat and humidity of the forest.

At my insistence, we stopped for a few minutes every hour. As soon as we did so, Njama sank to the ground and closed his eyes, his face grey. Each time, Layla examined him and checked his dressings; the wound in his stomach was beginning to weep again.

She met my gaze. 'He needs to rest.'

'We can't stop yet, we've too far to go. We can't risk using the tracks and there's nowhere I can set the helicopter down in dense jungle like this. We have to make it to where we've left the Huey.'

She bit her lip, then gave a reluctant nod. 'All right, but not much farther, then he must rest.'

The old man's frail voice cut through our discussion. 'I will make it,' he said. 'I will not let you down.' But I saw his anxious, desperate look as he peered ahead into the semi-darkness of the forest, where the ground sloped down towards the edge of the swamp glistening among the tree trunks.

We began to wade through the murky water. The other villagers, all uplanders, were as uneasy as I was in this environment. Their clothes were stained with sweat and their nervousness was almost palpable.

We paused often to look and listen behind us, and repeatedly had to check and skirt around an impenetrable obstacle. In places we waded chest deep through the brackish water, not knowing if the next step might plunge us in over our heads.

We tried to move in silence, but our feet slipped constantly on the slippery roots, so there was the noise of the splash of water and our gasps from the effort required to haul ourselves over obstacles or plunge into the next swamp pool. There were still no noises of pursuit, however, only the calls of birds overhead.

We stopped briefly to rest and drink a mouthful of water, trying to eke out the little we had left in our canteens, then we moved on again. The slow pace we were making was wearisome. I was soon exhausted from the effort of half-carrying, half-dragging Njama along, and I could hear his wheezing, rasping breath at each step.

We collapsed to the ground when we reached the low mound rising above the surface of the swamp, where we'd slept the previous night. Layla examined Njama again. 'He can't go any farther without proper rest,' she said.

I looked upwards. The light filtering through the forest canopy was bright; the sun must still have been high in the afternoon sky. I hesitated, then nodded. 'That's it,' I said to Rudi. 'We'll have to stop here. Njama can't go any farther until he's rested.'

Rudi glowered at me as the other mercenaries clustered around him. 'What the hell is this?' Reuben said. 'A patrol or a picnic in the woods?'

Raz took up the grievance. 'What are we doing here?'

'We're following orders,' Rudi said. 'We have a job to do.'

'Nurse-maiding kaffirs?' Hendrik said. 'Since when has Decisive Measures been interested in that?'

They looked on the point of mutiny. 'Maybe we should level with them,' I said.

Rudi met my gaze with a ferocious scowl and pulled me to one side, out of earshot. 'Need-to-know basis,' he said. 'They don't.' The tone of his voice was chilling. The others gave us sullen stares and I could hear them muttering to each other as we settled down to rest and wait for nightfall. Rudi posted Raz and Reuben as guards, keeping them apart, I thought, so that they would have no further chance to share their grievances.

I asked Hendrik for a cigarette. He stared at me for a moment, then rummaged in his bergen and pulled one out of a packet. He lit it with a disposable lighter and passed it to me.

'I didn't think you smoked,' Layla said.

'I don't. Do you know a better way to get leeches off?'

She followed me to a clump of trees on the edge of the mound, out of sight of Rudi and the others. I took off my shirt. Leeches were clustered around my neck, armpits and the crook of my arms, which were swollen with blood. I held the lit end of the cigarette against them and they writhed and dropped off.

I heard a rustle of cloth from behind me. Layla had pulled her shirt up and over her head. 'You'd better do me while you're at it,' she said, raising her arms.

I removed four leeches from her armpits and one from her neck. 'Anywhere else you want me to check?'

It was a feeble attempt at humour, but she made an effort to smile. 'Thanks, I'll get those myself.' She took the cigarette from me and disappeared behind a tree. She reappeared a few moments later. 'Three more,' she said. 'See if you can do better.'

I took her place behind the tree and unzipped my trousers. I shuddered as I looked down. Five black leeches were curled around my balls. I burned them away then stamped on the cigarette.

'Amazing that you don't feel them on you,' I said.

'Their bite contains a combination of a local anaesthetic and anti-coagulant,' she said. 'Stops you noticing them and keeps the blood flowing.'

We went back to the others. Rudi sat across from me and began cleaning his rifle, but I saw a cold, calculating look in his eyes as he studied me. I was sure that only the fact that I alone could fly the helicopter was keeping me, Layla and the villagers alive.

We had little food between us and though Raz and Reuben shared some of their rations, albeit with an ill grace, Rudi and Hendrik kept all theirs for themselves. I cut branches and brushwood and made a crude bed for the old man, raised a few inches above the sodden earth. I spread what spare clothes we had over his bedding, and he lay down, closed his eyes and was asleep at once.

Layla sat by him as the light faded, her face etched with concern. As night began to fall, we curled up together on the ground, tormented by stinging hordes of insects and biting mosquitoes. I had no chloroquine to take, but malaria was the least of my worries at that moment.

'I don't trust Rudi and his sidekicks at all,' Layla whispered.

'Nor do I. But we have something that they need – the helicopter.'

'They don't need the villagers, though.'

'I know, but they do need the helicopter and if the villagers are left here, then so are the mercenaries.' I paused. 'It's the only game in town, Layla. We have to go along with it.'

She studied me in the twilight. 'Why did you come back?'

'I finally realised that what you told me was true. You can't escape responsibility by sitting on the sidelines or looking the other way. You've got to take sides and get involved; otherwise you're no better than the rest of them.'

We lay awake listening until it was full dark. Then we fell into an exhausted sleep, our arms around each other, but we were awake again before first light. We packed our meagre belongings in the dark and lay motionless, listening for movement as the light strengthened.

Njama looked little better for his night's rest, but Layla pronounced herself satisfied that he could carry on, and we began moving on through the waist-deep water. Kaba and I supported Njama on either side, holding him as he stumbled over the mud and twisted roots and branches, and carrying him through the deepest parts of the swamp.

The air was thick with mosquitoes. Water snakes wriggled away from us through the murky water and leeches once more fastened themselves to our bodies. The trees blocked the sunlight and the floor of the jungle was in semi-darkness, but we paused constantly to listen, scent the faint breeze and scan the vegetation for any noise, smell or movement.

About two hours after first light, we stopped to drink a mug of swamp water, strained through a gauze dressing, and eat a biscuit and a piece of dried fruit. It was barely enough to dull the gnawing hunger pangs.

A couple of hours later we made another brief stop to drink a little more water and eat a few grains of rice and a piece of dried fruit. When we set off again, Rudi changed the marching order, putting the two younger mercenaries, Raz and Reuben, at the front of the column and bringing up the rear himself with the more experienced Hendrik.

I queried it with him. 'I told you before,' he said: 'you fly the helicopter and leave me to do the soldiering. The greatest danger to us is from rebels following our trail. That's why we're covering the rear.'

I inclined my head and said nothing more, as we moved off again, wading through the swamp in single file. In the gloom under the dense vegetation we could see no more than five metres ahead or behind us. Layla walked just ahead of me and one of the village women behind. The rest of the column might not have existed, even though they were only a handful of metres away.

We had been walking for almost two hours and I was about to call a halt for a rest, when there was a burst of gunfire from the forest behind us. We froze for a second, then hurried forward.

Raz and Reuben had stopped dead at the head of the column and indecision was written across their faces. They looked close to panic, but dropped into firing positions at either side of the animal track we were following.

Raz jerked his head at me. 'Take them on ahead,' he said. 'We'll follow when we've cleared the danger.'

I hesitated, looking from one to the other, afraid they might abandon us. 'There's a big reward on these guys, if we get them back to safety,' I said. 'A hell of a lot more than the few thousand dollars that Rudi mentioned.'

They exchanged a look. 'Get on ahead,' Raz said again.

Layla took over my role of supporting the old man as I moved to the head of the column, with Layla, Njama and Kaba immediately behind me. As I advanced, I clutched my rifle, with my finger resting uneasily on the safety catch, aware only too well of the danger all around as.

After the ferocious initial burst of firing there had been no more shots, but my ears were pricked for sounds from behind us as my eyes stared into the green wall of the forest ahead of us. I kept my gaze moving constantly to left and right, using my peripheral vision to look for sudden, unexpected movement among the tangled mass of foliage and undergrowth.

I had none of the skills of a trained jungle fighter. All I knew was what I had been told: that the lead scout had the lowest life expectancy and that in contacts with the enemy occurring at no more than five or ten metres' range, only those with the fastest reactions survived. It was not a reassuring thought.

I was barely able to concentrate for the fear rising inside me and the tension made my hands tremble as I moved aside each piece of vegetation, not knowing if a rebel soldier might lie in wait beyond it. If the rebels were planning an ambush somewhere ahead of us, they would have ample warning of our approach. I tried to move silently, but without the semi-instinctive skills instilled only by years of training and fighting in the jungle, my progress was continually accompanied by the faint snapping sound of dry twigs and the rustle of leaves.

As I had seen Rudi and the others do, I paused every few yards to watch and listen, and kept checking the GPS, trying to keep us on a direct bearing to the landslip where the helicopter was hidden. I lost all track of time as I inched forward through the swamp, my nerves jangling at each noise — the plop of a frog splashing into the water, the faint rasp of a snake's belly as it slithered away through the undergrowth of the cries of birds in the canopy high above us.

At last I could see the land beginning to rise ahead of us. We had reached the end of the swamp. I inched forward, making no sound, barely causing even a ripple on the surface of the swamp. As I looked down, I caught sight of my reflection in the water. A stranger stared back at me, filthy and unshaven, face gaunt and haggard.

I emerged slowly out of the water onto dry ground. The dripping rags I wore hung loose around me and my boots were torn, exposing my bruised and bleeding feet. I stood silent in the shadows at the edge of the swamp, listening intently. I took another look around and then signalled behind me. The others emerged one by one from the swamp.

There was a flare of brighter light ahead and we reached the edge of a natural clearing where a giant tree had collapsed, suffocated and eventually overpowered by the weight of a strangler fig, tearing a hole in the forest canopy.

I hesitated on the edge of the clearing, peering towards the shadows on the far side. A track ran through the middle of the clearing at right angles to our course. I crept forward, shading my eyes from the fierce sun. I stayed hidden in the undergrowth at the edge of the track, looking and listening in both directions.

Nothing moved and I heard no sound. After a couple of minutes, I raised my arm and waved the rest of the column forward, trying to cover them with the rifle as they crossed and disappeared back into the forest.

Layla, Njama and Kaba had just begun to cross when I heard a faint sound and saw movement from up the track to my left. I shouted to them, 'Take cover! Fast!'

They ran across the rest of the track and dived into cover. I looked back to my left. A woman was walking slowly towards me. I stepped out into the centre of the track and held up my hand, palm out, to show her she had nothing to fear from us. Her face remained nervous, frightened.

That was nothing unusual; these were desperate times, when every stranger was to be feared, but something made me look again. As I peered at her, I saw the black mouth of a rifle poking out from under her arm, and in the dust behind her I saw a double shadow – the woman herself and another figure crouching behind her.

I swung up my rifle and shouted at the woman, 'Get out! Get out of the way!'

She gave me a terrified look, whimpering with fright, but she didn't move. I saw the black mouth of the rifle swinging towards me and threw myself back into the cover of the undergrowth. There was the crack of a rifle and a bullet smashed through the vegetation a couple of feet from my head.

I rolled sideways and then belly-crawled a few more feet. As I did so I heard another single shot, and then a burst of gunfire shredded the undergrowth where I had been hiding. I slid my rifle forward and raised my head a few inches to peer out through the fronds of a fern towards the clearing.

The woman lay sprawled in the track, apparently stone dead, a pool of blood slowly widening around her. She had outlived her usefulness to the rebel soldier and he had disposed of the unwanted encumbrance with the single shot I had heard. Rifle levelled, he was now moving slowly forward again, towards the point where I had disappeared into the undergrowth. He walked erect, not even bothering to stoop, certain of his own invulnerability.

I took careful aim, then squeezed the trigger. The rifle was set on semi-automatic. The first couple of rounds ripped through his chest, hurling him backwards. The rest of the burst sprayed high and wide as the recoils threw the barrel upwards, but it did not matter. He was already dead, slumped over the body of the woman he had killed.

As the echoes faded, I reloaded with shaking hands. As I turned I saw Layla emerging from hiding. 'I had to do it,' I said.

She nodded mechanically, not meeting my eye, then turned and hurried on across the clearing and back into the forest. I waved the rest of the column through, urging them on, then I dropped back to the rear. We had gone no more than fifty metres when I heard the sound of pursuit.

I left the others shuffling along ahead of me and dropped to the ground. I wormed my way into the undergrowth, my rifle pointing back along the track we had made. I heard the sound of people moving fast, crashing through the undergrowth after us.

I eased off the safety catch and squinted along the barrel, drawing a bead where the track disappeared from sight, aiming about three feet above the ground. A figure burst into the open and my finger was already tightening on the trigger when I recognised the burly figure in camouflage fatigues. Rudi had only Raz and Reuben with him.

I called 'Rudi!' and, not wanting to be shot by reflex, I waited until I saw recognition in his eyes before I stood up.

'I saw your handiwork back there on the track,' he said. 'Not bad. We might make a soldier of you yet.' He paused. 'But I didn't think you English gentlemen killed women.'

'I didn't,' I said. 'The gunman killed her.'

He smiled. 'I believe you, English. I believe you.'

'What happened to you?' I said. 'What was the shooting?'

'Rebels. A small group. They won't be troubling us again, but they may have been the advance guard of a larger group.'

'There are only three of you. What happened to Hendrik?'

'Hendrik is dead. The rebels shot him.'

Something in the way he said it made the hairs on the back of my neck stand on end. He pushed past me and began to walk off up the track we were following.

Raz was white-faced and silent and I could see a muscle tugging insistently in Reuben's cheek, counterpointing the rapid blinking of his eyes.

'I'm sorry about your mate,' I said. 'Were either of you with him when it happened?'

Raz shook his head and turned away to follow Rudi. I stood staring at the ground, a growing chill in the pit of my stomach.

Rudi shouted back at me. 'There's no time to stand around. We have to get moving, fast. One thing is certain now. There'll be rebels round here, like flies on shit. If that old man can't keep up, we'll have to ditch him.'

I said nothing to him, but I made a private vow to myself that I would stick with the old man even if it meant that Rudi and his soldiers went on alone.

Chapter 16

We overtook the struggling column within fifty metres and pushed on together, finally leaving the swamps behind and beginning the long, slow ascent towards the mountain.

As the tree cover thinned, we began to advance more and more cautiously. I moved up alongside Rudi as he scanned the open hillside beyond the last of the trees. There was no one in sight, nothing moving on the whole expanse of hillside, but hampered by Njama's wounds, I knew that we would be exposed in the open for at least two hours before we could reach the landslip where the helicopter was hidden.

Rudi took a last look around, then turned to me. 'You go on with the others,' he said. 'We'll loop the track and make sure we're not being followed. If they catch us in the open out there, they'll cut us to pieces.'

Once more I had the feeling that his words concealed more

than they revealed. He paused, scanning the hillside again. 'Take them up the dry stream bed and then cut off along the contour line towards the landslip.'

'How long do we wait for you?'

He smiled. 'Oh, don't worry. I'll catch you up before you're halfway there. I wouldn't want you to have to make the awkward decision of whether to wait for me or leave me behind.'

He stood for a moment and touched his pistol, his ration pack and the grenades attached to his webbing, as if he was carrying out a mental checklist. Then he turned and hurried away. He hissed an order to the other two and they followed him back into the forest.

The rest of us moved out of the trees and into the glare of the sun. The heat of the full sun was overpowering. Our sodden clothes steamed and dried almost at once, then were soaked again with sweat as we laboured up the hillside, slipping and stumbling over the loose rock and scree.

Njama's head lolled on his shoulders and his mouth hung open. He still made no word of complaint, but it was obvious that he was exhausted, almost finished. I gave Layla a despairing look, then handed her the rifle and hoisted the old man onto my back. His arms hung limp around me and he was so weak that he could barely raise the strength to hold on as I stumbled slowly upwards.

Several times I had to pause and rest, gasping for breath as sweat cascaded from my forehead. There was a taste like ashes in my mouth and my head pounded from dehydration. We were still creeping slowly up the dry stream bed, climbing from boulder to boulder up the steep, almost sheer hillside. I looked up. We had another fifty metres or so to go to reach the contour line that would take us round to the mouth of the landslip.

Then there was an explosion from the forest behind us, a

single blast, followed by a burst of gunfire. I watched and waited for a minute, but the hillside below remained quiet and seemingly unoccupied. I urged the others on again and redoubled my own efforts, scrambling up the slope, my torn and bleeding fingers scrabbling for grip in the loose dusty rock.

Njama still clung feebly to my back. I climbed until I thought my lungs would burst, then set him down for a moment and turned around to look back down the hillside.

Rudi was just beginning to climb the stream bed behind us. He was alone and climbing fast, never once turning to look behind him. I picked up Njama again and carried him the last few metres up the stream bed. We were now level with the landslip, but half a mile from it. I set him down and Layla and Kaba took his arms and began to steer him along the ridge.

Rudi overhauled us just as we reached the landslip. 'Where are the others?' I said.

'We were followed. They threw a grenade. They killed Raz and Reuben. I shot those rebels, but there'll be others. We have to get out of here fast.'

I stared at him.

'What's up with you?' he said. 'Let's go. Let's go.'

I kept staring at him. There was a gap on his webbing where a grenade had been hanging when he'd gone back into the forest.

'I only heard one grenade and one gun firing, Rudi,' I said.

He looked down, following my gaze. When he raised his eyes again, there was a cold murderous look in his eye and I now found myself staring down the barrel of his rifle.

He studied me for a moment, chewing his lip as he pondered his options. Then he shrugged. 'Less people to share the diamonds with, Jack. That's all you need to worry about. Just fly this heli over the frontier, ditch it in the jungle near a city and we walk out with a few million in diamonds each.'

I shook my head. 'No way.'

'You don't have a choice, kaffir lover,' he said.

I glanced towards the others and he laughed at me. 'You think that coloured whore or those kaffirs will help you? If it means saving their own necks, they'll stand there and watch you die.'

Just the same, he moved slightly, trying to keep them in his sight as he confronted me. Njama's son just stood there blank faced, but I saw Kaba slink away from Rudi towards the rocks. I didn't blame him. I'd have run for it too, if I could.

'Kill me and you're trapped here,' I said. 'You can't fly the helicopter.'

'I don't need it. You think in twenty years' kaffir killing I haven't learned how to survive in the bush?'

'Then you'd better go ahead and shoot me, arsehole,' I said. 'Because I'm not going anywhere without these people.'

His jaw worked and I saw his knuckles whiten as he tightened his grip on the trigger. There was a moment of silence more deep than any I had ever experienced. Everything seemed stilled, motionless. I stared at his face, trying to read my fate there.

There was a thunderous concussion as the crack of a rifle-shot reverberated from the rock walls around me. A bullet smashed into my shoulder from point-blank range, hurling me to the ground. I tried to push myself upright, then collapsed again as my shattered shoulder gave way beneath me. I stared stupidly at the blood soaking my right sleeve.

I looked up. Rudi's mouth hung open in a silent scream of pain and rage. His head was tilted to one side as if listening intently, and his right arm hung at a strange angle. A dark stain was spreading over his fatigues. Then another blow smashed down into his shoulder. I saw his fingers spread and his hand fall limp at his side. The rifle dropped to the ground, its butt streaked with the blood running down his arm.

Rudi turned to face his assailant, but as he did so Kaba struck again, reaching up on tiptoe like a kid stretching for a sweet jar, except that in his hand he held a blood-stained panga. The blow hit Rudi in the side of the neck and a gout of arterial blood spurted outwards, drenching the rocks and undergrowth with a fine crimson spray.

Rudi let out a bellow and aimed a punch at the boy's head with his one good arm, but Kaba ducked underneath it and swung the panga again sideways, once, twice, at the back of Rudi's knees. His hamstrings snapped like guitar strings and he collapsed to the ground.

We stared at each other, both sprawled in the dirt, as Kaba advanced and stood over him, his face devoid of expression or emotion.

'Kaba! No!' I shouted, but it was too late. The panga was already rising again. He held it two handed, high over his head for a moment, then brought it whistling down with all his force across Rudi's neck, hacking his head from his body.

Kaba stood motionless, his face still impassive as he stared at the dead man's face. No one moved until Layla got to her feet, walked over to the boy and laid a hand on his arm. He started, but made no resistance as she gently eased the panga from his fingers, and turned him away from the dead body, cradling his head against her chest.

One of the old women led him away as Layla ran to my side. I stifled a yell of pain as her fingers probed the wound. 'It's badly broken,' she said. 'I'll tie off the bleeders and then I'll have to set it and strap it up. I'll give you some morphine. It's going to hurt like hell.'

'No morphine,' I said. 'I've got to fly the heli.'

'With a broken shoulder? You can't.'

'I have to. And you'll have to help me.'

'But I can't fly a helicopter.'

'You can if I tell you how to.' I tried to reach out for her arm, and cursed as the pain knifed through my shoulder. 'If we don't get out of here we'll die, Layla. Either the rebels will kill us, or we'll starve to death.'

'But Decisive Measures—'

I interrupted. 'Don't know where we are, don't have another helicopter to come and get us, and don't give a shit about us anyway. They want the diamonds, but not badly enough to mount a full-on rescue bid to get them.'

'What diamonds?'

'How do you think I persuaded Rudi and his boys to come along?' I said. 'They're in that metal case in the bottom pocket of his trousers. Now patch up my shoulder so I don't bleed to death on the way back and then let's get out of here. But, Layla,' I held her gaze. 'No morphine. I need to be alert or we're all dead.'

She gnawed at her lip. 'You can't imagine how painful this is going to be.'

'Just do it,' I said.

She gave me a twisted piece of cloth to bite on and then began to clean the wound, picking out fragments of bone and tying off the severed veins. I kept my eyes averted most of the time, but it hurt like hell and I felt waves of hot nausea sweeping over me.

She paused for a moment and our eyes met. She leaned down and kissed my forehead. 'Hold on,' she said. 'This is the really painful bit. I have to move your arm to set the bone, then I'll strap it across your chest. Shout, curse, swear, anything you need to do to get you through it. We're safe here, no one will hear you.'

She called to Kaba and one of the women. They knelt either side of me and held me down as Layla straddled my chest and took hold of my arm. Electric stabs of agonising pain shot through me. I heard the wet sound of blood and torn flesh and the dry scrape of bone on bone. The pain built and built until I thought my head would explode. I bit through the cloth clenched in my teeth, opened my mouth and screamed in agony. Then I blacked out.

When I came round, Layla was still crouching over me, watching my face. The worry lines etched into her forehead faded as my eyes flickered open and she gave a gentle smile. 'You had me worried there. Are you all right?'

My shoulder throbbed with a dull sullen ache. I glanced down. My right arm was strapped across my chest. 'I think so. Can you help me to get up?'

She laid a hand on my chest. 'Just give it a few more minutes first.'

I raised my head a fraction and looked around. Kaba and the others were squatting in the dust in a circle around us, watching me. Njama lay prone nearby.

'Njama?' I said. 'Is he—'

'He's weak, but he's okay,' Layla said. 'He's one tough old man.'

I took a few deep breaths. 'All right, I'm ready now. Help me up.'

Kaba came forward at a run and the two of them supported me as I struggled to my feet. The effort sent more hot waves of pain coursing through me and I had to steady myself against Layla and close my eyes until it subsided.

'It's too soon,' she said.

I shook my head. 'We have to get going. Help me get this net off the helicopter.'

We hauled at the camouflage net, dislodging the scrub branches that had helped to conceal it, and I sent Kaba up to remove the branches clear of the canopy and to wipe the thick layer of dust overlaying it.

Layla and Kaba then helped Njama to climb into the cab and laid him on the floor. The other villagers clustered around him. Kaba's face remained expressionless, but I could see the fear with which the old women regarded the helicopter. Layla spoke to them in their own language, trying to reassure them, and eventually we got them on board. There were so many people jammed in the back that one of the girls was hanging half out of the door, clinging to the outside as if she were a passenger on an Indian train, not a helicopter. At last she managed to squeeze inside.

I led Kaba over to Rudi's body. 'We need that case he's carrying,' I said. 'Can you break the chain with the panga?'

He studied it for a moment, then nodded. 'I can get it for you.' He raised the panga above his head and brought it down. There were no sparks and no sound of metal on metal, just a noise that was now all too familiar to me — a dull, wet thud like an axe chopping sodden wood. There was the scrape of a blade on bone as he pulled the panga out again. I looked down. Rudi's left foot had been severed at the ankle. Kaba reached down and pulled the bloodied chain over the stump and offered me the case.

'Just put it in the cockpit of the helicopter,' I said. I turned to Layla. 'Let's get airborne. I can still do most of the work, but you'll have to operate the cyclic for me.'

She stared at me. 'This is madness. I can't help you fly this. We'll crash and be killed. We can walk out instead.'

I shook my head. 'We'd be dead long before we reached the frontier. Even if the rebels didn't find us, how long would I or Njama last? Or the old women? Or you? Even Kaba would struggle to make it. It's the only way, Layla.

'I told you all this once before, remember? Of the four flight controls, I can still operate the rudders, the throttle and the collective, all you've got to worry about is the cyclic.' I tried a

smile. 'Think yourself lucky it's only a shoulder wound, otherwise you'd have to fly the whole damn thing. The controls are
duplicated for the pilot and the co-pilot. All you have to do is
move your cyclic when I tell you, but it has to be done in
synchronisation with the collective, and the movements required
are very small, absolutely minimal.

'Move it too far forward and you'll be spread all over the
Perspex, staring straight down at the ground rushing to meet you
very, very fast. Too far back and you'll be on course to be the
first inter-planetary helicopter. Too far to either side and we'll
drop out of the sky like a stone.' I paused. 'That's the bad news.
The good news is that I'll be six inches from you all the time. If I
see you do anything wrong, or feel, by the other controls, that
you've overcooked it, I'll get you to correct it. We may fly like a
drunken chicken on a rollercoaster, but we will keep airborne.
Trust me?'

She studied my face for a long time, then gave a slow,
reluctant nod.

I smiled with a bravado I was far from feeling. 'Then let's do
it, before either of us realises what fools we're being.'

Layla slid the cab door closed, then helped me up into the
cockpit. I couldn't get my flight harness over my injured arm, so
I remained unstrapped. She put on her own harness, then sat
back in the seat as far as possible and closed her eyes, unwilling
for the moment to engage with the void a few metres in front of
us.

'I hadn't thought of the little problem with the harness,' I said.
'It means we'll need to keep it as smooth and level as we can. If
we go down too fast I'll be going out through the roof.'

I settled my feet on the rudder pedals and gripped the
collective with my left hand. The pain in my shoulder had
subsided a little, but it was still bad enough to make the sweat

stand out on my brow, and any sudden movement sent a fresh stab of pain searing through my body.

'Right,' I said. 'Get the feel of the cyclic before we do anything else.'

She opened her eyes and took hold of the cyclic in front of her in a tentative grip, her forearm resting across her thigh.

'You have to hold the cyclic more firmly than that,' I said. 'When we fire up the engines it'll start to shake around like a vibrator in overdrive.'

She took a firmer grip on it.

'That's better,' I said. 'Now practise moving it around. Go left . . . right . . . forward . . . back . . . That's fine, except that you're moving it much too far. Try again, but no more than a quarter- or half-inch in any direction. Better to have to nudge it a bit farther than ram it right over and then drag it back again.' I paused. 'Right, helmets on.'

She helped me put on mine and fastened the strap under my chin, then fixed her own. I glanced over my shoulder into the crowded cab. Despite the press of people around him, Njama appeared to be either asleep or unconscious. He lay still and silent, his eyes closed, but when I looked again, I saw that his lips were working in what looked like a silent prayer.

'Say one for me, Njama,' I said. 'We need all the help we can get.'

I'd turned a little in my seat to look back at him and it caused an agonising stab of pain to shoot down my arm. I gasped and felt the sweat again start to my brow.

Layla shot me an anxious look. 'All right?'

I nodded. 'Let's get this thing airborne.' Reaching awkwardly across my body with my left hand, I stretched up and pushed the levers, feeling as much as hearing the click as they slid forward a notch into ground idle. I waited until the fresh jolt of pain in my shoulder had subsided a little, then pressed the starter. There was an electric whine over our heads and then the left engine began to turn over.

I stared at the RPM gauge, waiting for it to reach double figures. It seemed to take for ever, but at last I pushed the fuel switch. The engine roared and I let it settle into a steady throbbing beat before repeating the process for the right engine. When both were running sweet and smooth, I checked the gauges and warning panels again, and then pushed the control into flight idle.

I raised the collective gently until the heli lifted on its springs, poised to take flight. I looked at Layla. 'Don't worry. You'll do fine. Just don't panic and keep listening to what I'm telling you. Even if we seem to be out of control, we can pull it all back together as long as neither of us panics.'

I could see her hand shaking with the mechanical vibrations through the cyclic, and her knuckles whitened as she grasped it still more tightly.

'It feels strange at first, doesn't it?' I said. 'If anything on the mast is out of balance even a fraction, you can feel it through the cyclic, and there's never been a helicopter built that was perfectly in balance.

'Now, our first problem is to get out of this landslip without touching the sides. If we can do that, the rest should be a doddle. All we'll have to worry about then is landing at Freetown. So, in a moment I'm going to raise the collective, and as I do so, I want you to ease the cyclic forward a fraction. Don't move it to either side, just keep it absolutely in the middle, but move it forward a touch. There's a fractional time-lag before the heli responds, so don't think it isn't working and give it some more, or we'll be heading down again rather quickly.'

I turned my head to call into the back. Even that slight

movement caused another wave of pain. 'All right back there? Hold tight to the sides, we're taking off in a second and it's bound to be a rough flight.' I heard the frail voice of Njama translating what I had said.

'Right, this is it,' I said. 'Let's get airborne.' Still I hesitated for a moment. I looked longingly at Layla, so close to my side, then raised the collective again. 'Cyclic forward a touch.'

As the heli began to lift, sluggish under its heavy burden, Layla moved the control forward. She hesitated and then nudged it forward again. 'That's too much,' I said. 'Wait for the response.'

She corrected it, but the Huey clattered down again and bounced back into the air. Unrestrained by any harness, I was thrown up with it, and then crashed down again onto the seat, jerking the controls around in my hands. I bit my lip as a fresh burst of pain hit me.

The Huey was airborne again, but beginning to drift left. 'Ease it right a fraction,' I said.

'It's not responding.' Again she moved the cyclic further.

'Give it time,' I snapped. 'Move it left.' I saw the rock wall looming beyond her. 'Left now!'

She responded, but overcorrected and we began to drift towards the left-hand rockface. 'Forward,' I said, raising the collective again. The engine note and the beat of the rotors picked up, but we were now both dipping towards the rocky floor of the landslip and drifting dangerously close to its wall. 'Now back and right again. Right!'

We lurched away from the rocks and shot up into the air. I raised the collective to stop us from stalling, but Layla was already making a semi-instinctive correction, pushing the cyclic forward again. We hurtled down, caught the lip of the landslip with a thud that sent us bouncing back high into the air. The disc of the rotors scythed through the air by the right-hand rock wall, shredding the parched shrubs clinging to its face.

'Left, left!' I shouted. 'Forward!'

I raised the collective again and we lurched out of the mouth of the landslip. I heard Layla's indrawn breath as she saw the land falling away below us. 'It's all right,' I said. 'You're doing great.'

I risked a glance at her. Through the Perspex of her visor I could see her hair matted with sweat against her forehead. 'Now we need to pick up some speed,' I said, 'and climb to clear the ridge. Just hold it steady and give it a little forward nudge.'

This time I waited a fraction of a second before raising the collective, realising – not before time – that it was easier for me to adjust to her movement of the cyclic with a little more or less pressure on the collective than the other way round.

As I moved the controls, even above the thunder of the rotors, I heard the crack of gunfire. I looked down. 'Shit,' I said. 'Rebels.' The mountainside below us was black with soldiers. Bullets chipped fragments from the rocks around the mouth of the landslip and a moment later there was a whoosh, a crash and a starburst of smoke and flame as a round from an RPG streaked inches past the Huey and smashed into the cliff face.

'Climb! Climb!' I shouted. 'Back and left on the cyclic. Back and left!'

I yanked the collective upwards, twisting the throttle viciously as I stamped on the rudder pedal, swinging us around to face the cliff. There were cries and groans from the cab as the villagers were thrown around by the manoeuvre.

Rounds continued to smack into the mountainside and clang against the armoured underside of the heli. The only faint protection we had from the rifle fire was when they were shooting from almost directly underneath us, but if the soldier with the RPG got his next shot on target, it would pierce the armour as if it were paper and blast us right out of the sky.

We had to put the ridgeline between us and the rebel gunner before he could get off another shot, but an even more immediate danger was now threatening us. Taking me at my word, Layla had made the most minimal movement of the cyclic. It was not enough. The rock face just below the ridge loomed in front of the cockpit, filling my vision.

Cold sweat started to my brow. 'Back on the cyclic! Back! Back! Give it more!'

Slowly, ponderously, the Huey responded and the nose began to come up. Weighed down by the weight of people in the cab, the engines were screaming as they strained to deliver the power I was demanding through the controls.

Although we were climbing slowly, the ridgeline was rushing to meet us. Blue sky showed in the top half of the canopy, but the rest of my vision was filled with black, unforgiving rock.

'We're not going to make it,' I yelled, trying to brace myself for the impact.

There was a crash and a sickening lurch as the skids hit the rock just below the summit. More cries and screams came from the back and I almost passed out with the surge of pain from my shoulder. As the heli tipped forward, and even before I had time to speak, Layla had begun to correct, forcing the cyclic back to counter the dip of the nose.

There was another crash and a terrible scraping, gouging sound as the skids bit into the solid rock. The turbines climbed the octaves, shrieking at the strain imposed on them, then the Huey spun to the right and its momentum threw it clear.

At once we were climbing almost vertically, still with the sound of bullets smacking against the metal skin of the heli. The screaming engines faltered at stalling point. 'Forward, now!' I said.

The engines picked up again and we began to level, but rounds were still puncturing the fuselage. 'Forward again. More.'

The sounds of gunfire faded and stopped as we plummeted down the far side of the ridge, out of sight of our pursuers. I fought for control of the Huey and as soon as we levelled, I piled on the power again, putting as much distance as possible between us and the ridgeline before any rebel soldiers reached it.

I glanced at Layla. 'You were fantastic,' I said, as soon as I had got my breath back. 'You're a natural pilot. Now let's get the hell out of here.'

'Where to?'

'The airport,' I said. 'Where else? It's the only place we're certain is still in safe hands and it's also the only place we're likely to find the medical kit for you to patch up Njama.'

'And you.'

'And me. Let's hope we make it.'

Chapter 17

We flew on into the west. Layla tried hard to hold the Huey in straight and level flight, but we still kept drifting from side to side as she corrected, recorrected and overcorrected the cyclic.

'It's got a mind of its own,' she said.

I could still hear the tremor of fear in her voice. 'You're getting it. Give it time, it's hard to adjust to the delay in the response. But you're doing great.'

After a few more minutes she was able to hold it within a five degree arc of the direction I wanted us to be facing. We made slow progress, like a ship tacking into the wind, but with every minute we were cutting the distance separating us from Freetown.

I got Layla to push the radio button and spoke to the tower at the airport. 'Mayday. Mayday. Mayday. This is Grizzly One.

Pilot wounded, helicopter overloaded, request immediate clearance to land. I repeat, immediate clearance. Over.'

A voice cut through the hiss of static. 'Grizzly One, this is Freetown tower. We have operational military traffic flying from here in support of a ground offensive. Request you divert to Conakry.'

'Negative, tower. I have insufficient fuel and I repeat this is a Mayday. Over.'

'Can they turn us away?' Layla asked, as we awaited the reply.

'A Mayday takes precedence over anything,' I said. 'Including the Nigerian air force. Even if they try to refuse us permission to land, we'll just go in anyway. We'll circle over the tower to concentrate their minds. If they keep us waiting too long, the Huey might flake out and drop on their heads.'

I had kept us in a steady climb to above 2,000 feet, wanting plenty of space to recover if Layla should lose it and the heli began to drop, but the exertions of the take-off and the breakneck evasion were having their effect on me. The waves of pain were coming thick and fast and though Layla had staunched the worst of the bleeding, when I glanced down I could see a fresh crimson stain, spreading slowly out over the wound dressing. I had lost a lot of blood and, coupled with the exhausting route march to and from Boroyende and all the other deprivations we had endured, it left me feeling dizzy, light-headed and nauseous.

Without even realising it, I closed my eyes for a moment.

'Jack!' I jerked upright at Layla's warning and the knifing pain it caused shook me back to full consciousness. I had let the collective ease down, and we were plummeting fast towards the ground. I rammed the collective back up, then had to shout to Layla to push the cyclic forward as we threatened to flip over onto our backs.

'Sorry. I don't feel too great,' I said, when we had got it stabilised again. 'If you see me drifting off again, hit my wounded arm with something, will you?' Even as I spoke, I could hear my words slurring and felt my chin falling back onto my chest. I jerked upright again, provoking a fresh burst of pain – my solution to lapsing into wooziness.

I raised the collective and had Layla adjust the cyclic again, squeezing every ounce of speed we possessed out of the over-loaded craft. Then I began to make deliberate movements of my shoulder every few seconds. Each time, the stab of pain made me bite my lip to stop myself crying out, but it forced me back to consciousness.

'What are you doing?' Layla said.

'Trying to make sure we don't crash.'

'And if you black out from the pain?'

'I'll black out anyway if I don't give myself the pain.' I checked the GPS and stared ahead out of the cockpit. The manoeuvres to stabilise the heli had covered a considerable mileage. Already in the far distance I could see the blue of the ocean, its meeting with the land hidden by the surf haze hanging over the coast.

Nearer, there were pillars of grey and black smoke rising into the sky and I could see a couple of dark shapes, small and black as gnats against the immensity of the sky, wheeling and diving over the battle zone.

'Looks like the Nigerians have finally found the balls for a serious push,' I said.

The radio interrupted me. 'Grizzly One, this is Freetown tower. Emergency services standing by. Military aircraft using main runway, circle north of the airfield and make your approach from the north-west. Over.'

'Tower, negative. We're close to falling out of the sky and so overloaded we can't even hover. We're coming in from the east, repeat east, and we'll need a clear runway to set down. ETA five minutes. Over and out.'

The radio squawked again at once, but I ignored it. 'Here comes the tricky bit,' I said to Layla. 'Let's pray the rebels are too busy to spare any attention for us. I don't fancy any more one-handed attempts at evading anti-aircraft fire.'

Almost as soon as the words were out of my mouth, I saw streaks of red and orange tracer stabbing up into the sky. 'We've got to keep moving,' I said. 'And not offer a predictable target.'

'You mean keep flying it the way I have been?' she said. It was a brave attempt at a joke, but her voice cracked as she made it.

We were at 2,000 feet, a questionable range for an assault rifle, but well within range of anything heavier. The tracer bursts kept coming, lines of fire bright enough to show even against the afternoon sun. They began to get our range and the wavering lines cut through the sky towards us.

'Push it right and forward.' As I spoke, I hit the right rudder pedal and dumped the collective. The force of the diving turn pinned me against the side of the cockpit. I couldn't stifle a yell of pain. 'Sorry,' I said. 'But I'm all right, really. Now take it left and pull back.'

I waited until I saw her hand start to move, then raised the collective to the stops. Each manoeuvre was greeted by a chorus of screams and cries from the back for few of the villagers had any handholds and they toppled and slid from side to side as we threw the heli around.

As we continued the evasion, Layla moved the cyclic to send us lurching upwards and downwards, and drifting from side to side in a way that even I could not predict. 'If they hit us it'll be a sheer bloody fluke,' I said. 'No gunner in the world could track us through this pattern.'

If it was hubris, it got the punishment it deserved. A few

seconds later, the orange fires of bursting flak flared up across our track. I stamped on the rudder and shouted an order to Layla, but even as she moved the cyclic, I heard the tinny rattle of shrapnel against the fuselage and then a crack from the tail boom.

I felt the tail of the heli begin to swing left. The tail rotor countered the torque from the main rotor. If it was damaged, there was less resistance and the torque would force the body of the heli around. If it had been destroyed altogether, no power on earth could stop the heli from gyrating around its own axis until it hit the ground, or tore itself apart under the force of the endless, ever-quickening turn.

I stamped down on the right rudder, trying to turn into, and counter, the swing of the fuselage, but the ragged flight as Layla tried to bring the cyclic into equilibrium under this unfamiliar pressure made it hard to tell if it was working. There was a heart-stopping pause before I felt it begin to slow. We began to make forward progress again, but if I relaxed the pressure on the rudder even a little it immediately began to spin.

My calf muscles were already beginning to ache from the effort of holding it and as flak continued to burst around us, I found it hard to keep concentration on what Layla was doing with the cyclic. Our flight became ever more erratic, the Huey staggering across the sky like a drunk trying to get home, accompanied by the continued thuds, cries and groans from the back as people were thrown against the fuselage.

There was another burst of flak, another rattle as shrapnel knifed into the fuselage, cries from the cab and then the clamour of a warning siren. 'Shit, shit, shit!' I said.

We had to contend at the same time with the smoky, choking stench of burning oil, and the pressure gauge on the right engine registered a drop. Almost at once I heard it choking and banging.

The altimeter began to unwind in jerks, dropping a few feet, levelling as the engine caught and fired smoothly again, then dropping once more as it spluttered and almost died.

Each time the engine faltered, the low RPM warning added its own siren to the clamour. The oil and temperature gauges were moving in mirror symmetry, the temperature rising steadily as the oil pressure dropped still further.

I stared straight ahead, ignoring the flak and the tinny tick and rattle of smaller calibre rounds, willing the heli on towards the airport, now clearly visible ahead.

I called the tower once more. 'Mayday. Mayday. Mayday. Tower, this is Grizzly One. Now losing oil, engine failure imminent. Please clear the airfield and prepare for crash landing. Over.'

The flak faded away behind the heli and I saw below us the front line of the fighting. Nigerian armour was rolling along the airport road towards Freetown as the Hawk jets continued to strafe and harass the retreating rebels.

Now safe from ground fire, I was torn between the need to keep enough altitude to reach the airport and the knowledge that if the engines failed at this height no autorotative landing on earth would save us from being mangled and crushed as the heli plummeted to earth.

'Nudge the cyclic forward a touch,' I said. As Layla responded, the heli began what should have been a steady glide down towards the airfield, but the failing engine faltered again and set us sinking like a stone. The descent was now too fast. 'Pull back. Pull back,' I shouted, raising the collective and trying to twist a little extra power out of a throttle which was already locked against the stops.

The heli steadied, rose a little and then dipped again. We lurched from side to side as Layla tried to correct with the cyclic.

Fresh waves of hot pain jabbed through me as I was thrown around in my seat.

The airfield perimeter was now less than a mile ahead, but the oil pressure gauge had ceased to register, the engine was banging and clanking, belching filthy black smoke, and the smell of burning and hot metal was almost overpowering.

The effort of forcing down the rudder pedal was making my leg shake and tremble. I let the pressure slip for a fraction of a second and the heli at once slewed sideways. I gritted my teeth and stamped down again, counting silently to myself as I tried to hold it down despite the weakness in my leg and the mists of faintness and nausea that once more threatened to overwhelm me.

I heard Layla's voice from a long way off. 'Hold on, Jack, we're almost there. Hold on.'

We were fifty metres from the perimeter fence when the right engine exploded into flame. The heli gave a sickening lurch. 'Cyclic left. Left!' I shouted as we slid sideways and downwards.

Layla jerked it too far and we began to slip the other way. The perimeter fence loomed ahead of us. The drop had at least allowed a microsecond for the revs to build in the remaining engine. I squeezed another couple of feet of altitude from the feeble increase in power. Smoke began to fill the cockpit and the heat from the burning engine overhead was fearsome. If we didn't get it down in the next few seconds we might be blown apart in midair.

We had reached the fence. The heli jerked and almost stalled as it snagged the wire, then began to topple sideways. Spontaneously, I released the rudder pedal and kicked down hard on the opposite rudder. Driven by the torque, the tail boom whipped round like a striking snake. The force catapulted us clear of the fence, but the heli smashed down on its right-hand side, shattering the flailing rotors like toothpicks.

I howled in agony as I was thrown across the cockpit and landed full on my fractured shoulder, on top of Layla. As the wave of pain ebbed away, I shouted 'Out! Out! Out! Jump for your lives!'

Black smoke swirled around us and even through the visor of my helmet, I felt the searing heat of the blazing engine. The steel case containing the diamonds had been crushed by the impact. Its twisted lid lay ajar and half a dozen diamonds glittered in the dust of the cockpit floor. I began scrabbling for them. 'Fuck the diamonds,' Layla said. 'Leave them.'

'You get out, I'm right behind you,' I said. 'Run. Get away from the heli.'

As she dropped from sight down the side of the cockpit, the heli burst into flames. With the fire spreading and dense smoke filling the body of the Huey, the bruised and battered villagers scrambled, panic-stricken, for the cab door. I heard them crying and screaming in voices that were barely human, clawing at each other and trying to climb over the heads of those in front of them to reach safety. They began to tumble out of the door, many falling the few feet to the concrete and crawling away from the heli.

Coughing and choking, I fumbled with the steel case, then pushed at the cockpit door. It would not move. Only able to use my left hand, I heaved at it again, beginning to panic. It was stuck fast. Above the roar of the flames licking around the fuselage, I could hear Layla screaming for me to get out.

I crawled across the seats towards the other side, every movement sending surges of pain ripping through my shoulder. The heat was so fierce that I could smell the stench of burning hair – my own, smouldering beneath my helmet.

Gritting my teeth against the pain, I pushed again at the other cockpit door. It was also stuck, its metal frame swollen by the heat. I lay on my back, barely able to breathe for the stinking clouds of smoke enveloping me, and kicked out with my feet. There was a crack and an inrush of air as the door sagged open.

Still clutching the steel case in my good hand, I launched myself outwards and fell heavily to the ground. I lay there winded, my clothes smouldering, until Layla rushed forward and helped me to my feet.

'Did everyone get out?' I said.

She nodded. She helped me up and supported me, an arm around my waist, as I hobbled away from the stricken Huey. I was the last to leave it. The other villagers were strung out ahead of me in a ragged line across the concrete. At the rear of them I saw Njama's son, still wandering as if in a daze, and Njama himself staggering along, helped by Kaba.

I heard the clamour of a firetruck, but before it could reach the heli, there was a bang like a sonic boom. We were blown forward, hurled into the dirt as the blast wave flashed over us and burning fragments rained down around us.

I looked back. The Huey was a smoking ruin, a tangle of black, twisted metal. Layla helped me up and we moved on again to the dirt and parched grass at the edge of the airfield. Then I sank down, resting my head on my good arm.

Layla took my pulse and pulled off my helmet and laid a hand on my brow. Then she peeled back the dressing to examine my shoulder wound. 'It looks all right,' she said. 'Do you feel okay?'

'Never better.' I began to laugh at the stupidity of my remark, but it ended in a choking fit. 'My shoulder hurts like hell, of course, but thank God we all made it safely. You did a great job to get us here.'

She waved the remark away. 'Are you sure you feel all right? Your speech is slurred again.'

'I'm fine. Just dog-tired.'

I put my hand to my mouth, then pressed it against my shoulder, wincing as if another spasm of pain had hit me.

'You're badly dehydrated, you need fluids,' she said, as she reapplied the dressing. 'I'll set up a drip for you as soon as I can scrounge the kit.'

Over her shoulder, I saw Colonel Pleydell marching over the concrete towards us, flanked by a posse from Decisive Measures. I glanced back at Layla. 'I'm all right, really. Go and make sure Njama and the others are okay.'

I let my head sink onto my chest and half-closed my eyes, waiting until I saw the colonel's immaculately polished toecaps come to a halt in front of me before I raised my head again. 'Sorry about the Huey, Colonel,' I said. 'Hope it's insured.'

He stared at me for a moment. 'You left for Bohara two days ago. Where the hell have you been?'

'Engine trouble, Colonel.' I could hear my words slurring as I spoke. 'We were damn lucky I managed to patch it up enough to get back here at all.'

He gave me a dubious look, then waved his hand towards Njama and the others. 'Who the hell are all these people?'

'Human beings. Refugees.'

'Where are the others?'

'Rudi and the guys? They took off into the bush. Said they preferred to take their chances with the rebels than risk the flight back with me. Since I was coming back empty I took the opportunity of bringing these people with me.'

It took him a full minute before the implications of Rudi's disappearance hit him. 'Where are the diamonds?'

I handed him the steel case. He stared suspiciously at the

battered lid, then opened it and tipped out the diamonds to make a gleaming mound in the dust. He began counting them. When he straightened up again, his face was contorted with anger. 'There should have been seventy-four diamonds in this case. Six are missing.'

'Well, I haven't got any,' I said. 'Maybe they're still in the cockpit. You're welcome to go and search for them. Or talk to Rudi and those guys about it. They just handed me the case; I didn't stop to count them or ask how many were in it.' I paused as if the thought had just struck me. 'Maybe that's why they were so happy to risk it in the bush.'

He stared at me. 'Search him.'

His heavies manhandled me to my feet. I yelled in pain as one took my right arm.

Layla came running over. 'What are you doing?' she said. 'He has a serious wound and a fractured shoulder, and he's lost a lot of blood. Leave him alone and get him an ambulance.'

Pleydell swivelled to look at her. 'Who are you, pray?'

'I'm a paramedic with Medicaid International.'

He sneered at her. 'When I want advice from representatives of communist front organisations, I'll ask for it. This man is suspected of the theft of a number of diamonds and whether you like it or not, he will be searched.'

'It's okay, Layla,' I said. 'I'll be all right.'

They looked to Pleydell for guidance. 'Get on with it,' he said. 'Search him.'

Half-apologetically, one of them began to pat me down. 'Not like that,' Pleydell said. 'We're looking for diamonds not a pistol, for Christ's sake. Strip-search him.'

They stripped off my boots and trousers and searched every seam. Then they undid my shirt and body-searched me. They even began pulling back the bandages and peering at my wound, but I let out such a yell that they stopped at once. The sweat on my ashen face might have been enough to convince them that I was not faking, but Layla interposed her body anyway. 'That's enough,' she said.

They hesitated and then stepped back. Pleydell still directed his baleful stare at me. Then a faint smile crossed his face. 'His mouth,' he said. 'Search his mouth.'

His men stared uncertainly from him to Layla.

Cursing, he pushed them aside. I obliged him by opening my mouth. He peered into it, and felt between my teeth and my cheeks with his finger. 'Lift your tongue,' he said.

'What?'

'Lift your tongue.'

I made a show of hesitation, then did as he asked.

He felt around under my tongue then stepped back, wiping his fingers on his trousers.

'What if he's swallowed them?' one of his men said.

He studied my face as he replied. 'If he's swallowed them, they'll rip up his guts like ground glass.' He turned to face Layla. 'With the blood he's already lost from that shoulder wound, I'd say he'd be dead pretty soon, wouldn't you?'

She stared back at him, saying nothing, a look of pure poison on her face.

'Nice try, Colonel,' I said. 'But we both know that if I had swallowed them, they wouldn't rip my guts up. That's how people smuggle them, after all. But I haven't swallowed any. And if you want to prove that, you're welcome to personally search through every shit I do for the next week. It won't do you much good and it certainly won't gain you any diamonds, but if it makes you happy, who am I to stand in your way?' I paused. 'Tell me, Colonel. Why is it so hard for you to accept the obvious explanation? Rudi and three other mercenaries had control of the diamonds. They refused an order to ship them back on the previous flight, then gave me the box they said contained them, but forced me to drop them near the border with Guinea and went walkabout in the bush while I flew back to Freetown. Work it out for yourself.'

He gave me another long stare. 'Perhaps you're right. But don't think for a moment this is over. I'll have more to say to you when we get back to England. The charter's waiting. I want you aboard inside ten minutes.'

'That's impossible. He needs a transfu–' Layla began, but I interrupted her.

'You don't understand, Colonel,' I said. I looked from him to Layla. Beyond her Njama and the other villagers sat silent and watchful. Layla stared back at me, holding my gaze with a look that told me all I needed to know.

I turned back to face Pleydell. 'I like it here. So as far as I'm concerned, you can stick your orders, and your diamonds, up your arse. I'm going nowhere, I'm staying here.'

Pleydell's mouth worked. 'To hell with you then. You're in breach of contract, and your wages are forfeit. See how long you last without money in this stinking shithole of a country.'

He turned and marched away, followed by his men. As our ragged band made our slow, shambling progress around the perimeter towards the airport buildings, I saw the Tristar's doors close. The engines fired and it taxied to the end of the runway. A couple of minutes later it took off towards the setting sun.

As the rumble of its engines faded, I turned to Layla. 'Could you change my dressing for me? Those diamonds are bloody uncomfortable.'

She stared at me for a moment and then began to laugh. She carefully peeled back the dressing and a few moments later she dropped six perfect, if blood-stained, diamonds into my hand.

I turned them over, watching the light shimmering through them, and then passed them to Njama. 'These belong to you,' I said. 'You'll need them. Once the rebels are beaten, we've got a lot of rebuilding to do.'